The Marriage Bargain

Sandra Edwards

PUBLISHED BY:
Sandra Edwards

The Marriage Bargain
Copyright © 2012 by Sandra Edwards

Print ISBN: 978-1478273981
Digital ISBN: 978-1452474236
Kindle ASIN: B007JNWCRA

Cover by Sandra Edwards
Photos used to make the cover obtained from fotolia.com

ALL RIGHTS RESERVED. No part of this book may be used or reproduced in any manner, or by any means (electronic, mechanical, photocopying, recording, or otherwise) without the prior written permission of the copyright owner, except in the case of brief quotations in reviews or critical articles.

This book is a work of fiction and all characters exist solely in the author's imagination. Any resemblance to persons, living or dead, is purely coincidental. Any references to places, events or locales are used in a fictitious manner.

There is only one happiness in life: to love and be loved.

~ George Sand

Chapter One

JULIAN DE LAURENT had lost faith in his plan. He thought the ad he'd placed in the L.A. Trades, looking for a *regal-type actress for an extended gig abroad*, would bring out the finest America had to offer. So far that hadn't happened, at least in Los Angeles.

Evident by the young lady who'd just left his table in the back corner of Donato's, a high-end bistro on the coast just south of Malibu. The scent of her cheap perfume lingered long after she'd gone and snuffed out the more pleasing aroma of the fresh grilled Panini Julian had dined on for lunch. Between her fragrance and her appearance, Vanessa Indigo had failed miserably at meeting Julian's standards.

Not that there was anything wrong with her blue-tipped hair and excessive tattoos, but Julian needed a woman with an air of sophistication. His choice had to look and act like she'd been groomed for one thing—to marry into the de Laurent family.

In addition to her savoir-faire, it would help if she had fine hips and long legs. He didn't particularly care about the size of her breasts. They could be small, medium or large. Her mouth was more important. Kissable lips, or the lack thereof, was a deal-breaker. Her hair color wasn't a factor. Neither were her eyes. He just had to look into them and see love.

The girl he chose would have to be one hell of an actress if he hoped to convince Papa.

Julian was ready to wind up the interviews when a young blonde walked through the entrance. Every physical trait he'd deemed important was wrapped in cultured class.

She's perfect.

She stopped at the hostess, and Julian dared to consider that she might be there for him. He sighed when the girl pointed Ms. Perfect toward Soren, Julian's valet, sitting at the bar patiently waiting to greet the applicants.

She was here for him. Thank God.

Soren glanced his way, and Julian nodded. He'd told Soren no more today, but that was before she'd waltzed in. She was the answer to his predicament.

Ms. Perfect followed Soren to the table and Julian stood as she stopped in front of him.

"Mademoiselle." He pulled a chair out for her. She *looked* ideal for the part. Hopefully she'd be as refined as she appeared.

"My name is Camille Chandler," she said, dropping into the chair and perching her purse onto her lap and a briefcase at her chair's side.

"Julian de Laurent." He snuck a peek at her hands, her left hand in particular. No rings. Good.

She thumbed through the satchel and offered him a single piece of paper. "Here's a bit of my acting history." A shadow of insecurity darkened her turquoise eyes so briefly he questioned its realism. She settled her gaze on him and his heart danced with excitement.

Julian didn't care about her acting history. He was more interested in whether or not she'd come across as convincing. It was one thing to act like his wife, and completely another to look the part.

He took the resume, glanced over the paper and dropped it onto the table next to his plate. "Are you hungry, Miss Chandler? Can I order you something?"

"No thank you. Nothing to eat. But I wouldn't mind having an iced tea." Her voice lulled him into a relaxed mood.

Julian motioned the waiter over. "Could you bring the lady an iced tea?" he said, and glanced at Camille. "Sugar or unsweetened?"

"Unsweetened," she said, reaching for the sugar substitute.

Hm. Did women as young and softly rounded as her worry about their figures? He saw nothing wrong with hers. It belonged in a Ferrari.

Another waitress passed by with a piece of apple pie.

"Ooh, is the apple pie fat free?" she asked.

"No ma'am. But we do have a nice low-fat custard."

"I'll have a piece of the apple pie. And can I get a scoop of vanilla ice cream on the side?"

She fiddled with a couple of Splenda packets, waiting for the iced tea. Julian tried to figure the odds against her putting the sugar substitute in her drink.

The waiter returned and set a glass in front of her. "Your pie will be right out." He paused just a second or two and then moved away from the table.

Camille ripped the Splenda packets open and dumped the contents into her tea. Fascinating.

"Have you been able to earn a competent living as an actress?" He began fishing for information just to get a feel for her potential as an actress.

She gave an impromptu shrug. "Not as much as I'd like, but I do okay." She paused as the waiter appeared with her ice cream and pie. Once he'd left, she continued on. "I get enough commercials and bit parts to pay the rent," she said with a hint of laughter and then scooped her ice cream and pie together onto her fork.

The most satisfied look crossed her face as the sweet treats mixed together inside her mouth. It wasn't a depraved expression, but said *I really like this and I'm not worried about over-indulging*. She picked up her iced tea and washed the remnants down with her artificially sweetened drink.

The whole concept confused Julian. He drew a breath. A sweet soft scent, one that reminded him of lavender, invaded his senses. It wasn't an overwhelming or an expensive perfume, but it did its job effectively.

He summoned the bravado to discuss her odd eating habits. "I've got to ask about your method of sweetening your tea."

"Artificial sweeteners melt easier in iced tea," she said. "There's nothing worse than bitter, under-sweetened tea." Her features contorted in an expression of distaste.

This girl's major complaint was unsweetened iced tea? That suggested an easy-going demeanor. He liked that.

He also liked her wholesome good looks. She was dressed simply but smartly in a plain, skirted suit of pale blue. Designer labels wouldn't be found on the garment, and it wasn't as chic as a snug custom-made fit, but it was adequate for her station in life. And, it complimented, brightened her blue eyes.

"So what's your deal?" she asked.

"My deal?"

"Yeah." Her fingers, tapered and delicate, caressed the glass. "What exactly is this acting gig?" She gave him a scrutinizing look. "I take it you're not a movie producer."

"No, I'm not a producer," he said. "You won't win any Oscars with this role, but it pays well."

Her face drew into a terribly serious expression and she peered at him shrewdly. "Well, if I'm not going to get an Oscar nod...then it'd better pay damn well." She took another bite of her dessert.

"The part also requires the actress be single."

Her head shot back and she hit him with a lethal glare. "Not that I see how that matters, but I am not married."

"The location is in Europe."

Her gaze traveled off to the side. "I've got a passport."

"Let's have dinner this evening," he said. "We'll discuss the part in further detail then." He wanted the chance to show her the benefits of the acting assignment. Just a taste of what accepting his offer would involve before revealing the particulars. If she saw the luxury in which she'd be living, perhaps it would induce a positive reaction.

"Okay, sure. Why not?" she said, after a second of thought.

"I'll have a driver come for you at six?" he suggested.

"How about if I meet you?"

"All right," he agreed, impressed that she was so easily evasive. The trait would come in handy if she accepted his proposal. "Come by the Montage in Beverly Hills."

She gave him one of those raised eyebrow looks that wasn't so much about his extravagance as her vigilance.

"We'll meet in the lobby." He hoped his calm demeanor was enough to satisfy her concern.

Her face relaxed and melted into a smile. "Okay."

Julian reached for the pocket inside his blazer and drew out a business card and an ink pen. He jotted down the hotel's name and his room number on the back. "Here's my hotel information. My cell is on the front." He offered her the card. "My room number is on the back."

She took it, glanced at it and slipped it inside her purse. "I don't have a card," she said, as if it was the most natural thing in the world.

An actress without a business card. Odd. But she was a struggling actress. Perhaps it came down to food or business cards. He could understand why she'd choose the former.

"A cell phone perhaps?" he asked. "In case I need to contact you."

She rattled off a ten-digit number and he keyed it into his phone.

She pushed the empty plate away, sighed and then smiled. "I've got to go. I have another appointment." She grabbed her purse and brief case as she stood. "Thanks for the food."

Julian rose, out of habit more than anything else. "Well, Camille, it was a pleasure meeting you." He reached for her hand and kissed it. "Please don't accept any other acting jobs without giving me a chance to make a counter offer."

If she landed another role in her afternoon appointment, that would be disastrous.

♡

The setting sun cast its golden hue across the Santa Monica Mountains and showered the city in a honeyed haze. Luckily, the cab she'd gotten into had tinted windows, and shielded her from the glare ricocheting off the Pacific Ocean.

Camille looked at her face in the lighted compact mirror. She painted red lipstick on with practiced precision, for all the good it would do. No amount of makeup would make her as appealing as her friend Tasha claimed she needed to be.

"*If you want to get the dirt on what he's doing here, you need to entice it out of him,*" Tasha had insisted when Camille objected to the slinky black dress.

In case Tasha hadn't noticed, Camille wasn't the enticing sort. Her breasts were too small. Her butt was too big. And her legs were too thin.

She tugged at the dress self-consciously as the car rolled to a stop in front of the Montage. Even though Tasha had told her not to, she pulled the sheer wrap up over her shoulders, clutching it tight against her chest in hopes of hiding at least one of her flaws.

She paid the driver, and before she could step out, a doorman appeared instantly and helped her out of the taxi. She thanked him and moved indoors.

Soren was at Camille's side within a few steps. Damn. This guy was efficient—and not too bad on the eyes, in a clean cut sort of way.

"Ms. Chandler, it's a pleasure to see you again." He walked beside her, his hands clamped loosely behind his back. "Mr. de Laurent is waiting with a car at the back entrance."

Nothing about Soren raised red flags; still she couldn't shake the uncomfortable feeling suffocating her. But that probably had more to do with her reticence than Soren or Julian's potential to be a threat.

She followed Soren through the lavish lobby and into a back corridor that, although toned down, still reeked of extravagance. The pair walked in silence. Approaching the exit, Soren stepped a few paces in front of her and held the door open.

Julian was waiting outside, leaning against the white limousine. Camille's heartbeat pounded in overtime, pushing those pheromones through her system. This guy was serious eye candy, with jet-black ringlets hanging nearly to his shoulders. His hair was a little long for her tastes, but it suited him well, complementing his broad shoulders and masculine frame as if it, along with each portion of his body, had been handpicked by the gods. And those aqua eyes, they stood out against his bronze skin like Mediterranean jewels.

He pushed himself off the car and stepped toward her.

Not knowing what to say, she smiled. Julian reached for her hand and brushed it with a kiss. "Chéri, I am honored to have the pleasure of your company for dinner this evening."

Is this guy for real? An involuntary snort rumbled up her throat and she tried to subdue it by holding her breath. No such luck. "Yeah. Likewise, I'm sure," she said, and moved closer to the car.

Julian chuckled and waved the driver off before opening the car door himself. With an elaborate hand gesture, he beckoned Camille inside the vehicle. "Chéri, I can assure you my intentions are nothing less than sincere."

Sure, it was probably a line. But Camille got the impression it was a line he genuinely meant, even if it was fueled by ulterior motives. Julian de Laurent wanted something, and in a bad way. Otherwise, she doubted he'd be in L.A. looking for an actress on the sly. Her boss, Margo Fontaine, had made it clear it was Camille's job to find out what.

The longer he stalled, the more worried she became. What was he up to? She drew a breath, wanting more than anything to enjoy the luxury of the evening. Nights like these didn't come along very often for Camille. But until Julian was ready to reveal his motive, she saw no relaxation in sight.

Julian climbed inside the limo and scanned her seductively before scooting up against her. The smell of his aftershave, cool and slightly erotic, and their close proximity melted her insecurities and prompted her to consider other, more appealing activities. Activities that involved kissing and touching and....

A delicious shudder heated her body, embarrassing Camille. She was too smitten to look at Julian as the car pulled away from the curb. For her own sake, she needed to get a hold of the attraction quickly. She wasn't sure what he was looking for, but she had a good idea it wasn't love.

"You know, you seem like a really nice guy, Julian." Camille kept her focus on the red sequined clutch she'd borrowed from Tasha, and tried to ignore the feel of Julian's silk suit as it caressed temptingly against her bare leg. "If you're not in movies, what can you possibly want with an actress?"

Camille wished she could be this inquisitive with her boss, Margo. If she questioned that woman's intentions, she'd be shot down before the words ever settled in the air. But with Julian, it was different. He didn't seem to mind her wariness. Ever the gentleman, always on the verge of courtesy.

He paused, his expression softening, his eyes closed and lingered shut for a brief interlude. "Chéri." He looked back at her. "May I tell you about my family?"

"Sure."

His demeanor was young, hip, and fresh but his words were old-fashioned, shaped in old-world charm, at least the kind of old-world charm she was used to seeing in the movies. If it was truly an act, he was a savant.

"My family is deep-rooted in France. I will be honest with you because, if you accept my proposal, you will find out anyway." For the first time he fidgeted, appearing uncomfortable with his forthcoming information. "The de Laurents are, how do you say tactfully...a very wealthy family." He shrugged as if it meant nothing. "The money is old and the principles are set in the ways of the past."

"How do you mean?"

"Decades ago. Hundreds of years even, in noble and elite circles, arranged marriages were, and still are, quite common. They worked well back then, and some Europeans aren't ready to give up their old-fashioned ways."

"Kind of like the old saying...if it ain't broke, don't fix it?"

"Exactly."

"Are you telling me that you suffer from an arranged marriage?"

Julian's eyes lit up. "Of sorts." He exhaled and his woes seemed to blow out with his excessive breath. "It's more like an arranged engagement that hasn't yet been announced."

Could he possibly be after what it sounded like? Was Julian looking for a wife?

Camille dismissed that notion, as tempting as it was. It didn't make sense. "Okay, but I'm not really getting how hiring an actress is going to help you."

"My father thinks it's his God-given right to choose a wife for me." His brow drew together in a conflicting frown. "I disagree." His demeanor faded into defeat. "But you can only push a man like my father so far."

"And you're too rich to be poor?"

"Precisely."

Was Julian trying to pull a fast one on his father? Camille insisted her brain not go there. It didn't listen. "A man who's already married can't get married." She laid it out there in the vaguest terms, just in case she was wrong.

"It's not quite that diabolical." He chuckled. "You see, my father feels he also bears a certain sense of responsibility for my happiness, as well as securing a future heir—"

Whoa! Nobody said anything about heirs.

"He wants a daughter-in-law." Every muscle in his face tightened. It seemed hard for him to say the words, much less consider making them happen. "But I'm not ready for a wife." He paused with a wide-eyed innocence that Camille suspected was a smoke-screen. "Not a real one, anyway."

She shrugged to hide the bit of disappointment behind her growing confusion. "So, you think getting an actress to pretend to be your fiancée will fend off your father long enough for him to get over his fascination with you getting married?"

"No." Julian shook his head with a calm resolve. "My father can't be placated so easily."

A soft gasp escaped her. "You want somebody to actually marry you?"

He remained silent, and his mouth curved into an unconscious smile. She'd finally stumbled upon the root of Julian's purpose.

"Okay, I'm missing something here." Her breath caught in her lungs and she forbade herself to lose her sensibility. "You don't want to get married so you think it's a good idea to hire an actress to marry you?" She paused, trying not to let her composure falter. "How is that going to fix your problem?"

"It's temporary, Chéri," he said with a bit of complacency. "Six months, long enough for my father to move on to my younger brother. Then my wife and I can divorce amicably, and I'll be free from the confines of a *real* marriage."

"Why would anyone agree to that?"

Julian rested his arm along the back of the seat and wound his hand in her hair. "Perhaps five million dollars would be an ample inducement?"

Five million bucks? Hell yeah. Camille knew a ton of would-be actresses who'd practically kill for half that.

Camille suspected her boss, Margo Fontaine, enjoyed her throne perched high upon the eighteenth floor. Who could blame her? A corner office with two walls of windows displaying, almost smugly, a commanding view that overlooked downtown Los Angeles.

On this day, Margo ignored the scene outside. Instead, her face fell into exaggerated melancholy as she stared at Camille. "What do you mean you told him *no*?" Margo's voice shrilled across the desk and withered Camille's self-assurance.

Disbelief twisted and knotted in Camille's gut. How could Margo expect her to agree to this charade?

"Margo." Camille's nervous laughter fogged around her like a thick, suffocating vapor. "You really can't expect me to marry some stranger just to get a story?"

Margo stiffened and displayed short-tempered impatience. "Of course I don't expect you to actually go through with the marriage." She heard a heavy dose of sarcasm in Margo's voice. "You can change your mind the day before the ceremony," she added, as if that was okay.

A dense tangle of ideas swarmed inside Camille's head and tightened her muscles with dread. Was Margo serious? She had to be joking. But Margo Fontaine rarely joked about anything. Especially assignments.

"Margo—" Camille stalled, long enough to find her credible voice. "—I can't do that. Not even to a stranger."

Julian de Laurent had come across as a little eccentric and he was most likely a pain in the butt because he was probably used to getting his way, but toying with him just didn't seem right.

"Sure you can." Margo crossed her arms defensively. "And you will."

Stunned surprise yanked Camille back. She shook her head with an air of resignation. "No." Camille's voice cracked with her failing optimism. She studied Margo's stark face, feeling increasingly uncomfortable as she began to realize the severity of her boss's resolve. "I'm sorry, but I can't do that."

Margo waited, letting the silence linger on the space between them. A tactic to let fear of the unknown build in her enemy. "Camille." Her tone was calm. A little too calm. That couldn't be good. "How long have you been interning at Disclosure? A year now?" She grabbed a fountain pen and rubbed her thumb along the edge. "Our internships typically last a year. Then I decide whether or not to offer a full-time position, or quite possibly to offer recommendations elsewhere, if I'm so inclined."

"Margo, I'd love a permanent job with the magazine." Camille leaned forward and rested her arm on her boss's desk. "But I'd also appreciate a recommendation if that's your decision."

"Camille, how would you like to come on board with your own column?"

"That'd be a dream come true."

"You get me that story and the column is yours."

Tempting as that was, Camille wasn't prepared to play the game by those rules. She stifled her cynicism and retreated back into her chair. "I'm sorry. I can't." She dared to raise her gaze and look at Margo. "Is there anything else? Other positions available?"

Margo stared at her in a forceful, gritty way. "Camille, your continued employment with Disclosure is contingent upon your accepting this assignment and getting me that story." Her tone hardened to match her cynical words. "People like de Laurent make me sick. They think they can come over here and buy people at will."

Wasn't that what Margo was trying to do with Camille?

"Well, I guess I'll have to decline a position with the magazine then." Camille wanted to go back to the beginning, before the ad showed up in the L.A. Trades. That was the beginning of the end of her basic belief that her employer abided by the rules of human decency.

Julian de Laurent's actions, as far as Camille could see, were no worse than the average superrich guy who'd gotten himself into a bind and was trying desperately, albeit foolishly, to wriggle out of a disagreeable situation. That didn't mean he deserved to have some reporter disguised as an actress spying on him and his family to write a juicy tell-all.

Not that Camille wouldn't mind helping out Julian. She wouldn't mind living the luxurious life for few months, except she'd probably get too used to it. That'd be her luck. She'd become too attached to the life and Julian's charms.

Margo cleared her throat. There was no mercy in her countenance. "That's really unfortunate," she said with a faint bitterness. "I guess I was wrong about you."

"Wrong?"

"I thought your career was your top priority." Her comment was no question. "As opposed to protecting the privacy of someone you don't even know."

Maybe Margo had a point. Why did Camille care about the ramifications for Julian and his family?

Why? Because she wasn't raised that way. Granny Mae had made sure of that. Camille had lived with her grandmother ever since she could remember, after being deserted by both her parents, and Granny Mae had infused Camille with some old-fashioned values. Values that wouldn't allow her, in good conscience, to do something so underhanded.

"I'm sorry Mar—Ms. Fontaine. I guess there is a line I'm not comfortable crossing."

"That's too bad."

"Might I perhaps garner a letter of recommendation?" Desperation pushed the hopeful inquiry out of her mouth. Camille would have to find another job and quickly. The bills for the student loans she'd acquired while putting herself through college would soon inundate her. She didn't want to have to compete in a job market that was overcrowded with aspiring actors and actresses. Not that there was anything wrong with waitressing, but that was supposed to be a temporary gig for college students and people like Tasha, who were waiting for that big break. It wasn't meant to be an option for people with college degrees in journalism.

"Recommendation?" Margo's ridiculing laughter shattered what little esteem she had left. "Camille, it's all or nothing."

"All or nothing?" Camille's light tone failed to fit the moment.

Margo leaned over her desk and propped herself up on folded arms. "How's your serving skills?"

"Serving skills?" What the hell was she talking about?

"Well, actresses who can't act, waitress. Reporters who can't report, well, they waitress too."

What? "Waitressing?" Surely she'd misunderstood Margo's meaning. Camille had graduated from Stanford University with honors. It shouldn't be that hard to land a job with some sort of publication in southern California. "I think I'll be able to do better than that."

"Not when I'm done, you won't." Margo pushed herself up and marched around in front of her desk. She leaned against it and folded her arms and crossed her legs, staring down at Camille from behind a mask of artificial sympathy. "In case you've convinced yourself that I'm nicer than people have tried to warn you in the past year, by the time I'm done, you'll be lucky if you can get a job at a fast food restaurant."

Chapter Two

BANG. BANG. BANG.

Camille Chandler rapped on the hotel room door so hard her knuckles hurt. But damn it, Julian de Laurent owed her. Big time. *He'd* gotten her fired. Well, sort of. He was definitely the reason she wasn't going from an internship to a permanent position with Disclosure Magazine.

Granted, that wasn't his intent when he placed his ad in the L.A. Trades. She was just supposed to find out what the mega-wealthy Frenchman was up to, and boy, did she ever. Not in Camille's wildest dreams would she have ever imagined her hard-nosed boss would make such demands. Who knew rejecting a proposal for an arranged marriage was shunning her job duties? She'd missed that memo.

A little piece of Camille—the part that found Julian de Laurent as fascinating as he was handsome—had pushed her to his doorstep. But mostly, her fear of being homeless, not to mention broke and in debt, was her main motivation for relenting and giving in to his business proposal.

She glanced down at the red fitted skirt and tailored jacket she'd snagged off the clearance rack at JC Penney, the best an intern at Disclosure Magazine could afford. Should she have worn something sexier?

Sexier? Who was she kidding? Sex appeal didn't come easy to Camille, not like her friend Tasha. The most flattering comment Camille had ever received was that she had nice eyes. Not very gratifying when the same guy told Tasha, "*God, you're gorgeous.*"

Julian de Laurent must have liked something about her because he'd said she was perfect for the part. If he'd changed his mind, she was screwed.

Just breathe. Her stomach churned with the misgivings of her well-intended but ill-conceived scheme. Maybe this was a mistake. She considered a turn-and-run tactic before someone answered the door.

Too late.

Soren, de Laurent's shadow, appeared from behind the half-open door. The two times she'd met with Julian, this guy was with him. It made her wonder.

"Ms. Chandler, what a pleasant surprise." Soren's stoic expression showered Camille with intimidation.

"I'd like to speak with Mr. de Laurent." The words trembled up her throat, right along with the desperation.

"Please come in." Soren stepped back, moving aside. "I'll let Mr. de Laurent know you're here. Please make yourself comfortable." Heading toward a closed door on the other side of the room, he gestured about the suite's living area decorated with plush couches and chairs and other opulent furnishings that probably cost more than her car.

I was comfortable until he waltzed into my life. She stormed to the nearest couch and plopped down. The sofa melded around her like a cloud. Damn. Of course he lived in luxury. God takes care of children and fools. Anybody who'd place an ad in the L.A. Trades looking for an actress to pretend to be his wife for six months had to be crazy.

Mr. Crazy—AKA, the extremely hot Julian de Laurent, as Tasha would call him—entered from an interior room. The suit he wore, custom-tailored and no doubt silk, clung to him and maneuvered with his athletic frame as he moved toward her with laid-back grace.

Although a bit on the arrogant side, he was all about making those around him as comfortable as possible. Julian's attentiveness was sexy as hell. His assumption that he knew what was best for everyone was just as exasperating.

Camille shot up from the couch, tried to feign indifference and waited for his lead.

"Ms. Chandler. To what do I owe the pleasure?" he asked in a low voice that sounded a lot like how chocolate tasted. Divine. "Have you changed your mind, perhaps?" His inquiry hadn't come off as a question so much as an insinuation.

Was she that obvious? Did she have the words *I'm desperate* blinking above her in pink and green neon?

Camille shifted her shoulders and arched them back. She drew a breath that needed to contain both the confidence and the capability to get her through this nutty scheme. "I've been thinking about your...offer."

"Really?" he said in a polite but patronizing voice. She had little time to think about his arrogance as he lured her back to the couch with a persuasive, cajoling gesture. "I took your rejection of my project proposal yesterday as your final word."

Project proposal? God, he made it sound like a damned business venture. Something she had to convince herself of if she wanted to avoid failure. Failure wasn't an option. Neither was stupidity.

"Let's just say that given a little time, I was able to see some of the hidden benefits of your proposal." Camille paused as a whiff of citrus and light spices danced through the air and played with her senses. The manly aroma, an effective calming agent, had her dreaming about cool refreshing breezes on warm summer evenings. "I'm willing to negotiate." She pushed her anxiety and the temptation aside. "Unless you've come to an agreement with someone else."

Julian's arm stretched across the back of the couch behind Camille. He didn't touch her, but she had a corporeal reaction to his nearness. It shivered through her like an arctic chill when he flashed his to-die-for smile.

"No. The position is yours if you want it."

She sucked in a breath of relief and doused it with logic. "We have to set a few ground rules."

"Such as?"

Like, you can't change your mind once you meet Tasha. Letting him meet her bombshell friend was probably a mistake. Nix that idea.

Camille cast her insecurities and attraction to Julian aside in favor of a stereotypical cold and heartless business persona. Julian de Laurent could not find out about the recent change in her employment status, or that she had a slight 'thing' for him—which she fully intended to conquer. She had no intention of falling for him. Her mother had fallen for her father, and look how that turned out. The man deserted her long before Camille was born.

"I have some loans that need to be paid off before I leave the U.S." She hoped her monotone voice came across as a shrewd negotiator, instead of a desperate fraud. "I don't want to ruin my credit," she added, hoping to downplay the loans' significance.

"Done," he said without asking how much.

That set Camille's worry back in motion. Who would agree to such a thing without knowing the particulars?

"Our marriage must appear real." The seriousness in his voice drew her focus back to him, just as his lips curled into a goading smirk. Camille couldn't decide if she wanted to smack him or kiss him. "You and I will have to share a bedroom wherever we go."

She nibbled at his baiting comment, trying not to let it get to her. "Wherever we go?"

"My family is very well known in Europe. The media lurks around every corner. You'll have to be mindful of every move you make, including those in front of my family." His aloofness siphoned the confidence from her soul, leaving her too spooked to do more than nod. Julian continued like he was relating a P&L statement. "Above all others, my family must believe the marriage is real."

Was sex part of the bargain? Not that Camille found the thought of sleeping with him out of the question, but she wasn't ready to start trading her favors for money either.

"You can't buy me." Defiance rumbled through her like a runaway train. "Not like that."

"Chéri, if we make love, it will be your idea." With a wink, he tilted closer and his devilish grin ignited the allure of temptation.

"We won't. And I won't." She hoped he bought the resistance.

"Whatever you say, Chéri." His mischievous smile gave way to roguish laughter. He turned her on. She didn't mind that so much as not being able to control the desire itself.

Calling her by the wrong name bruised her ego and earned him a vengeful tone. "My name is Camille."

"I know that," he said, undaunted. "Chéri is, how do you Americans say…a term of endearment. I called you *darling*."

"Sorry." The bitter tang in her apology stung, but she didn't give him time to exploit her blunder. "So, once we're married, as long as I don't leave you or tell anyone the marriage is merely a business contract, at the end of six months we'll go our separate ways and I'll get five million dollars for my troubles?"

"That is the deal," he said through a half-smile with nothing behind it but teeth.

Damn. This guy must be really loaded.

"What do you want to pretend to be married for, anyway?" she asked. The reason he gave seemed a little extreme. "Why can't you just tell your dad to get off your back?"

Julian stood. "Chéri, you will understand that better after you meet him." He buried his hands in his trouser pockets and towered above her like a hungry vulture eyeing his cornered prey.

"I see." The words tumbled from her mouth. But frankly, she didn't see at all. It made no sense.

"So, do we have a deal?" he asked, carefree and smoothly. He slid his hand out of his pocket and volunteered it as a gesture of good faith.

"There's just one more thing." She evaded his handshake overture. "We have to get married before we leave the States." Considering she was born to distrust people, she insisted on a formal guarantee before her feet left American soil.

"If that makes you feel better. Sure." He shrugged, way too calm, or foolish. "But we have to keep the American marriage under wraps."

"Why?"

"There will be another, more elaborate wedding when we arrive in France. The six months will start after that one—"

"Wa...wait." Camille flew up like a bottle rocket and teetered at his side. "When will the French wedding take place?" she asked, intrigued by the lengths he'd go to in order to pull off his ruse.

"Two weeks. A month." His eyebrow quirked as if amused. Apparently he'd seen disapproval in her reaction, rather than intrigue.

Displeasure clamped her mouth shut and bulleted her head back.

"Surely, Chéri, for five million dollars an extra couple of weeks won't matter?" Julian said, reading her all wrong.

But since he had, maybe she should just go with it. Evidently, it was what he expected and Camille thought it better to please. "You said six months." She made it up as she went along. "Not six months and two weeks, or seven months." Agitation echoed in her voice, unnerved and alarming. It scared even her. She added for good measure, "Six. Months."

The rant made her question the whole crazy notion more than it solidified her decision to hop on board. *What kind of idiot agrees to become some stranger's wife for six months, anyway? One who's lost her job, thanks to him. One who has a ton of student loans coming due, and no way to pay them. One who was afraid of being penniless and forced to live on the streets. That's who.*

Margo's promise to blackball her on the L.A. circuit hadn't done a thing to temper that fear. In fact, it magnified it. Whether her ex-boss could do that kind of damage or not was overshadowed by the possibility. And when she added all that to Julian's vulnerable expression when he talked about not wanting to get roped into a loveless marriage, Camille found saying 'no' impossible.

That settled it. She was a desperate idiot who was about to agree to marry a hopeless fool.

♡

Julian wanted to distract his father, and Camille Chandler was the perfect facade as well as a most agreeable diversion.

"Chéri, I can promise you it won't be as bad as you imagine." He'd stop calling her Chéri, but he liked the way it angered her and brightened her eyes.

Feistiness was the one quality she'd need, the spunkier the better, to mount a satisfactory defense against his father and Madeleine, Papa's choice for Julian. Camille would have to be warned, he couldn't risk them blindsiding her. But not until they arrived in France.

Acutely aware of his selfishness, Julian decided to wait because he didn't want to begin his search again for a suitable replacement. It wasn't like he was doing Camille a disservice. She'd held her own against him and she'd hold her own when confronted by his nemeses.

He eased back down onto the couch and gestured to the empty space at the other end. She looked at the vacant gap between them, at him and then back at the sofa again. Her hands nervously smoothed her skirt before she grudgingly sat and folded her hands in her lap.

"I promise it won't be that bad," he said again, not quite sure if he was trying to reassure her or himself.

"Yeah, so you say." Her tone told him all he needed to know. She didn't trust him.

"All right. Care to make a little wager?" The suggestion was nothing more than a means to ease the tension. Besides, a side bet might be fun. And who knew, if she'd enter into wagers so easily, then perhaps she'd end up in his bed just as effortlessly.

She cut her eyes at him. "What kind of wager?"

"Of course it will require that you declare complete honesty." He let the mystery linger a little longer, simply because it aggravated her.

"How will you know I'm being completely honest?"

"I trust you, Chéri." He held back the snicker, only releasing bits and pieces.

She let out a snort and rolled her eyes. "Yeah, I'll be as honest as you are sincere."

"Aren't they the same?"

She skewed her face into a twisted knot. "Can we get back to the point?"

Ah, good. She wouldn't let his father or Madeleine trick her into disclosing information. "The point is that Pacifique de Lumière is well-known throughout Europe. You won't be able to resist its charm and beauty."

"Pacifique de Lumière," she repeated, not nearly as fluently or confidently.

"It's my family's home near Marseilles."

"So, what do you...live in a castle or something?" She snickered, as if her words were funny. "You know, I hear those things are like cold and damp."

"No, Chéri. Not a castle." A happy memory from his childhood, of his mother chasing him and Andre through the grove, paraded through his thoughts. A mild, pleasurable chuckle rippled up his throat. "Just a chateau that's been in my family for about four hundred years."

She sighed and frowned again.

"Oh, it's been fully renovated and updated with all the latest modern-day amenities."

That didn't get her either. Her stoic expression suggested she couldn't care less about his family's home.

"Yeah, whatever." She rolled her eyes and her voice faded, losing its steely edge. "What's your point?"

"If you are not entirely mesmerized by the view, if not the chateau itself, I will double your pay."

Finally, her jaw dropped. "Are you serious?"

"Entirely."

"And just so we're clear." She paused, fidgeting in her seat. "What exactly do you get if I am somehow mesmerized?" She covered her mouth and coughed out something that sounded a lot like, "*Bullshit.*"

"Nothing quite so dark and lurid." He propped his elbow atop the couch and chuckled before taking on a more serious tone. "Our six month marriage will begin on the day we are wed in France."

She reached for his forehead like his mother used to do when he was a child, but Camille's touch was different. It sparked hunger, warm and soft and unfamiliar, and sent it surging through to his core. He grabbed her wrist, a feeble attempt to distract himself from his intense emotions.

"I haven't known you for very long," she said over a half-giggle rippling through the air, "but I think there might be something wrong with you."

He laughed and laced their fingers together. "Camille, you are going to drive my father insane."

Her face relaxed into a knowing expression. "I thought so." She made no move to withdraw her hand.

"You may not know as much as you think."

"You may be surprised."

"Hm...that'd be a first." He wasn't being terse. Women rarely surprised him. They were an open book, one that could be read from cover to cover in about five seconds but were seldom worth the time. Until now. Every word, action, hint and suggestion about Camille Chandler held him captive. He hoped he didn't end up disappointed.

"Well that's a pretty cynical outlook for a guy who's got the world at his feet." The spunk in her tone had returned full-force.

"The world at my feet?" he asked, more for amusement's sake than curiosity.

"Well, anybody that'll wager five million dollars on a bet that can easily be fixed has to have the world at their feet."

She had a point. She could lie. He'd be surprised if she didn't. Money had a way of motivating people to do strange things. His motivation was freedom. Luckily, he had a virtually unlimited supply of cash to support his quirks.

But more than that, he got the impression she could use a break.

"Being me is not all it's cracked up to be."

"And why is that?"

"Enough about me." He leaned toward Camille and looked her over seductively. How he'd like to tangle his hand in those golden tresses and draw her to him. "Are you ready to leave the United States?"

"Just as soon as we're married."

Oh, that. "All right. I'll leave the arrangements to you. It's probably more efficient that way." Julian had no interest in supervising the tedious preparations. The only thing he cared to oversee was the pre-nuptial agreement.

"Vegas."

"Vegas?" *What?* She wanted to gamble? Perhaps his instincts had failed him and he'd made a bad choice.

"Vegas. It's the quickest, easiest, simplest way to get hitched."

Hitched? Oh, yes, an American idiom. Relief washed over Julian and relaxed his shoulders. Thank God. He'd hate to think he'd lost his edge.

"Vegas. That's where we want to go." Her eyes lit up, like she was enjoying herself. He liked it. "When do you want to go? Today? Tomorrow? I'm not sure when we can get a flight out."

"Oh, we can go anytime you're ready—"

"Let me guess." She cut him off. "You have your own plane?"

"That I do, Chéri."

"Look." Her shoulders dropped and she blew out an exasperated sigh. "You've got to stop calling me that."

"Why?"

"I don't know. It just doesn't seem right."

"Why?"

"I'm not really your *darling*. It's not like we're a real couple or anything."

"For the next six months, Chéri, we will give every appearance of being just that."

And if she succumbed to his charms during that time, so much the better.

She was beginning to blush a little and when she started to fidget, Julian grew anxious. He didn't want her to get antsy and have second thoughts.

"Would you like to pack a few things, or purchase a new wardrobe?"

"Is that really necessary?" She paused, as if letting the idea of her clothes being inadequate settle into her thoughts. "Well, I guess my JC

Penney look isn't quite up to par for the de Laurent family, huh?" She opened herself up for a shot at ridicule. A quality only for the brave. She didn't take herself seriously. Another trait Julian could appreciate.

"Camille." He used her name purposely this time. "I think you look great no matter what you wear...but, as the wife of Julian de Laurent, certain responsibilities and expectations come with the arrangement."

The look on her face said she understood. It also said she wouldn't want the job for good.

"And being your wife includes dressing the part."

She caught on quickly. Another positive. "You'll wear the latest fashions from the finest designers. You'll be draped in jewels that most people can't even imagine. Those who can will envy you. Enjoy it, Chéri." He went back to calling her by the French endearment. She needed to get used to it, because people would expect nothing less from a member of the de Laurent family.

"Are you going to make up some fantastical yet completely bogus background for me as well?" Her brittle tone oozed out and she stiffened with a disinterested, casual lack of concern. Clearly, she felt belittled and didn't like it. That wasn't his objective.

"You are who you are. The story is yours to tell."

Julian had to make sure Camille was as comfortable as possible, because soon enough she'd learn about the couple of bulldogs waiting in her near future. It just couldn't be right now.

♡

Sure, the story may be mine to tell...but is he going to end up dictating it to me?

Even though Camille had her reservations, she intended to go through with his charade. What other choice did she have? Life on the streets in L.A. wasn't pretty, and she didn't want a firsthand look.

Marrying Julian wasn't a jail sentence or anything. She'd love to know what it was like to slip into a one-of-a-kind Christian Dior, if only for a little while. And slipping into Julian's arms wasn't a bad idea either.

She peered at him, trying to find a reason to back out while sifting through all the advantages of following through at the same time. Money. A hottie husband—who cared if it wasn't real? No worries for six months. Some potentially great sex. Luxuries beyond anything she could envision.

"Well, it might be fun to *play* rich for a little while," she said, selling herself on the idea.

"On the contrary, Chéri, you will be rich, moderately so anyway. Remember, I am paying you five million dollars."

Julian did have a point. But Camille had a feeling the degree of wealth she was about to experience was beyond her wildest dreams.

A fun prospect, but she was more concerned about ending up homeless and unable to find a job in the field which she'd spent tens of thousands of dollars on in educational fees.

She just wanted to get on with it and secure her future. And right now, marrying Julian de Laurent for the whole of six months seemed appealing for more than one reason. Of course, the option would cruise out the window real quick if he knew why she'd changed her mind.

No way could she tell him she'd lost her job at Disclosure Magazine when she refused to accept his proposal and turn the experience into a story. Like he'd really believe that now.

The question was, could they get to a wedding chapel in Vegas before he found out she and her employer had parted ways—or worse yet, ran across her bombshell of a friend Tasha?

Chapter Three

CAMILLE HURRIED CLOSE behind Julian as they ascended the stairs up to the aircraft. He paused long enough to grab hold of her hand before entering a private jet that rivaled the size of most commercial airliners.

Her stomach churned with the uncertainty of not knowing if she was doing the right thing. Too late now. Her career was already ruined. And Julian owned at least part of that blame. If only he hadn't come to America in search of a temporary wife.

Geez, weren't there any gold diggers in Europe? Did he have to travel halfway around the world to buy himself a temporary wife?

Julian's redeeming quality, besides his appeal, was that he seemed like a nice enough guy. *Yeah, and they say Ted Bundy was charismatic too. Trusting him had gotten a whole lot of women killed.*

Good Lord. Camille shook the insecurities out of her head. Julian was no killer. Unless you counted kindness and his to-die-for good looks as a weapon.

He stopped just inside the cabin and turned to face her with a gorgeous smile curling on his lips. "Make yourself comfortable." He fanned a hand about the cabin. "I must speak with the captain, but I'll return momentarily."

Julian disappeared through a door near the plane's entryway, leaving Camille alone with her paranoid insecurities.

Just breathe. Camille scanned the cabin. She should take a seat but she questioned her choice to be there. Did she deserve a five million dollar reward for perpetrating a fraud?

Probably not. But she didn't deserve to be forced out on her ear either. She had no prospects of employment here in L.A.—thanks to Julian—and thousands in overdue student loans that he had agreed to pay off as part of their arrangement.

She'd bet the plush couches, even the chairs, were sumptuously comfortable and would lull her into a quick nap. The prospect of an uncertain future in L.A. lured her toward a beige leather chair. Easing down, she felt like she was settling into a cloud. She'd never experienced such luxury or comfort and welcomed it, encouraging it to settle her nerves.

Camille opened her eyes and studied the door where Julian had disappeared. She grabbed her purse and dug out her cell phone. Not that there were too many people who'd be looking for her if she came up missing now that she'd lost her job, but there was Tasha. She'd make a big fuss. Camille didn't want that. She'd better contact her but not on her cell. She brought up Tasha's home number and set the call.

After a couple of rings, Tasha's seductive voice greeted her caller. "Hey, it's Tash. If you don't know my cell then leave me a message and I'll get back to you." Her flirtatious delivery was overshadowed by her cutting words pointing out that some callers had limited access.

"Hey, Tash, I tried your cell but got nothing." The lie came easily since it was for the greater good. "Listen, Margo gave me that big promotion I've been waiting for. The catch is, I've got to go out of town on a story. I don't know how long I'll be gone but it'll probably be an extended assignment." She stopped talking when Soren entered the cabin and approached her.

"Ms. Chandler, may I get you something to drink during our short flight to Las Vegas?" He paused, resting his hands behind his back. "Mr. de Laurent asked if the Bellagio will be satisfactory until we leave the U.S.?"

"I'll call you later, okay?" she said into the phone. "Don't worry. Everything's cool." After a bit of hesitation she disconnected the call.

After a brief interlude of silence she turned to Julian's valet. "Soren. Is that your first name?" she asked, slipping her phone into her bag.

"Yes ma'am." He stood waiting for her direction.

"Can I just get some water or something?" Alcohol and her empty stomach weren't a good match.

"Of course." He moved to a small bar on the far side of the cabin. "And I take it the Bellagio will do?" Behind the counter, Soren prepared to serve her request.

Not used to having someone wait on her, Camille went to Soren's side. Politely, she slipped the bottled water and the ice-filled glass from his hands and filled it herself.

"Sure." She tried to hide her surprise and anticipation of a visit to the ritzy hotel. "The Bellagio is fine with me."

The glass chilled quickly, frosting her fingers. She hurried back toward her seat and sipped the water before setting the glass on a nearby coffee-like table.

"Can I get you anything else?"

She shook her head. "Will Julian be joining me during the flight? I don't really like sitting out here by myself."

Soren's sympathetic smile said he felt sorry for her. "I will inform Mr. de Laurent." He bowed his head and backed out of the cabin.

The last couple of days had been long and stressful. Camille's eyelids grew heavy and she scrutinized her chair and the sofa nearby. She moved to it, wanting to rest for a moment or two. The couch melded around her, lulling her into slumber.

Julian exited the cockpit and headed toward the cabin, fully aware of the haughty smirk spreading over his mouth.

Camille Chandler, soon to be de Laurent, was a force to be reckoned with. No doubt she could easily handle anything papa or Madeleine threw at her, but more than that, she had the makings to become a wildcat in bed.

Before the marriage was over, he would have her, and it wouldn't happen out of a sense of obligation.

Watching her sleeping on the couch, he appraised her with more than mild interest. Her nubile body filled him with an inner excitement. Blonde hair strewn across her delicately carved face beckoned him to her side.

"Chéri." Gentle fingers swept her hair back.

She stumbled out of the sleepy fog and when her gaze settled on Julian, a hint of pink stained her cheeks.

"We're about to take off. The seatbelt is a good idea."

She sat up and, to his dismay, inched away from him.

"Gee, I didn't realize I was so tired." Camille fumbled for the seatbelt.

He placed a hand on her shoulder, hoping to calm her. "No worries, Chéri. Once we're in the air there's a state room where you can rest."

The color in her cheeks deepened and a bewildered smile touched her face. "Do you have any food? I'm kind of hungry."

"Food? Of course. What would you like?"

"What do you got?"

"Soren," Julian lifted his voice slightly.

His assistant appeared. "Sir."

"Miss Chandler is hungry. I trust we have something that will meet with her approval once we're in the air?"

"Most of the dinners we have will take longer to prepare than we will be in the air," Soren said. "We do have sandwich meals. Turkey or ham, I believe."

Julian looked at Camille.

"Turkey." She nodded.

"Excellent." Julian's smile turned on at half-power as he leaned back against the sofa.

Camille reached for her water glass and glanced at Julian.

He stretched his arms along the back of the couch. "Will our U.S. wedding take place this evening or tomorrow?"

With a shrug born in indifference she waved and said, "How about this evening?" She didn't say anything more until his gaze met hers. "Do you think we can get someone from one of the chapels to come to our suite instead of going there? I know you want to keep it under wraps."

"If that's what you want. I'll make it happen." He touched her cheek in a wistful gesture. "We'll want to wait until my legal counsel drops by, of course."

There was no way they'd be tying any knots before they'd signed prenuptial agreements and business contracts. Julian was a lot of things, but he wasn't stupid.

"We can wait until tomorrow if it helps."

Soren came in and the mild scent of turkey filled the cabin. Julian's stomach ached. Perhaps he should've ordered something.

Camille straightened and clasped her hands in her lap. Soren placed a tray with everything she could possibly want on the table before them. She opened the sandwich and tossed aside the lettuce and tomato, painted the bread with a thin layer of mayonnaise, dusted it with salt and pepper, and slapped it back together again. She cut the sandwich in half and grabbed a portion.

"You want the other half?" she asked, raising the sandwich to her mouth.

"You go ahead." Not that Julian wouldn't mind it, but he didn't want to take food from her. He could have Soren bring in another but his instincts said they'd be landing soon. "I'll get something once we get to the hotel."

Her face darkened with rebellion. She dropped her half of the sandwich onto the plate and picked up the other. "You want some mayo or mustard on this?"

Julian shook his head.

"Look, we can both get something at the hotel," she said. "But for now, we'll just have this to tide us over."

A chuckle ventured up Julian's throat. Trying to resist her was futile. He accepted the sandwich, as is, and took a bite. The bread was void of moisture and not appealing taste-wise. "Pretty dry," he said with a wink.

They laughed.

"I think room service should be at the top of our list once we're settled into the hotel." Her infectious grin set the tone for fun.

The phone on the table beside Julian rang. He snatched it up before it had the chance to jingle a second time. "Yes."

He listened and after a brief interlude, hung up the receiver and turned to Camille. "We'll be landing directly," he said. "You have your seatbelt on?"

She nodded with a flicker of amusement in her eyes, as if she found his attentiveness both invigorating and irritating.

Julian fastened his seatbelt. The puzzle pieces of his future were starting to fall into place. Everything would be fine so long as Camille didn't go running for the hills once she met Papa and Madeleine.

♡

Camille and Julian registered in the Bellagio's executive suite lounge rather than the hotel's front lobby. She had no idea that high-profile guests were accommodated in this privileged manner. There was a lot to learn about Julian's world.

After the party checked in, including Soren and Julian's pilot, they rode the private elevators up to the thirty-fourth floor to one of the hotel's Villas.

The five bedroom suite's décor captivated Camille with its plush bright red couches and chairs, fine furniture in tan and gold and topped with black marble. On the far side, a wall of windows draped in red and gold curtains caught her attention and landed on a fireplace smack-dab in the middle. Wow. Outside a terrace boasted immaculately groomed gardens and a private pool. Double wow.

Julian grabbed her hand and she floated along as he pulled her toward one of the rooms. "This will be your bedchamber," he said, opening the door.

He knew his way around. He'd been here before. She couldn't imagine paying for this place one night, much less multiple times.

Camille stepped inside a room that borrowed its theme from the suite's outer area. Red leather chairs and a matching bed frame were happily situated amid the grandeur of old-world European elegance. The king-size bed, covered in a pink and red floral print, looked inviting.

"You look tired, Chéri." Julian brushed Camille's bangs out of her face. "Why don't you rest for a bit?" He leaned against the doorframe, and the smile in his eyes glowed with a sensuous flame. "When Davis gets here, I'll let you know."

She exhaled a long sigh of admiration. Julian was respecting her space and not making demands or assumptions. His thoughtfulness was winning him points.

"All right." She looked down and backed away from him. He turned and closed the door as he left.

A cry of relief broke from her lips. Thank God he'd left, before she had the chance to throw herself at him.

Julian returned to the suite's living room and Soren handed him a scotch, straight up. He needed it. He was close, but any minute things could fall apart. Julian was a firm believer in Murphy's Law. If something could go wrong, it would happen to him.

He drained the glass, set it on the marble-topped wet bar and moved toward the wall of windows overlooking the garden and the pool. The Nevada sky was in the midst of a desert twilight and the terrace lights were beginning to flicker on in a warm, subtle hue.

Soren was at his side instantly, handing him a refill. Julian took it and gave his valet a quick nod. "I think it's going to work."

"You have seen to every detail."

"Yes, but sometimes that doesn't help." He shook his head and glanced out the window at the darkening sky and brightening poolside lights. "Things have a way of falling apart easily."

"But you're quite adept at not letting that happen," Soren reminded him. "You think things through thoroughly. You see every aspect down to the last detail." Soren paused, catching his breath. "I'm sure this will be no exception."

"Well, Soren," Julian said, "let's hope you're right." The doorbell rang, grabbing both men's attention. "I'll get it," Julian said, stepping in front of Soren and moving toward the door. Hopefully it was Davis.

Julian hurried across the room and opened the door. Davis greeted Julian with a handshake and a smile they only taught at law school.

Julian stepped back and gestured him inside the suite.

"I have the paperwork you've requested. It's ready for signatures."

"Can you get it filed today?" Julian asked, leading him to the wet bar.

"Yes, I can get it filed this evening."

"Good." Julian gestured to the counter. "You can prepare the papers, I'll get Ms. Chandler." He moved toward the hallway behind the dining area.

At Camille's bedroom door, Julian knocked softly and waited for her vocal response. After the second knock, he heard her voice drift through the door. "Yes."

"Chéri, may I come in?"

The door opened. Camille was in a bathrobe, her hair wet and clinging to her face. God, she looked sexy. Julian wanted to know what was under the robe. Nothing, he'd guess. He'd sure like to peel it off, discard it onto the floor and run his hands through her damp tresses before exploring every inch of her naked body.

She smiled, tousled her hair with a towel and gestured him inside. "I decided to take a shower."

"The prenuptial agreement is here and waiting for our signatures. If we can sign it now, it can be filed directly and we are free to wed before leaving tomorrow. If that's still your wish."

He didn't know what her wish was, but his was to have his way with her. But that wasn't going to happen tonight. It would take some finesse to woo her into his bed.

"That is our deal," she said. "I'll just slip on some clothes and be right out."

He wrenched himself away from his ridiculous fixation with her arresting body. His heart thudded a couple of times and then settled back to its natural rhythm. "Of course." He backed out of the room and closed the door.

You idiot. Acting like a teenage boy who'd never seen a half-naked girl was not a winning attribute.

Julian forced himself back out into the common area where Soren and the attorney were waiting. He smiled and summoned his confidence. "She will be out directly. She's changing clothes. You know how women are."

Both Soren and Davis laughed. The attorney offered Julian a fountain pen. "You can sign now and we'll get her signature when she comes out."

Julian stepped forward and took the pen, turning his attention to the papers on the bar. Three sets. One for him. One for her. And one for the American courts. He picked up a copy and scanned it quickly but with expertise. Satisfied that it was all there just as he'd stipulated, he signed the copies one by one.

When he was done, Camille entered the room dressed in a pair of blue jeans and a skintight red t-shirt. She walked across the room with sunken shoulders, possibly self-conscious about her breast size. But Julian, being a leg man, was preoccupied with her long, shapely legs. They more than made up for her small breasts.

She moved to the bar, scooped up one of the documents and began reading it. She took her time reviewing each page carefully, and finally when she reached the end of the last page she looked at Davis. "So, this basically says if we stay married for at least six months, I'll get five million dollars?"

"That is what it says in a nutshell." Davis rubbed his nose.

"Good." She grabbed a pen and signed the copy she'd been reading. Then she proceeded to compare it to each of the other two copies before signing them. Clearly, she didn't trust people, and Julian wondered what made her so suspicious. Perhaps it had something to do with the fact that people were always letting her down.

People, as a general rule, were unreliable. Julian knew that to be true. It had happened to him. It had happened to his mother—his real mother. She'd died, killed herself, when he was five. His father had remarried shortly thereafter, and it was as if his natural mother had never existed. Claudette, his stepmother, had taken her place, and even though she'd always loved Julian and Andre just as much as she'd loved her own child Lecie, Julian had never forgotten his *real mother*.

Chapter Four

BRIGHT AND VIVID SUNLIGHT painted the first hues of the day, awakening Camille from her cozy slumber. The lavish bedroom suite at the Bellagio reminded her where she was and of yesterday's events. Considering she'd spent her wedding night alone, her sleep had been surprisingly restful. She forced herself up and out of bed and stumbled into her private bathroom. A quick shower would put things into perspective.

Too bad it didn't work.

Half an hour in the shower hadn't done anything except give her insecurities time to awaken and fester. She stared at her reflection in the mirror and raked a comb through her damp hair.

When was Julian going to wake up and take a long, hard look at her? There was nothing regal about Camille. Or refined. She was pretty sure Julian could secure the hand of just about anybody in marriage. Why her?

Because it isn't real. She had to keep reminding herself of the conditions that brought about this union. For her own sake, she couldn't get lost in the fairytale factor that emanated around Julian. Her mother had probably seen it, although to a lesser degree, in dear old dad. Camille was painfully aware of how that turned out as she'd never met her father. Her mother had come around a couple of times when Camille was little, but she never stayed long. She was constantly off on some other adventure, always too busy to take on the task of raising her own child.

Camille slipped into a pair of jeans and a loose-flowing print blouse. She drew a breath and summoned the courage to face her first day as Mrs. Julian de Laurent.

Inside the suite's dining room, her new husband was sitting at the table, all decked out in one of his tailor-made suits.

He looked up, smiled when their eyes met and stood, pulling a chair out for her. "Good morning, Chéri." His deep voice filled with amusement. "I trust you slept well?"

Smelling the faint citrus scent of his aftershave, she settled into the chair next to him. She propped one foot up and reached for the coffee mug, disappointed by its emptiness. Soren was at her side immediately and filling her cup. "Good morning, Mrs. de Laurent."

She glanced at Julian, who seemed utterly amused, and then let her gaze travel to Soren. A shadow darkened the valet's face and Camille realized she'd frowned at him. She tried to offer an apologetic smile, but wasn't sure it'd come out right. Then she saw him grinning.

"Thank you." She reached for the sugar bin.

"I asked specifically for some of your Splenda," Julian said.

"Well, it isn't *my* Splenda, but thanks." She stacked a couple of packets together and ripped off their ends. Pouring the contents into her cup, she glanced at Julian. "So, what's on the agenda today? When do we leave here?"

"Perhaps this evening." Julian played with his food, dancing the fork around his plate. "The hotel has several boutiques. I thought perhaps you'd like to go shopping." His unquestioning tone reminded Camille of their lifestyle differences. She wore what she could afford, and he wore whatever he wanted.

"Oh yeah, the clothes thing." She stirred uneasily in the chair and distracted herself by grabbing a plate. Not that she bought into the notion his money made him better than her, but it was hard to ignore Julian's mega-success. It magnified her less-than-spectacular start in life. Camille's fingers tensed around her fork as she stabbed a piece of ham off the serving dish.

He looked as if he was weighing the options, but didn't appear the least bit aware about her insecurities. "Be sure to procure a full wardrobe."

Camille's gaze froze on Julian and her fork stalled in mid-air. "What constitutes a full wardrobe?" What an odd choice of words. It sounded so old-fashioned.

Julian hesitated, probably rethinking his choice. Too late. They'd already signed the papers. The deal was done. The marriage had happened. And besides, he owed her.

"Would you like Soren to accompany you on your shopping excursion?"

Soren? Well, okay. Maybe. "I guess. Sure." But why wasn't Julian going with her? *Because he's not really your husband, that's why?* "But what about you?" She paused, knowing she was probably sticking her nose in where it didn't belong. "Doesn't he take care of things for you?"

Julian chuckled. "Yes, he does. And by helping you out today, he will be helping me."

"Can't argue with that."

Soren grabbed a plate and moved around the table, filling it, and then went to the nearby kitchen counter. Camille didn't understand why he had to eat over there. She didn't like the separation.

Julian stood, wiped his hands on his napkin and dropped it onto the table. "I have some business to attend to before we leave the country. Would you like to meet for lunch downstairs at the Café Bellagio?"

She gave a one-shouldered shrug. "Sure."

Julian kissed the top of her head and moved toward the door.

Money? How was she supposed to pay for the clothes. "Julian..." She rested her wrist on the edge of the table and perched her hand in the air. "I, ah..."

As if he sensed her dilemma, he said, "Soren has all the necessary bank cards." Julian paused, letting his gaze travel to Soren. "Just let her buy whatever she wants."

"Of course, sir." Soren spoke without glancing up from his plate.

Julian left, and Camille turned her focus on Soren. "Hey, why are you sitting over there?"

"It is not my place to eat at the same table as my employer."

"I'm not your employer. Come sit with me?"

"You are my employer's wife." He gave her an exaggerated look of reproach. "Same thing."

"Okay, so if I'm like your employer...then I'm telling you to come sit with me."

Soren laughed as if sincerely amused. "Nice try."

Camille stood, grabbed her plate and headed to the counter. "If you won't join me...then I'll join you."

"Dining with the hired help." He let out one of those ironic laughs. "You're going to fit in nicely at Pacifique de Lumière."

"Don't get ahead of yourself. I'm the hired help, too."

Soren stopped and his demeanor turned to stone. "You must never say that again."

"It's just a joke."

"Not even joking." He paused, no glimmer of sympathy showing on his face. "No one can ever suspect that this marriage isn't real."

"Geez, Soren...you're one loyal guy." She envied it from Julian's perspective, but felt sorrow from Soren's standpoint. His loyalty seemed unappreciated because he and Julian weren't friends. They had a working relationship and nothing more. Soren felt himself beneath Julian, evident by his own judgment that he didn't deserve to eat at the same table.

Camille didn't understand the ways of the wealthy.

"It's all part of my job." Soren nodded and cleared his throat, clearly uncomfortable with the comparison between himself and Julian.

"Do you ever worry that your efforts will be in vain?" she asked, thinking of her own misplaced loyalty in Margo Fontaine.

"No." Soren's head shook in defiance. "Julian de Laurent is an honorable man. And I'm certain he'd never put me in a position that would require me to compromise my values."

"Really?" That surprised her. "So you're okay with this little charade of ours?"

He paused for a moment, as if thinking it over. "It's not like either of you are hurting anyone. He's not taking advantage of you, and you're not taking advantage of him. You've simply entered into a business deal where both of you are in complete agreement on the details."

"That's true."

"And in the long run, I do believe this is what is best for Mr. de Laurent. He would never be happy...." Soren's words trailed off and a look crossed his face suggesting he'd said too much.

"He'd never be happy...?" Camille repeated Soren's words, turning them into a question.

He hesitated, as if guarding a secret. When he finally did speak, it was evasive. "Mr. de Laurent's freedom is what will make him happy."

"How can you be so sure of that?"

"Because he told me so."

Camille chuckled. "Man, I need a friend like you, Soren." If only Tasha listened this effectively.

"Does Mrs. de Laurent have a knack for picking fair-weather friends?"

Camille snorted. "That's one way to put it."

"Perhaps Mrs. de Laurent is searching for friends in all the wrong places?"

"Sounds like a country song."

Soren chuckled. "I see what Mr. de Laurent finds so fascinating about you."

"He finds me fascinating?" Her voice escalated, like those cheerleaders did in high school when they just found out the captain of the football team was into them.

Soren looked at her with an absent stare. "Yes, I do believe those were his words...'she's simply fascinating'."

Camille couldn't fathom why that pleased her, but it did. "Soren..." She hesitated and then leaned toward him touching his arm. "How do you feel about going shopping with me?"

"Oh, I never miss a chance to spend de Laurent money." He held a stoic face for about ten seconds and then burst into laughter. "Seriously, I also never miss a chance to see a pretty girl in fine clothing." His amusement showed on his face. "It will be my pleasure."

Pretty girl, huh? He's definitely been listening to his employer, and taking notes.

"Does Julian have a favorite color?" Camille's inquiry touched something inside her. For a wild moment she wanted to please Julian, and then she wondered why she cared.

"I believe it's red." A smile curled on the tips of his mouth. "A color that will no doubt suit you beautifully."

A blush warmed her cheeks even though red wasn't anywhere near the top of her favorite color list. She preferred electric blue or a spring green, both colors that brought out her eyes. But she'd make an effort to look like an obliging wife because that's what was expected. She was just trying to meld herself into the part and nothing more.

Camille had given her loyalty to too many people who didn't deserve it. Like her parents for instance. Her father had split when he found out her mother was pregnant. And her mother hadn't lasted three months after Camille's birth. At seventeen, a baby was too much trouble. Camille had forever after had a love-hate relationship with her parents, resenting them for not caring enough to stick around, thankful they'd left her in the care of her maternal grandmother. And still she carried them in her heart, waiting for them to prove she wasn't a waste.

Those days of misplaced loyalty were over.

♡

Julian entered the Bellagio's main lobby and approached the front desk, fiddling with the jewelry box in his pocket. He hoped she liked it. He probably should've gotten her opinion on the rings but there wasn't time, and he was old-fashioned about that sort of thing. It was his gift to her, not her gift to herself through him. But most women, he'd come to learn, weren't overly picky as long as the rock was big.

"Is there a package for me?" he asked the concierge.

The lady's polite smile offered confirmation before she answered. "Yes sir, a messenger dropped it off moments ago." She stepped back and moved toward the cubicles behind her.

At the other end of the counter a stunning—artificial, but stunning—young woman was in the midst of an altercation with the clerk. Her blonde hair had been perfectly coiffed. Her dress was nice but gave the appearance of being more expensive than it really was. Her shapely body was too perfect. She'd spent a lot of money to look the way she did. Definitely not Julian's type.

A girl like her would be too high maintenance. Not that he couldn't afford it, but he didn't want a woman who was so centered on vanity that nothing else mattered. No, this girl was more Andre's type. Little brother loved sporting a trophy on his arm.

"Look, I know she's here," the Barbie doll said. "She said she was coming to this hotel specifically."

"I'm sorry, Miss..." The clerk waited for her name.

"Ms. Gordon. It's Ms. Gordon." An irritated tone edged her voice. "And I know my friend Camille Chandler is here, in this hotel. Somewhere."

What? She's looking for Camille. *But why?*

The concierge handed Julian a large manila envelope. He took it and closed the gap between himself and the girl. "Excuse me, Miss..."

She gave him one look, smirked and raised a defying hand. "Are you hotel security? I'm not going anywhere. I know my friend is in this hotel, somewhere."

"I can assure you that I'm not hotel security." Julian laughed inside. Of course she was a friend of Camille's. Neither of them took shit from anybody. "But I do know where Camille Chandler is."

"You do?" she said, almost grateful.

"I'll just call her," he said, going for his cell phone.

"I already tried to call her." She inclined her head in defeat. "She's not answering her phone."

Julian hit the speed dial. "One second." He waited for Soren to answer the call.

"Soren." The valet answered immediately.

Julian thought about asking for *Mrs. de Laurent* but thought better of it. It was probably best to let Camille tell the girl, whoever she was, about their arrangement herself. "Is Camille close by? I need to talk to her."

Within seconds Camille said with a gentle softness, "What's up?"

Did Camille have any idea how sensuous her voice sounded?

Julian discarded his wandering thoughts and focused on the girl before him. "There's someone here who'd like to speak with you."

"Who?" Her voice was edgy and filled with conjecture.

Julian's gaze traveled up to meet the feisty girl's. "Your name?"

"My name?" Her eyes widened with an impatient glare. "Give me that damn phone." She yanked Julian's cell from his hand. "Camille?"

♡

Oh shit. "Tasha. What are you doing with Julian?" Camille said quickly over her choking, pounding heart.

Soren and Camille exited one of the Lobby Shops at the Bellagio.

"What am I doing with Julian?" Tasha asked in a subtle, mocking tone. "The better question is...what are *you* doing with Julian?"

"We'll talk about that later." Camille used a tone she knew Tasha would recognize as a discreet warning to keep her mouth shut. "Where are you?" She and Soren entered the lobby where she saw Julian and Tasha at the registration desk across the way. "Never mind. I see you." She disconnected the call and handed the phone to Soren.

Camille had a couple of bags in her hands and Soren toted the rest. He'd protested over her carrying any of them, but she'd insisted. Soren hadn't handled it very well, but she hadn't given him a choice. Now that they'd come face-to-face with Julian, Soren's posture seemed to crumble right along with his composure.

Camille's first stop was Julian, rather than Tasha. "Look," she whispered against his ear. "Don't say anything to him about me carrying the bags, okay? I insisted."

"Chéri, you really should let him do his job." Julian's response was kind, but firm.

"He did do his job." Camille's gaze followed Julian's until she'd wrangled it into submission. "He helped me pick out some great clothes." She acknowledged the bags in her hands before turning her back on Julian and moving toward Tasha. "What are you doing here?"

"What's going on, Camille? I called your work and Margo said—"

Camille shushed Tasha, cutting her off. She flashed her friend a look that she hoped was oppressive before turning to face Julian. "This is Tasha, my best friend. She and I need to talk."

"May I take your bags?" He held out his hands. "Why don't you go into the cafe and have a drink. I'll join you in about half an hour and we'll all have lunch."

Camille gladly gave Julian her shopping bags, happy to get rid of him so she could smooth Tasha's curiosity without giving herself away.

Julian looked her over with an inspecting glance. His lips curled into a faint smile as his gaze traveled up to meet hers. "Nice outfit. The color suits you," he said of the red and black designer clothing.

She prayed Tasha had kept her mouth shut. Julian moved closer, his intention to kiss her cheek clear. Camille froze. Warm lips brushed against her face and sent chills roving over her body.

Julian turned to Tasha. "I look forward to getting to know Camille's friend over lunch." He offered a friendly smile and bowed.

Soren dipped his chin and followed Julian.

Camille's gaze got stuck on Julian for a moment. A little distance lightened the weight on her shoulders. She drew a breath and turned to her friend. A few wrong words from Tasha and Camille's plan would be ruined.

Chapter Five

TASHA DRAPED HER ARM around Camille's and they walked toward the Café Bellagio. "What the heck's going on?" she whispered. "And where on earth did you get this outfit?"

Camille drew a breath and held it. "I told you I was doing a story. Undercover."

"And Margo told me you're no longer with Disclosure."

"She did, did she?" Camille shuddered inwardly. "Did she also tell you that she's an unreasonable shrew?"

Tasha's eyebrows shot up.

Camille cleared her throat as they approached the maître'd, signaling Tasha to keep quiet.

"Ah, Mrs. de Laurent. Will you and your companion be joining us for lunch?"

"Yes. Could we have a private table? Somewhere out of the way?"

"But of course." He led them out to the garden area.

"Mrs. de Laurent?" Tasha whispered.

Camille shushed Tasha, and turned her attention to the maître'd, saying, "Mr. de Laurent will be joining us shortly."

"Thank you," the girls said in unison.

He pulled out two chairs at a table surrounded by plants and foliage in the café's exquisite botanical gardens. While daffodils and snow drops were in full bloom behind their table, Camille recognized the scent of jasmine lingering in the air.

"Unsweetened iced tea?" The waiter confirmed her choice.

Camille nodded.

He turned to Tasha, "And what would you like? A pomegranate martini perhaps?"

She hesitated, in thought. "Yes," she nodded, "I believe I will." She watched him walk away and turned to Camille. "I believe I'm going to need it."

"Why are you here?" Camille asked again. "I told you I was on a story. You could've easily blown my cover."

"You're not on a story. You were fired."

"I wasn't fired. I quit."

"You say tomato. I say tomato," she said, using the American and English versions of the pronunciations. "Did you marry that guy?"

She thought about lying, but it wasn't a good idea. Camille was knee-deep in lies as it was. "Yes."

"What?" The long lashes shading her cheeks flew up. "Where'd you meet him? I didn't know you were seeing anybody, much less thinking about getting married." Tasha studied her suspiciously. "Is that why you quit?" she said, with a flash of curiosity. "Where's he from anyway? Somewhere in Europe, I bet." An enlightening smile curled on her plump, red lips. "Ooh...that's why Margo's so mad because you up and quit."

Maybe the best thing for everyone was to let Tasha think the marriage was real. "Look, don't say anything to him about my employment at Disclosure Magazine or what happened. I don't want him to start thinking he's robbed me of my career."

"Yeah, that's not a great way to start a marriage, is it?" She paused, reaching for a goblet of water. "Maybe you should just tell him you're an aspiring actress. That way, it's easy enough to explain away your lack of *real* work." Tasha was reiterating her parents objections to her acting career, or lack thereof, as Tasha was the epitome of an aspiring actress who hadn't caught her big break.

"I'll keep that in mind."

"I am curious about one thing though?" she said, with a hint of questioning in her tone. "When you called, why'd you say you were on a story?"

"I thought you'd try to talk me out of marrying Julian."

"Why would I do that?" she asked. "It's obvious he's crazy about you."

Surprise blasted through Camille. Tasha didn't need to see her composure crumbling. She held her breath and arrested the astonishment, holding it inside.

"When were you going to tell me?" Tasha threw an accusing glare at Camille.

"When I called to invite you to be a member of the wedding party for the ceremony in France." Well, it sounded good anyway.

"France?" Her mood changed, turning buoyant. "Are you shitting me?"

Camille shook her head. "His family lives in Marseilles. Most of the time."

She looked at Camille's attire again and drew a sharp breath, like she'd discovered the queen's jewels. "This guy's like super rich, isn't he?" The words came out like a question but there was no inquiry in her tone.

Camille considered lying. Again. But abandoned the idea. "Yes."

"Oh, man, no wonder you didn't tell me about him." Her devilish laughter validated Camille's reservations.

"Precisely."

"I wouldn't have hit on him, though. Not when you're so clearly into him."

Camille snorted. "Since when did that ever stop you?"

"Well okay, there was that one time," she said, as if it wasn't as important as Camille had deemed. "But he provoked me."

"Just stay away from Julian, okay."

"Oh, no worries there." Her mouth pulled into a tight-lipped smile. "He's not into me. He's all about you."

Good. She was glad Tasha saw it that way—no matter how distorted her view was. It saved Camille a lot of grief in the long run.

"Okay, so, remember not a word of Disclosure or any of that stuff." Camille hoped her stern voice was effective.

"Mum's the word." Her friend nodded her head slyly. "So, when's the French wedding?"

Camille had no idea. But she knew the European wedding needed to take place soon because of the pre-nup provisions. So, the sooner the better. "Probably a couple of weeks."

"I'll bet there are some hot guys in France. When do I get to come?"

"We'll see what Julian says. I don't even know where we're going to live." She laughed, her confidence wavering. "He said something about a family home in Marseilles."

"Oh, God, you're not going to have to live with his parents, are you?"

"Geez, I hope not."

Camille hadn't really thought about that, but she should've when he told her about his family home. Maybe she could talk him into leasing a place in Marseilles. If not, hopefully his family home was a really big house. The last thing she wanted was to feel like she was under someone's scrutinizing eye.

She saw Julian crossing a gardened path and straightened in her chair. "Oh, here's Julian."

Camille's gaze followed Tasha's to Julian who'd stopped a waiter in his path. After a few verbal exchanges the waiter walked away and Julian moved toward them, smiling at Camille. Sitting, he scooted his chair close to hers.

"Well, are we all set now?" he asked.

"Yep," Tasha said. "We're all on the same page." She reached for her glass. "I am invited to the wedding, right?" She asked Julian in particular.

"Of course you're invited to the wedding." He draped his arm around Camille's chair. "I'm sure Camille will want you by her side."

"Since the wedding isn't going to be for a couple of weeks, could Tasha join us in France in maybe a week or so?" Camille's insecurities leaked out as she spoke to Julian.

"Sounds perfect. Whatever you want." Julian glanced at Tasha. "I can send a jet for you when you're ready to come."

"A private jet?" Tasha's eyes lit with excitement, but she masked it with smooth composure. "Cool."

Uneasiness knotted inside Camille and escaped in her nervous laughter.

"Say, Julian...?" Tasha asked. "You got any brothers?"

"I have one brother."

"Older or younger?"

"Younger, by two years."

"Is he married?"

"No." Julian smiled.

Camille kicked Tasha's shin under the table.

"Ouch!" Tasha yelled and glared at Camille. She bent over, rubbing her leg.

Julian hid his chuckle behind a cough.

The waiter Julian had stopped to talk to earlier appeared with a tray of food, including a plate of hamburger and fries for Julian—he'd told Camille that he loved the American delicacy—and a slice of apple pie with a side of vanilla ice cream for Camille.

After serving them, the waiter hesitated over Tasha with a plate of cheesecake. "Mr. de Laurent asked me to choose something from the dessert menu for madam." He sat the dish in front of her. "I'm sure you'll find it to your liking. Or, if madam prefers something else...?"

"No, this is fine." Tasha smiled politely and grabbed her fork, ready to feast on the café's sweet treat.

As the trio munched, they reserved the conversation to minimal small talk until they'd nearly finished with their desserts.

"Well, Tasha, are you going back to L.A. tonight?" Julian asked, pushing his plate aside. "If you'd like to say in Vegas a couple of days, I can extend our villa upstairs for you." Julian paused, catching his breath. "I do hate to risk looking like a poor host, but we are due at the airport soon. We'll be leaving for London this afternoon."

"Well, Vegas ain't exactly London," she said in lighthearted quips. "But okay, I'll take it."

The three of them stood and went back inside the hotel lobby where Julian made sure the staff knew Tasha would be staying on through the end of the week—four days away. They were to see to her every need and desire.

Camille was surprised to learn that while they were lunching, her belongings inside the suite had been packed into brand new designer luggage. A notion that made Tasha swoon.

The girls said their goodbyes. Tasha went upstairs and Camille climbed into a limo with Julian, Soren, and Heinz, Julian's pilot. During the drive to the airport, uneasiness crept over Camille and left her with a troubled feeling. Leaving the country with three men she'd known for less than a week might not be construed as prudent.

She knew her qualms were crazy. Julian and Soren were honorable men; even though they came from two separate classes of society, their morals and principals were the same. Maybe that's why each was able to put so much faith and trust in the other. They got as good as they gave.

♡

At the airport, Julian showed Camille the stateroom on the plane. "Once we're in the air," he said, "you can rest in here if you'd like."

He wondered about Camille's friend. She was loud and flashy. The exact opposite of Camille. How had they become friends? But no matter, if Camille wanted her to come to France, he'd bring her there. Better yet, he'd send Andre to get her. That'd serve him right.

"So, we're going to London and then on to Marseilles?" she asked, as if she was just trying to fill the silence.

"We will spend a day or two in London where you can do a little more shopping." He felt an eager attraction coming from her and it pleased him. "Then we'll head to Paris where you'll meet with a designer or two."

"Designer? Why?"

"To make you the wedding dress of your dreams." One way or another, Julian was going to charm his way into his new wife's good graces. And at the end of six months, when he'd grown tired of her and she of him, they'd go their separate ways and he'd be free. Free from the bonds of matrimony his father was so sure he needed.

Her mouth opened in dismay, but she remained silent.

"What is it, Chéri?" Seeing the uncertainty in her eyes, a flash of loneliness stabbed at him. "A dress designed specifically for you does not please you?"

Her faint smile held a touch of sadness. "Julian, that's very generous of you." Camille's face went grim. Something was on her mind, and judging by the demure smile, she wasn't talking.

"But..."

"I guess dressing properly comes with playing the part, huh?"

"Well, you might as well enjoy it." Her lack of enthusiasm surprised Julian and somehow pleased him at the same time. Not that he didn't want his wife attired in the finest designs, but her indifference was appealing. There was something comforting in the notion that Camille was unmoved by designer fashions.

Julian wanted to see her smile though. "Someday, when you do it for real, you can just think of this as a...how do you Americans say it? A dry run?"

Camille's smile fell into laughter.

He thought he knew her problem. Camille was about to have the wedding of her dreams for a marriage that wasn't real. Women got that way about weddings. All mushy. Julian knew he should have considered the ramifications of their 'pretend marriage'. "Well, at least I can make you laugh."

She squared her shoulders and plastered on an overzealous smile. "From here on out I will play the part with complete enthusiasm and absolutely zero regret."

Julian wasn't sure if she believed what she'd told him. But it didn't matter. He trusted his instincts and they assured him Camille was the solution to his troubles. She held a certain appeal with her sentimental mind-set over a real dress for a faux wedding. No matter how hard she tried to hide it, Julian sensed her disappointment.

A soft knock in the hallway accompanied Soren's serene voice. "Sir, we're next in line for takeoff. We should take our seats."

Julian gave Camille a carefree shrug. "Shall we?"

She followed him into the lounge and they sat together on the couch.

"Did you tell your friend the truth?" he asked, fastening his seatbelt.

"No." Camille didn't bother looking his way until her belt was fastened. "I thought it was best to let her think it's real. Besides, wasn't that part of the deal?" she said in a peculiar searching way. "Everybody's supposed to think we're married in more than name only?"

She had a point. The fewer people aware of the scheme, the better their chances of success. So far, only three people knew. Julian, Camille, and Soren. If word did get out, it wouldn't be hard to unearth the culprit.

Julian fiddled with the jewelry box inside his jacket pocket. Camille was looking a bit disenchanted, but this might raise her spirits.

"Speaking of believability." He paused and pulled out the trinket box. "I thought you should have these," he added, offering her the gift.

Her eyes radiated joy. She accepted Julian's present and opened it as if it was made of fragile glass. She gasped and one hand flew to her chest. Her jaw dropped as she stared at the diamond-studded rings inside.

Julian slipped the box away from her and put the marriage symbol onto her ring finger. "Every beautiful bride deserves beautiful rings." He backed up his statement with a wink and a smile. "No matter the circumstances."

Her face softened into a desirous *I-want-to-believe-you* look.

She was caving; he could see it happening. In no time, Julian would win her over with his charms.

"Why me?" she finally said. "I know you said 'I'm perfect for the part'. But why?" she asked, as if she thought she was a speck of nothing. "What makes me perfect? And say, not my friend Tasha?"

"I'm sure your friend Tasha is a nice girl." He paused to stifle the derisive laughter charging up his throat.

A glint of understanding sparked in her eyes. He could see, deep down inside, she knew why even if she wasn't ready to admit it. Tasha was, in a word, *unrefined*.

"But..."

"She is, how do you say...?" He hesitated, searching tactfully for the right words. "A trophy wife."

Camille's entire body seemed to relax, as if she got it. "And Julian de Laurent wouldn't be caught dead with a *trophy wife*."

She did get it.

"If it's to be believable, my wife has to be a woman of substance and eloquent beauty." He waved his hands before him in a grand gesture. "She is the bride. Not the young lady who jumps out of the cake at the bachelor party."

The makings of a serpent's stare quickly gave way to a stony gaze before her eyes settled with approval.

"Underneath all that fluff Tasha has her moments." Camille's tone, hesitant and weak, suggested she was digging for something good to say. "She's been a good friend."

Julian sensed there was a 'but' lost in her thoughts and struggling to get out. It was up to him to help her forget about it. "Yes, and just the kind of girl my brother Andre will fall madly in love with." Julian laughed in a deep, jovial way. "Tell her to go easy on him."

"You keep your brother in check, and I'll do the same with my friend."

Always the diplomat. Julian liked that about Camille. He also liked that she was able to remain composed while under pressure. She'd need it, especially when it came to Papa and Madeleine. Julian would love to shield her from both. But for six months? It didn't seem possible.

"I doubt they will be half the problem that Papa and Madeleine will turn out to be." He eased it in there, half-hoping she wouldn't notice.

She did. Indicative of her head whipping in his direction.

"Who's Madeleine?" The inquiry clawed its way out, as if crawling over mountainous terrain.

"Madeleine is my father's choice," he said with a trivial, dismissive tone.

"That doesn't sound good." She stiffened and pulled away.

"But she'd is not my choice." He leaned closer to Camille. "All you have to remember, Chéri, is, *you* are my choice."

"Oh, I get that," she said with a touch of irritation. "But, just how far are your father and Madeleine willing to go?" Her eyes narrowed as she peered at him. "Will they be out for revenge?"

Denial shook Julian's head. "My father...no. But he will have a sharp eye out though, which is why we must appear real."

"And what about Madeleine?"

"Well, she's not going to be happy."

"Will she get violent?"

Madeleine? Violent? The notion was laughable. She wasn't the physical type, but that wouldn't stop her from trying to cause trouble. "She's not going to take this well. But you aren't in any physical danger, if that's what you're asking."

"So, I'll just have to be on my toes around Madeleine, because she's going to be out to sabotage me." She seemed to be filing informative tips away in her brain.

"Us. Sabotage us." Julian didn't want Camille thinking or feeling like she was in this alone.

She had to know and understand they were in this together. Julian couldn't afford to have her back out on him now. It meant the difference between six months of make-believe with a woman he found simply delightful, or a lifetime of nothing special with Madeleine.

Chapter Six

CAMILLE CHANDLER WAS AFRAID of the unknown. That fear fueled her continued support of Julian's harebrained scheme. She was terrified to start over. She had nothing to start over with. And Margo wasn't likely to ease up on her threats.

With five million dollars, Camille could go to some nondescript little town Margo had never heard of and get a job at the local paper—or hell, with that much money she could probably even buy the town's newspaper. That's it; she'd purchase a house and run the newspaper. Any money she had left over, she'd put the rest away for a rainy day.

That dream sounded better than the alternative: living on the streets and hoping to land a job at the local diner—a job she'd never worked in her life.

The stopover in London had been quick. Too quick, considering Julian's jilted lover and his father, who wasn't getting the daughter-in-law he desired, were waiting in France. The layover was also expensive, but probably not from Julian's point of view. No doubt, he was used to spending thousands on a single suit.

Not Camille. She considered anything upwards of fifty bucks a splurge. After stopping at a few of the finer boutiques, they were back on Julian's jet and headed for Paris. The afternoon spending spree—

dozens of outfits ranging from several hundred dollars to a few thousand—was a little unsettling.

In Paris, they made another quick stop and had a brief meeting with some designer, Marie something-or-other. Camille had never heard of her, which didn't mean much. Her wedding gown designs were supposed to be all the rage.

Julian promised Marie's questions, strange and off the wall, would give her insight into Camille's true personality and in the end, she'd be rewarded with the wedding dress of her dreams. Camille had her doubts, but five million bucks was ample motivation to yield to the designer's quirks.

After the appointment with Marie, Julian and Camille dined at a sidewalk café before returning to the airport.

Funny, the closer they got to Marseilles, the tighter Camille's nerves twisted in her gut. She almost wished she didn't know Julian's father and the girl he'd slighted would be out to get her. Well, probably not the father, but definitely the girl.

Camille was determined to disregard this new development and not give it a second thought. Julian had pledged to be on her side. He had just as much at stake as Camille, even if their motives were born from entirely different reasons.

She followed sheepishly behind Julian as they descended the stairs out of the aircraft. A light breeze blew a whiff of salt through the air. Camille looked around. Were they near the ocean?

Julian grabbed her hand at the bottom of the steps. "Remember, Chéri," he whispered in her ear. "From here on out, in public, we must appear in love."

His fingers remained tangled with hers. "I'll be so convincing—" She looked at Julian and smiled. "—even you'll think I'm in love."

They jumped into a Mercedes limousine waiting in the pickup area. The chauffeur, a tall, gangly fellow in a driver's suit, sprinted around the car and climbed behind the wheel. This time, Julian and Camille were alone in the limo. Where Soren and the pilot had gone, she didn't know.

Julian raised the glass partition between them and the driver. When it completely closed, he turned to Camille. "There will be times when you may not be able to find me. If that's the case and you need something, seek out Soren. Otherwise, don't be too open with the staff."

A quick and disturbing thought assailed Camille. Julian thought he'd hired an actress. Camille was no actress. What if she blew it? "Look I know this whole plan was born because you want to retain your freedom." The fear of being left alone with his family pushed her words out in a brittle, broken tone. "But you're not going to leave me alone for weeks on end, are you?"

"No, Chéri. If I go away on business, you will accompany me, just as it would be expected of any newlywed couple in love."

Camille's relief escaped in a quick deep breath. The further Julian kept her away from his father and Madeleine, the better.

"Don't be nervous." Julian's arm encircled Camille and snuggled her close.

"I know, I know. I'm perfect for the part." She was glad he thought so, but she had her doubts.

Camille's gaze traveled outside the window, her eyes drawn to the crowded city looming ahead. Old-World architecture peeked through the modern-day lampposts, traffic lights, and automobiles lining the paved streets. The ancient city had been effectively transformed into a twenty-first century metropolis.

As they left the jumbled urban center, the buildings diminished becoming sparse, replaced by rich, lush countryside. Camille was impressed with the winding roads and the grand estates perched atop rolling hills. The beauty of the landscape made the near-hour trip pass quickly.

The limousine turned off the main road and followed a tree-lined avenue twisting and winding its way up a hill. At the top, a barricade of ancient stone walls and massive pine trees guarded the fortress. When the path cleared, a sprawling chateau, three stories high in some places and with turrets on either side, sat majestically against the countryside. The site stole Camille's breath away.

Damn. Did this mean Julian had won that silly bet?

The car slowed to a stop in a covered archway where a group of people, presumably Julian's family, were waiting. Camille felt like she was in the midst of some strange foreign film.

An older couple stood alongside a man about Julian's age and a young girl. And behind them, a row of servants—Camille figured them for servants because of their attire. The men were dressed like Soren and the women had on maids' uniforms.

Camille climbed out of the car with Julian's help. He rested one hand against the small of her back and led her to the older couple first. His parents, Maurice and Claudette de Laurent.

Julian's brother—and if Camille remembered correctly, his younger brother—peered at her with cold, judging eyes that were almost the same color as Julian's bluish-green, but maybe a little paler.

His sister Lecie was maybe eighteen and the epitome of the beautiful girl-next-door. Camille knew the type. With her blonde hair and blue-eyed good looks, she was everything all the other girls in school detested yet desired to be. And she was probably nice as hell to boot.

She hated it when she was forced to like those drop-dead gorgeous types—like Tasha.

Camille fidgeted, lacing her fingers together behind her back. Julian slipped a hand comfortingly around hers. How was she ever going to convince his entire family? There were so many of them. Parents, a brother, a sister. She'd never experienced the chaos of a big family. It'd always been just her and Granny Mae. Even holidays were quiet.

Lecie stepped toward Camille. Julian must have sensed her discomfort and slipped between them, making small talk with his sister and asking about her latest endeavors and if she'd chosen a university to begin her studies in the fall.

"Somewhere far away from here," she answered in near-perfect English.

Camille laughed, thoroughly amused. She remembered feeling that way when she'd headed out for college. Now she'd give anything to talk to Granny Mae again.

"Tell me," Lecie turned to Camille. "Where did you two meet? Was it romantic? I want to hear all about it." The enthusiasm in her voice fueled Camille's mounting fear.

She and Julian had never talked about where they were supposed to have met. They had to have a story, didn't they? Asking people to believe they'd accidentally fallen in love after she answered his ad in the L.A. Trades was probably asking a bit too much.

Camille squeezed Julian's hand, hoping to impart some of her worry to him.

"We'll talk about that later." Julian's promising tone was convincing, even for Camille. "Right now, let's let Camille settle in so she can rest before dinner." He guided Camille up an outdoor set of stairs that looked like it was made of marble, and led to an impressive set of double doors.

Lecie trotted up the steps after them, her devilish laughter tapping the worry receptors in Camille's brain. Camille sought to push the alarm aside.

"You'll both need to rest up," Lecie said, as if she was privy to some secret information. "Guess who's coming to dinner?"

If she said Madeleine, Camille would just burst.

Julian raised an eyebrow. "How many guests are we having?"

"Just a small party," she said, with a teasing wink. "About thirty."

Camille's heart jumped into her throat. It didn't take a genius to realize Madeleine would be seated next to Julian while Camille, his supposed fiancée, would be at the other end of a very long table.

Julian opened the double doors to the most elegant and extravagant foyer of marble and granite Camille had ever seen. Lecie grabbed her free arm and Camille clung to Julian with the other. He wrapped her arm around his. The strength of his hand atop hers was so male, so agreeable.

"Over here," he said, pointing to the right, "are a couple of salons, a library, and my father's office." Julian focused his attention in the opposite direction. "And over here are several dining rooms and the kitchen. It's fully modernized now, but the old hearth my ancestors used is still intact and in working order." He chuckled. "Not that today's servants relish the idea of cooking over an open fire."

The fireplace in the kitchen intrigued Camille, but Julian led her to a spiral staircase just in front of them. Somewhere along the way they'd lost Lecie, and Camille found herself alone with Julian as they climbed the stairs.

"You and I are on the third floor. Technically, the entryway is on the second." He wrapped his arm around her midriff and her body tingled from the contact. She wondered what it would be like getting locked in Julian's embrace, but she didn't dare voice the thought out loud.

He led her around a corner and swung a door open, gesturing her inside. From out of nowhere, Lecie appeared behind them.

Camille put forth extra effort to push her doubts aside. She needed a friend in this place. The next six months might be unbearable without one. She stepped into the room, surprised to find her recent purchases and her luggage already inside the suite.

Julian stopped in the doorway, blocking his sister's entry. "We will see you in a little while," he said, and closed the door between them.

The most sorrowful look crossed his face when he turned to Camille. "I am sorry, Chéri. The thought of where or how we met never crossed my mind," he said, extending his arms.

Outstretched arms. Too tempting.

She rested her forehead in the palms of her hands. Doubts over the mess wobbled her head. There were too many holes. Their story hadn't been thought out clearly.

"How are we ever going to make anyone believe you came to America last week, we fell in love and now we're getting married?" Camille flung her hands into the air. "France would have to be full of a bunch of idiots for us to pull that off."

"Your friend believed it." Julian beamed at her with a look that was as soft as a caress. A dizzying current raced through her. She had to get a hold of that emotion, and quick.

"Well, not exactly. I didn't tell her we just met."

"And I didn't tell anybody we'd just met either."

Camille dropped onto a couch by a massive wall of windows overlooking an infinity pool that appeared to spill into the gardens below. Off in the distance, coastal mountains gave way to the Mediterranean.

Now she understood why Granny Mae called them picture windows. This one, in *her* room, held the grandest view of all—especially when Julian stepped into the scene.

"What did you tell your father?" Camille wanted to minimize the impact his presence was having over her, but she wasn't having much luck. "You said he wanted you to marry Madeleine. What'd you do? Tell him you had a girl stashed away in the States?" She laughed at the ridiculousness of that notion.

"Something like that."

"What?"

"Last year, I spent some time, several months in New York City on business." He showed no signs of relenting to his father's wishes. "I told him that I couldn't marry Madeleine because I was in love with someone else, a girl I'd met while in America."

Talk about lame.

"And he bought that?"

Julian's smugness escaped in his complacent shrug. "I'm told he has a soft spot where I'm concerned. He wants to believe the best about me." He tightened his lips to hold back the laughter and sat beside her. "I'll admit, I have used that to my advantage more than once."

"You'd better remember that when you become a father."

♡

Her laughter crawled up Julian's leg and smacked him in the gut. *When I have children.* Julian wasn't going to have children. But if he did, he could see Camille as their mother.

Suddenly, the topic wasn't funny anymore. This girl, an actress, was supposed to be a means to an end—not somebody that started him thinking about children. Realizing he was sitting too close for comfort, he backed away from her.

Her eyes grew openly amused. "Uncomfortable talking about kids?"

"It's a little scary," he admitted.

She pushed aside the fleeting thought to wonder why. Adding to his anxiety wasn't conducive. "So, you and I met when you were in New York last year."

"Yes."

"Where'd we meet?"

"Hm...."

"We can say I worked for one of your associate firms, writing technical reports."

Julian was surprised at the validity of her suggestion. Nobody would ask her about a job like that. "Perfect."

"But I need to say that I'm from L.A., because I don't really know anything about New York."

"How would you like to abstain from tonight's party?" he asked, hopeful. First, they'd ditch the millions of questions they weren't prepared for. And second, he wouldn't mind some alone time with his new wife.

Her whole face spread into an energetic smile. "Could we?"

"You bet we can." He leaned toward her and brushed his lips against her cheek. Her skin was so soft, intoxicating. "We'll sneak out a couple of hours before dinner." Devilish laughter rose in Julian's throat, allowing him to regain his senses. Disappointment rolled over him at the thought of not being around to see Papa's face when he realized they were gone.

The possibilities of where to take her, where to woo her, filled his mind and chased away his fleeting regret. Wherever they went, it had to be special because it would take more than ordinary wining and dining to charm her into his bed.

♡

Julian slipped quietly through the chateau's hidden passageways. He knew all the routes and intersections well, as he'd played in them as a child. The tunnels hadn't changed. They were still dark, damp and daunting.

He slipped into the east salon. It was empty. Thank God. Julian poured Scotch into a chilled glass and strolled to the window overlooking the east pool and rose gardens.

Camille had caught him off guard when she said something about him having children. That'd never crossed his mind, much less the notion to settle down with just one woman. Least of all Madeleine.

What was wrong with Madeleine? She was pretty enough. She'd been conditioned for the part since childhood. She was educated, polished, and personable. But Julian felt nothing when he looked at her. No spark.

That's why his decision to formulate this orchestrated marriage was the right thing to do. It'd save Madeleine some grief, his sanity, and a ton of money in the long run.

Julian drained his glass and moved back to the bar. He poured another drink as a passageway door opened. A different one than he'd used.

Andre. Julian found it ironic that his younger brother by three years had outgrown him by a couple of inches.

Approaching Julian, Andre laughed. "Well, big brother," he said, reaching for a bottle of bourbon and a glass. "You do have the market cornered on the shock factor."

"What do you mean by that?" Julian poured the drink into his mouth, savoring the whiskey's cool bite.

"You and father have an argument. The worst I've seen yet." Andre studied Julian and took another drink of his liquid courage. "He wants an heir. And since you're the oldest, he expects you to give him one."

"What's your point?"

"So you do what you do best," he said, his tone growing bitter, less tolerant. "You disappear. Then, mysteriously, you return a week later with an American fiancée."

"Again. What's your point, baby brother?"

"Are we really expected to believe this is real?"

"You think I'd marry someone if it wasn't?" Julian asked.

"You? Sure."

"If that were the case, it might as well be Madeleine."

"Anything not to marry Madeleine." Andre reflected with grim amusement. "I hope you know what you're doing."

"What's that supposed to mean?" Somewhere deep down inside, Julian hoped his brother understood.

"How well do you know this girl? How do you know she's not—"

"I've known her since last year, Andre. And make no mistake—" Julian waved a finger in Andre's face. "—be very careful what you say about my wife."

"Your wife?" Andre gave him a sideways glance of utter disbelief.

"Yes." Julian sat the glass down and slid his hands inside his pockets. "Between you and me, Camille and I are already married."

"Married?"

"Married."

Andre gave him a dismissive gesture. "You know Papa's going to be furious. And he's going to want a French wedding."

"Well, he can be pushy." Julian was casually amused. "He won't believe it's real unless he witnesses it for himself." He laughed to hide his discomfort over Papa's control.

Andre shook his head. "Man, I hope you don't end up regretting this."

"There are no regrets."

"You just up and got married? I can hardly believe that." Andre stroked his chin and studied Julian. "Pre-nup?"

"Yes. We have a pre-nup." Sarcasm crept into Julian's voice. "I know what you're thinking, but you're mistaken."

Andre couldn't be more wrong. Julian knew exactly what he was getting with Camille and how much it was going to cost him. Five million dollars.

"For your sake, big brother, I hope you're right." Andre smirked and poured himself another drink. "I certainly don't want her dipping into my children's inheritances."

"You don't have any children."

"Not yet. No." Andre paused, sipping his bourbon. "But someday I think I might. And I don't want your gold-digging wife stealing from them."

Rage almost choked Julian. Curses fell from his mouth as he grabbed his brother's lapels and slammed him against the wall. He didn't care whether he hurt Andre or not. Nor would he tolerate trash talk about Camille. He'd take that from no one.

"Julian...!" Andre's voice cracked.

"Be. Very. Careful." Julian's jaw clinched as he tried to contain his anger. The fury quaked through him, diminishing as it rippled out. He reached up and gave Andre a light slap on the cheek. "Watch what you say about my wife."

Heated anger burned against Julian's face. He was a fragile thread away from the breaking point, and by the looks of Andre—eyes widened with a mixture of fear and uncertainty—he saw it too. And when Julian snapped, nobody wanted to be in his path.

Andre raised his hands in surrender. "All right. I'm sorry. I shouldn't have said that about your girl." He tried to squirm out of Julian's grasp. Julian let him. "It was rude and inconsiderate."

Julian shifted his focus to his glass. He needed a refill. Why had he done that? He'd never raised a hand to his brother. "I'm sorry." He overfilled his glass with more than the usual double shot. "I'm sorry," he repeated himself, feeling like a heel. He'd always protected Andre, never threatened him. Julian drained his glass.

"I hope she cares about you, half as much as you care about her." Andre cleared his throat around his fragile, shaking voice and perched his hands on his hips. "If she does, you two will be all right."

Care about her? Disbelief and confusion muddled Julian's brain. He didn't *care* about her. What Julian cared about was his freedom.

"You might be interested in knowing that Papa's not taking this lying down." Andre's confidence returned with an agreeable nod. He slid his hands inside his pockets and stepped toward Julian.

Andre's words bothered Julian more than his closeness. He looked at his little brother. "What's he doing?"

One could never feel too comfortable when Maurice de Laurent implemented one of his crazy, harebrained schemes. Julian was well aware of where he'd acquired that trait. His own scheme had Papa written all over it. And if not for the fact that the idea was born to dupe him, his father would probably be proud of the ingenuity.

Julian didn't like the stark look on Andre's face.

Not Madeleine. "No...." The word ground out like tires bouncing over ruts in a gravel road. "Please tell me he hasn't invited Madeleine here as our guest?" Even though he doubted his chances, he still held a flicker of hope that he was wrong.

"That he has." Andre's reluctance was overshadowed by the message.

"Why would he do that?"

Was Papa really that sadistic? Sure, Julian didn't want to marry Madeleine, but he didn't have anything against her either. Not enough to induce him to force her to sit around and watch him marry another woman.

"I suspect he thinks he can thwart your efforts to marry your American...wife." Andre snickered, as if finding perverse pleasure in Julian's predicament. "But, before you start feeling too sorry for Madeleine, remember...she and Papa are cut from the same cloth." His voice took on a warning tone. "She won't accept your engagement lightly either."

All the more reason to avoid this evening's dinner party. Especially if Madeleine was going to be there, which she obviously was since she was in the house.

Julian was going to have to intensify his efforts to shelter Camille now that Papa and Madeleine were obviously up to no good.

Chapter Seven

JULIAN GAZED AT CAMILLE in her black dress with its crocheted look. It was sexy. An approving moan rumbled up his throat and he grabbed her hand, moving toward an inner wall inside the third floor salon. He glanced at her, winked and popped a wall panel open.

A soft gasp escaped her. "What the...."

"There are tunnels all over the estate." He coaxed her inside. "We'll make our escape through here." It beat running into Papa, Claudette, or Madeleine in the hallways.

"Ooh, I feel like a spy." She giggled as they enter the dimly lit tunnel.

Julian chuckled. "Yeah. A spy whose sanity depends on her escape." He quickened his pace. He wasn't the only one well-versed in these tunnel paths. The quicker they got outside and through the gardens, the better.

They hurried through corridors, descended steps cut into the ground and rounded corners, all in near-darkness. Camille tightened her grip on his hand.

"Don't worry, Chéri. I know this place inside and out."

"God, I hope so." Her rich laughter wrapped him in amusement.

"We're almost there," he said in a low, husky voice.

After a few more feet and another curve to the left, Julian gave Camille a tug and pulled her closer before stopping to push his way through the outside exit.

The twilight of a setting sun filtered inside, casting a flattering glow over Camille. Her golden hair glistened like strands of lustrous glass, and he felt a ripple of excitement when her mouth curved into a tempting smile.

"What are the chances somebody's going to be waiting for us out here?" she asked, and he got the feeling she was trying to be funny. And she would be, so long as she wasn't right.

"I'll let you know." He checked the immediate area just outside the exit.

All clear. Good. Not that he was afraid to face them. But this was more fun. Sexy even. A faint light twinkling in her blue eyes told him she was just as excited.

Julian latched onto Camille's hand. Joy bubbled over in her laughter as they raced along designated paths through the rose garden. Her happiness brought Julian a sense of satisfaction. It'd been a long time since he'd had this much fun.

Adrenaline sped through him, increasing ferociously when the tunneled gateway to the river came into view. Just as he'd arranged, a speedboat was waiting at water's edge, ready to assist them in their escape.

Julian helped Camille before climbing aboard. The boat thundered to life and the engine's vibrations roared through him, stimulating his adrenaline and his aspirations. He'd taken plenty of boat rides, and with a number of girls including Madeleine, but none had aroused him like this ride with Camille. Maybe it was just the thrill of the escape. Yes. That had to be the reason.

Camille sat on the seat next to him, perched in a model-like pose. Her legs, long and tanned, rose from red shoes and traveled seductively up until they disappeared underneath a black cocktail dress riding midway up her thighs. He liked the dress when they'd bought it in London, and he liked it now—especially now, as he envisioned slipping his hands beneath the fabric in an exploring fashion.

The boat charged down the winding river and a warm summer's wind whipped Julian's hair around wildly. Raking it back, he looked at Camille. Their gazes met, and a faint delicate flush glowed against her face.

"You okay?" He reached over, laying his hand at her knee.

"Yeah," Her breathless declaration murmured out from behind a smile. "Where are we going?"

"Where would you like to go?"

"It's your country. I'm leaving it up to you."

Was she always this complying? Maybe he'd test that theory. "So, if I said, we're going to see the symphony or an opera...you'd be up for that?"

"You didn't say, '*what do you want to do*'." She challenged him with her dauntless blue eyes. "You said, '*where would you like to go*'."

"Okay." Julian laughed. "What do you want to do?"

"Well...how about dinner and then maybe a walk on the beach or something?" An alluring smile implied she was inviting trouble.

Not that Julian wanted to tempt fate. He just wanted to explore what was underneath that little black dress. It couldn't hurt. They *were* supposed to be in love.

"Good call. After all, we are thought to be lovers, are we not?" He reassured her with a soft caress over the bare portion of her thigh. But he didn't push it. He didn't invite himself to further exploration. Not yet.

"I'm just trying to cover all our bases," she said, her voice strengthening as if she'd regained some of her confidence.

"What are you in the mood for?"

"What do you mean?"

"What kind of food?"

"How about something local?"

Good answer. Not too specific, but she narrowed it down just the same, and complimented his hometown by keeping it 'local'. Very pleasing.

Maybe he'd take her to L'Epuisette. That way, he could sate her palate with the best food around and reduce her inhibitions with some good champagne. He cut the boat's engine and coasted alongside the pier, landing near his driver waiting by the car.

Julian stood and helped Camille to her feet. He liked the way the boat ride had tousled her hair, leaving it all windblown and sexy-looking. Their exhilarating escape reddened her cheeks.

He handed her off to Sebastian, his driver, who helped her out of the boat. She climbed up onto the landing and Julian enjoyed the advantageous view for admiring her assets. Her legs, bare and gleaming, continued to arouse him. Her dress hugged her hips, teasing him. Her laughter filled him with not just joy, but hope. Hope that when this was all over, he'd surface as the victor.

Camille could've gone straight to the car, but she didn't. Surprisingly, she stood on the edge of the dock, waiting for him to emerge from the boat. She was the first to do that. There had been plenty who'd traversed the river with him, but none had ever thought of him. Not once. Until Camille.

For someone who was in it for material gain, she was doing a hell of a job at making Julian feel like she was here for him.

♡

Camille waited for Julian on the landing. Mainly because she wasn't about to get into the car without him. The suspicious sort, there weren't many people she trusted. But she trusted Julian—sort of—yet there was no reason to offer blind faith to his employees.

Julian grinned at her and grabbed her hand. His manly grasp settled a warmth over Camille that she wasn't used to. She followed him to the car and Sebastian opened the door. Julian laid his palm against the small of her back, guiding her inside.

He slid in beside her and loosened his tie. The citrus scent of his cologne intoxicated her. Feeling a bit overwhelmed, she smoothed her dress and rested her hands in her lap.

"Would you like a glass of champagne?"

Her first thought was to say no. Drinking on an empty stomach had never turned out well in the past. But a sip or two wouldn't hurt, and it might help her lighten up. She wanted to enjoy the evening, not worry about what she was doing right or wrong.

But what could she do that would chase Julian away?

He wasn't going to up and leave her. Not yet anyway. For the next six months she could count on Julian more than she'd ever been able to count on anybody else—except maybe Granny Mae.

"Maybe a touch," she said of the champagne.

Julian grabbed a bottle, popped the top and poured the overflowing spirits into two glasses. He handed one to her and kept the other for himself.

She sipped the liquor, bubbles tickling her nose. She didn't care much for the tart taste, but she supposed people put up with it for the buzz. Still, there had to be a better way. At least a better tasting way. Maybe a Pina Colada, a Daiquiri, or something made with melon liqueur. Yeah, that sounded good.

She might get one of those during dinner, but for now she'd go with what was on hand.

Julian downed his drink, and it didn't go unnoticed by Camille. He turned to her, draping his arm along the back of the seat behind her. "If Papa or Madeleine get to be too much, just tell them to talk to me."

He was beating around the bush about something, what she wasn't sure. "Are you expecting them to get out of hand?" Her fingers stiffened around her glass.

"No, I don't think so. But Papa has invited Madeleine to stay through the wedding."

Camille shrugged to hide her confusion. "She must be a glutton for punishment."

"I wondered about that myself."

"Why would she want to attend a wedding in which she aspired to be the bride?"

"Papa is probably to blame." Julian refilled his glass. "I think he's probably put it in her head that she can somehow thwart the wedding." He glanced at Camille with the champagne bottle in the air, as if waiting for her to request or decline more.

She did neither. "So, I should keep a sharp eye out?" Camille fidgeted, not liking the idea that Madeleine could smash her dreams beyond repair.

"Couldn't hurt." His fingertips caressed her hair back from her face. His touch was suddenly almost unbearable in its tenderness.

She drew her head back, facets of desire shuddering through her.

"Will I be catching the two of you in bed?" She laughed, mostly because she'd come to believe that Papa and Madeleine would be the main topic of all their conversations. It reiterated the fact that Julian de Laurent would never be interested in *her*. She was just a means to an end. A way out of real matrimony.

"If Madeleine has her way...I wouldn't doubt it." Julian's laughter wrapped its cold tips around her heart.

But why wouldn't Julian sleep with Madeleine. He'd already said he didn't have anything against her. Just like most men, Julian probably wouldn't mind sleeping with a girl he wasn't interested in marrying.

And Julian and Camille? They were merely in a business arrangement. He had no real alignment to her, and thinking otherwise was crazy.

Prepare yourself, chickie. She heard her warning loud and clear. Julian had all but told Camille she'd be finding him in bed with his mistress.

But no matter. Camille was prepared to play the dutiful wife to the hilt. The payoff was worth it. And in the meantime, she was going to enjoy being the wife of one of the richest men in the world—for as long as it lasted.

"Have you decided where we'll be eating?" she asked, trying to keep the mood light.

"Since you expressed an interest in the local cuisine, I thought we'd dine at L'Epuisette."

I say eat; he says dine. The subtle differences in their vocabulary wrapped her in a straitjacket of unworthiness. Suddenly she felt unintelligent, uneducated, and undeserving, even though she'd graduated from Stanford University with honors.

"It sounds lovely." Her words drifted off into a hushed whisper.

"You'll enjoy it. I promise." That chocolaty tone of Julian's voice returned, sounding more enticing than ever. She was caught up in his enthusiasm.

"It has to be awesome," she said with conviction. "You've never let me down yet."

He studied her, like he was amazed—or maybe it was amused. "You keep that up and Papa will fall in love with you." His statement, bold and brassy, skittered her pulse.

She felt her face burn, and she hoped the dim, almost nonexistent light hid her weakness.

The car rolled to a stop in front of a wood-planked building on the edge of the sea. The doorman stepped forward and opened the car door.

The warm night air breezed past and caressed her bare arms as Julian nudged her from the limousine. Tantalizing thoughts invaded her head. Julian grabbed her hand and she prayed he didn't notice her shivering reaction.

"Are you cold?" he asked, draping his arm around her shoulders as they strolled toward the restaurant's entrance.

"No." She smiled, hoping to convey that she didn't mind his touch. "Everything's perfect."

Julian rested his hand on the small of her back as they entered the restaurant's lobby.

"Mr. de Laurent." They were greeted with smiles and hellos and handshakes. "Your table is ready."

They followed the maître'd through the restaurant. Tasteful wall hangings and pleated drapes divided the dining area into intimate sectors and the privacy they afforded more than made up for the establishment's overcrowded popularity.

The dimly lit ambiance mesmerized Camille as they followed the maître'd up a short flight of stairs and out onto a private balcony, amply shrouded in shrubbery and foliage. They were led to a secluded table against a tall banister overlooking the sea. She guessed this was Julian's *regular* table.

Camille sighed, happily relieved over the privacy. Pretending to be in love was going to take some adjusting. Easy for an actress, but not Camille.

Julian remained standing while the waiter seated her. Nobody had ever done that for Camille. With just two chairs at the small table, he sat with his back to the railing and reached across the table for her hand.

She succumbed, but reminded herself this was Julian's staple for wooing the ladies. He probably brought all his conquests here to fill their tummies and get them in the mood so he could win their favors. And he'd brought her here just to keep up the charade. But she wasn't one of his conquests. She was his business partner.

"Would you care to see a wine list?" the waiter asked.

Julian rattled off something in French, and Camille didn't doubt they'd soon be drinking the finest champagne France had to offer.

But damn. She'd just as soon sip on a cocktail. Something sweet, exotic, and intoxicating.

The waiter walked away and Julian fiddled with his jacket and tie and beamed at her with an overdone smile. "What's your pleasure? Chicken, seafood or steak?"

"I have to choose one?"

Julian howled. But it was a good kind of laughter. An enjoyable one. "Chéri, you can have everything on the menu, if that's your desire."

Her desire was a Pina Colada. And why couldn't she ask for one? Why was she trying to appear so agreeable? She didn't need to impress Julian. She just needed to stay put and not leave.

She leaned toward him. "Julian," she whispered, "do they serve cocktails here? I'd so love something fruity and sweet."

He looked crushed. "I'm sorry, Chéri."

The waiter appeared, ready to take their order.

Julian focused on Camille. "What would you like to drink? Margarita? Pina Colada?"

"A Pina Colada would be awesome."

Julian turned to the waiter and rattled off some directions in French. She thought she caught a few of the words, French terms for chicken, beef, and some kind of fish, crustacean maybe. Was he ordering a little bit of everything, just to please her? She could see why Madeleine wasn't willing to let Julian go so easily.

Madeleine was the least of her worries, so long as the girl didn't expose Camille and Julian's scheme. Camille tossed the potential threat aside and contemplated the dessert menu.

One waiter left and another appeared with her drink, topped off with fresh strawberries, pineapple and maraschino cherries. She went for the fruit, devouring the strawberry and savoring every morsel.

Camille glanced at Julian. He was ranging his glance up and down, gauging her with a seductive gleam. She'd swear he had x-ray eyes. Desire danced with her heart. She wavered and looked away, grabbing her Pina Colada.

"Is this your first time in Europe, Chéri?" Julian looked as surprised by his question as she felt.

"Yes." Overwrought with feelings of inadequacy, she siphoned her drink up the straw.

"Is there anywhere special that you'd like to see while you're here?" he asked. "We have ample time. Would you like to tour?"

Camille wasn't comfortable saying, *yes, I'd like to tour Europe*. It reeked of *taking advantage*. But they would be going on a honeymoon, wouldn't they? She drained more of the Pina Colada and a relaxing sensation warmed her. "You know," she said, half encouraged by the liquor's temporary confidence. "I've always wanted to see the Greek Isles."

"By ship?"

"A cruise?" She absent-mindedly chewed on her straw.

"How about a yacht?"

A yacht? That sounded wonderful. "If you're trying to win points, de Laurent, you're well on your way." She smiled, laced her fingers around the shapely cocktail glass and slurped the bottom of the empty frozen treat.

The waiter brought them an appetizer plate of pan-fried prawns and cannelloni. He glanced at Julian, who motioned to Camille's glass and then nodded him away post-haste.

"How many points do I need to get something good?" Julian asked Camille, and then drained his champagne glass.

"Just two more." She giggled. The liquor kept her from blushing. "So pay attention."

She laughed and reached for a prawn. Not only did it taste divine, but she needed to put something on her stomach since she wasn't a big drinker.

"Speaking of debts." He let the words linger on his tongue.

Camille got the feeling this wasn't going to be good. Was he going to claim his prize for their bet over Pacifique de Lumière?

"Okay. Okay." She laughed it off. "I was suitably impressed. You win." She forced her gaze up to meet his. "So, what's your reward?"

"Nothing more than the pleasure of your company, Chéri," he said with a smile that could melt Antarctica.

Damn. This guy was good. If he made a pass, Camille doubted she'd be able to resist.

A smorgasbord of food arrived just in time to keep her from throwing herself at him, and filled all the vacant space on the table.

Julian was invitingly attentive, filling her plate with samples from all the dishes, a variety of lobster, escargot, lamb, duck and filet mignon.

She nibbled on lobster dipped in butter, savoring the sweet, creamy flavors. "So, when exactly are we getting married here?"

"I think the sooner the better," he said between bites of lamb and steak. "I'd like to send my brother for your friend in a day or two, and then we can have the ceremony at the end of the week." His sea-green eyes studied her face. "How does that sound?"

She propped her elbow on the table and rested her chin in her hand. Excuses danced across her mind, none of them viable enough to stick. "Sounds fine." Not interested in finding a reason to say 'no', she turned her focus to the delectable fares. "What's this?" she asked, pointing to a bowl of small shells in butter sauce. She had ideas about the dish's identity but refrained from passing judgment.

"Escargot," he said as if it was no big deal, but there wasn't any on his plate.

She swallowed hard and tried to push the confirmation out of her head. "I'm not really in to snails." She took quick short breaths, nausea setting in. "In fact, they're kind of gross."

Julian laughed. "My sentiments exactly, Chéri. You're probably the first person I've met who doesn't enjoy the delicacy."

Camille giggled. "Care to make a wager on how many people eat these things and actually like them?" She tossed her hair back over her shoulder. "I know a lot of people who wouldn't touch that stuff with a ten foot pole." She scooped the shell up between two fingers and inspected it. *Ugh!* Distaste rattled her shoulders.

Julian laughed again, picked up the plate of Escargot and passed it to the attendant waiting near the door. "Please, take this to the kitchen," he said, with an impersonal nod.

It bothered Camille, the way he talked to the restaurant's staff. How long before he'd start talking to her that way? She too, after all, was hired help.

♡

Camille had grown quiet all of a sudden. It bothered Julian when she did that. He didn't like wondering if he'd done or said something wrong. Her disappointed looks showered him with feelings of inadequacy.

Even so, her hearty appetite was refreshing. Dining with a girl who wasn't afraid to eat was pleasing. Julian was going to enjoy the next six months.

An attendant cleared away the last of their nearly empty plates.

Julian wondered what else he could do to charm Camille. Of course, she had asked to go for a walk along the beach, but what else would make the occasion special?

The waiter approached the table. "Would the lady care for some dessert?"

Excellent idea. Julian gave Camille a 'would you?' look.

"Oh, man." A smile touched her lips and her features softened. "Would I."

She perused the menu, and as Julian anticipated, she couldn't decide on just one, so they ordered an English Trifle and a Chocolate Crème Brulée to go. Julian envisioned a midnight picnic on the beach, complete with sweets and champagne.

He discreetly took care of the bill and they headed outside with their desserts. Camille's laughter filled the air as they scooted into the limo. He flipped a small refrigerator compartment open and popped the containers inside.

"You still up for that walk on the beach?" he asked, leaning back against the seat.

"You bet I am." She giggled, smiled and snuggled close to him.

"Great, I know just the place." Julian hit the intercom and rattled off something in French to the driver.

Instantly, Sebastian navigated the car into the street. Julian glanced at the city lights streaking by as they sped down the roadway. It was a view he'd seen many times, but tonight it seemed better somehow.

Moments later, the car rolled to a stop in a deserted parking lot and Sebastian stepped out and opened the door. Julian rolled out and extended his hand to Camille. Delicate fingers latched onto his and she emerged from the vehicle.

She adjusted the wrap around her shoulders and Julian draped his arm around her, trying to offer her comfort.

"I have a surprise for you." His voice held a rasp of excitement.

"Really?" She looked at him and flashed an eager smile.

"Yes. I think you'll be delighted." He let the mystery linger on his tone as he motioned to the driver.

Sebastian fiddled around in the car for a moment and then followed them with a blanket, the desserts and a bottle of champagne.

"You do this often?" she asked, half in anticipation, half in dread.

"No," he said sharply, abandoning all pretense. Julian drew a calming breath and comforted his mind. "You said you'd like to go for a walk on the beach, so while we were having dinner Sebastian secured the blanket. I thought you might like to do a little stargazing while we relaxed to the soothing sounds of the sea."

Julian didn't blame her for being suspicious of his motives. He would be, too. Most people had an angle. He was no exception. But Camille sure was. He'd have to tread lightly if he wanted to win this prize. And, he prided himself on being an expert in the art of wooing a woman into his bed.

After a few steps, she stopped, used him as a prop and slipped off her shoes. She dangled them in one hand, clung to him with the other and let him lead her forward.

The beach was as deserted as the parking lot, and Julian saw no sense in journeying far. This spot was just as good as any further down. He stopped and made a grand gesture toward the water. "How's this?" He waited for her answer. "Shall we have our dessert here, do you think?" Getting the lady's approval was always best. That way, she never felt like she was being backed into a corner.

"Sure. This is great." She glanced back at the car, a relieved look crossing her face.

Sebastian spread the blanket over the sand in front of them, and Julian removed his jacket and shoes. He laid lengthwise on the edge of the coverlet and patted near him on the blanket.

With a bit of reluctance, she dropped to the ground and readjusted her wrap again. She must be cold. Julian draped his jacket around her and coaxed her back against his torso.

Sebastian readied the desserts and handed plates and a fork to each of them. He popped the top on the champagne and poured two glasses. "Here you are, Miss Camille."

She took one glass, and Julian the other.

"Will there be anything else, sir?" Sebastian directed the inquiry to Julian.

"No, Sebastian. That'll be all."

The driver didn't hesitate. He backed a few steps away, turned and put his usual twenty feet between them.

"How is your Trifle?" Julian asked, trying the Crème Brulée.

"This is so-o-o-o good." She made an almost erotic sound. "It ought to be illegal." Her laughter reached out and wrapped him in a tender desire. He'd never wanted a woman quite so badly. "How's the chocolate?"

Julian cut a small bite from his dessert and scooped it onto the fork. "Try it."

She willingly accepted a taste of his treat. Her demeanor pleased him. She was open to his advances, yet independent enough to speak her mind. Like with the snails at dinner.

Thanks to Camille, Julian now knew he didn't want a 'yes woman' in his life. Still, he'd appreciate one who followed his lead once in a while.

"Oh, man...that's awesome," she said, pointing her fork at Julian's plate. "Here, try this." She scooped the trifle onto her fork and fed him.

He let the food melt in his mouth, savoring the sweet flavors.

"Isn't that great?" she asked with a lingering smile.

"Wonderful." He stared at Camille. She was an absolute treasure.

Julian drew a deep breath and reminded himself of what they were doing. Pretending. Pretending to be in love so he could keep his freedom. He had to remember to act the part but not feel it. How did she do it? She looked totally enamored with him. Why wasn't she some big-name actress making twenty million a film?

Camille sipped the champagne and studied at him with her intense blue eyes. "So, you're going to send your brother for Tasha soon?"

"Yes. I think tomorrow." He checked his watch. Nine o'clock. It was probably about noon or so in L.A. "You should give her a call later."

"I will."

"How about your parents?" Julian set his plate on the ground. She did the same. "Should we invite them over?"

Her response was a resounding headshake. Why didn't she want her parents there? Because it wasn't real.

"It would look more authentic if they were to attend." The urge to caress her face overwhelmed Julian. "Besides...they'd forgive you, if it involved a trip to Europe, wouldn't they?" Julian threw imperatives at her disguised as choices, hoping to distract her while he let his desires get the better of him. Her skin was soft. So soft.

She stiffened and inched back. He didn't like that.

"Chéri...?" He reached out to her, risking touching her again. Risking being rejected. Again.

Camille shook her head and turned so slowly toward Julian that she seemed to be running out of steam—or hesitating. The latter was most likely the case since she avoided looking at him. "I don't have any parents." Her voice broke, and splintered Julian's soul.

"I'm sorry, Chéri." Julian paused, feeling a chip had been taken from his heart. "Your parents have passed away?"

"I'm afraid it's worse than that." She broke into a bitter laugh that Julian was eerily familiar with. It was the same laughter he and Andre had often used when they were trying to cover the pain of their real mother's demise.

"My father, and I use that term loosely." Camille dragged Julian away from his bitter memories. "Dear old Dad took off when he found out my mother was pregnant." Her unforgiving tone filled him with sorrow. "Never heard from him. Never met him." She avoided looking at him. "My mother...and I use that term just as loosely...the only difference was, she took the trouble to actually let me be born, rather than taking the easy route and opting for an abortion." Her body jerked, with tears bathing her eyes. He suspected her grief was well on its way to escaping, and that saddened Julian. "Mommy dearest didn't bother sticking around afterwards, though." Camille's empty gaze finally met Julian's. "I wasn't worth the time and trouble."

The near-full moon cast a glow over Camille, emphasizing her mouth as it tightened and a tear spilled down her cheek.

Julian skimmed a hand up her arm and nudged her closer. Sitting up, he pulled her to him. "Chéri...you are definitely worth the time and *effort*."

Camille was anything but trouble, and absolutely worth the effort.

She let the tears pour, and he tightened his embrace. Her head moved until their faces met. Their lips brushed, accidentally, and desire swept through Julian. He wanted, needed to shower her with kisses. To comfort her, to let her know just how much she was wanted and needed. Camille welcomed his overtures with warm, inviting enthusiasm. Their lips met again, their tongues danced, their hunger ignited.

And then, like a bad dream, she let out a disapproving groan, broke the kiss and backed away. Avoiding eye contact, she said, "I'm sorry, Julian. I didn't mean to..." She sprang up and moved toward the surf.

Julian followed her to the warm, soothing water's edge. "Chéri." He struggled with the urge to touch her. Embrace her. Comfort her.

But the girl was truly troubled, and he couldn't in good conscience take advantage of that. Nor did he want her thinking she'd have to spend the next six months enduring unwanted sexual overtures from him. He needed a wife. One that was temporary and make believe. He needed Camille.

"It was just a heat of the moment kind of thing on both our parts. No worries." He tried to sound reassuring and unaffected. "And besides, if Papa's watching...and he probably is...our kiss, however impromptu, was a good thing."

Julian smiled, kissed her forehead and drew her back into his arms, having found the perfect excuse.

Papa was watching.

Chapter Eight

CAMILLE AWAKENED TO BRIGHT SUNSHINE and the chaos of loud voices filtering in from Julian's adjoining room. Although muffled, she was able to identify the voices and their words.

"Julian, how could you do that to your father?" a woman said. Camille thought it might be Claudette.

"How could I do that to him? How could he do this to me?" If Julian's tone was any judge, he wasn't holding back, even though it might have been the gentlemanly thing to do.

Camille shoved aside her fledgling concern over his insensitivity.

"What exactly has Maurice done to you? Except provide you with a caring and stable home?" Her scolding tone was just as passionate as Julian's. "Let's not forget the birthright your father's built for you. A legacy that most of Europe envies."

Julian's laughter traveled through the walls but nothing about it indicated amusement. "The whole of Europe might not envy me quite so much if they were privy to the strings that come attached to father's legacy."

"Oh, Julian." Her voice blasted Camille with its impatient tone. "Don't be so dramatic."

"Dramatic...?" Julian rumbled like a volcano. "Papa brought Madeleine here. Why would he do that, knowing I'm coming home with the woman I'm about to marry?"

Camille leaned against the wall separating her room from Julian's. A touch of the old childhood fear washed over her, leaving her with feelings of abandonment. Again.

"Tell me, Julian..." The woman's voice softened. By now, Camille knew it was Claudette. "Who are you more upset for? Madeleine's feelings or your new bride's?"

Yeah, Julian? He'd kissed Camille last night like nobody's business. But she wanted to know right now if she was getting dumped.

His response came through in low, barely audible, muttering. He had an opinion but damned if Camille heard what it was. She sighed and wandered to a plush chair facing the window.

God, this place was beautiful. It was impossible for the view *not* to calm her insecurities—at least it overshadowed them for a moment or two. Camille understood why Madeleine wanted to be mistress of Pacifique de Lumière. Between the house, the grounds, and Julian's to-die-for kisses...a girl could get swept off her feet.

Under ordinary circumstances. But these weren't ordinary circumstances. Camille could never let herself forget that. The world was not her oyster. Maybe somebody like Madeleine's, sure. But not Camille. She'd had one painful reminder after another since birth that she had not been smiled upon by fate.

Oh well. She did have a contract with Julian. One that'd make her a multi-millionaire. She might never be truly content, but she'd bet she'd be a lot happier with five million bucks than without it. Money might not buy happiness, but she wagered it'd soften the blow.

A strong knock at the door between her room and Julian's invaded her thoughts. Camille straightened in her chair. "Yes?"

"Chéri..." His voice was strong, but calm. "May I come in?"

"Sure, Julian." Her voice rattled and she checked herself, staring down at the knee-length Mickey Mouse jersey-type nightgown. Not the sexiest garment she could've been sporting. She made the most of it, leaned back in the chair, pulled her stomach in and crossed her legs.

He strolled in like he owned the place, wearing a pair of dark trousers and a dark blue pullover tee. The tailor-made clothing looked like it'd been molded over his body. Perfection. The man was aesthetically faultless and his manners weren't too far behind.

Julian smiled and closed the door behind him. "Good morning, Chéri. I trust you slept well?"

His smile touched some untapped portion of her psyche. He was always concerned about her comfort. At least, that's the way it appeared.

"I slept fine, thanks." She lied. She hadn't slept well. She'd tossed and turned all night. Ridden by dreams of him—maybe desires was more like it—because his kiss had affected her, a virgin. A virgin who was quickly turning into a wannabe sex kitten.

"I hope my disagreement with my step-mother didn't alarm you."

Step-mother? Camille wondered how to tackle that one delicately. Of course it bothered her, the argument and the revelation that Claudette was his *step*-mother. But did she want to say so? No. "Well, I'm not really used to family arguments." For one awful moment she let the past consume her. "There was always just me and Granny Mae. Arguments can only go so far when there's just two people in the mix."

A relieved look crossed his face and he stepped toward the door leading to the hallway. "Then you're going to think it's pretty noisy around here. But don't let it get to you. We're mostly harmless."

"All talk and no action, huh?" She tried to lighten the mood, but the possible repercussions wouldn't leave her alone.

Julian chuckled and reached for the door. "If there's anything special you'd like to do today, talk to Soren. I've got business to attend to." He opened the door and stepped into the hallway. "I'm sure Claudette and Lecie will commandeer your time regarding the wedding."

With a pert smile, he was gone. No mention of last night. No regrets. No promises.

The kiss meant nothing to Julian. It wasn't worth talking about.

There's nothing like a little dose of eye-opening reality to put things into prospective. Camille gave herself an imaginary kick in the pants. She couldn't fall for Julian. It wasn't smart. Even if he was her husband.

Julian made his way down the hallway. He'd wanted to say something about the kiss, but Camille was already uncomfortable as it was. She'd blamed it on her inexperience with a large family, but Julian suspected she was trying to be polite. Clearly, she didn't feel the same way about the kiss.

There was plenty of time to change her mind, if Papa and Madeleine didn't run her off. He'd nip that in the bud, though, starting with Papa.

Julian jogged down the stairs, dashed through the first floor hallway and didn't stop until he reached his father's study. He hesitated, holding his fist in the air before knocking.

After a triple tap, his father's voice filtered through the door. "Come."

Julian readjusted his posture and entered the lion's den. He doubted Papa was happy about last night, but he hoped the charm he possessed over his father hadn't diminished.

Papa groaned as Julian crossed the spacious room and settled into one of the two chairs in front of the desk. Groaning couldn't be good. Julian forced himself to raise his gaze.

The senior de Laurent's icy glare sliced through Julian and hung on the silence between them. Papa's attention dropped to the desk and he leaned over. A rattling told Julian he was unlocking *the drawer*, the one he always went for when faced with a situation he couldn't control.

Three. Two. One.

Papa withdrew a bottle of whiskey and two glasses. The bar had been removed from his father's office five years ago, on Claudette's orders, after he'd suffered a heart attack and the doctors advised him to stop drinking. Sometimes, Julian thought Claudette knew about *the drawer*, but if she did, she wasn't talking.

The liquor bottle clinked as he set it on the desk, the sound resonating in Julian's head. This undoubtedly meant an argument was about to ensue. He didn't see why skipping last night's dinner party was such a big deal.

Papa cleared his throat and poured the amber liquid into each glass. He remained silent on purpose, knowing it unnerved Julian.

"None for me, thanks," Julian said, in that same old weakened tone his father had a way of commanding.

Papa bellowed and sat the bottle down with a thud. "Your restraint is ill-timed."

He was making jokes. That was a good sign.

"What did I restrain at the wrong time?" Julian struggled to regain his composure, but Papa had a way of making him feel like a wounded lion. "And when exactly was that?"

"This is not funny, Julian." Papa's glare cut through him as he raised the glass and dumped the liquor into his mouth.

Julian's shoulders jumped as he tried to come up with witty words that didn't leave him looking like a fool. He couldn't find any, so he shook his head.

"What's that?" His father asked, mocking him. The senior de Laurent stared at Julian for a moment and then admonished him with quiet laughter.

"Is this about dinner last night?" he said.

"Don't minimize it, boy." Papa pointed his finger at him.

Julian hated it when Papa called him "boy". It made him feel helpless and useless. Just like he'd felt when he found his mother's cold, lifeless body. Julian shifted in his chair. "What's the big deal?"

"Is this what America has done to you? Turned you into an insolent cad?" Papa's gaze traveled up to meet Julian's. Intolerance darkened his eyes. He was blaming it on America, but Julian knew it went much deeper than that. Papa was looking at it like he'd lost because Julian had chosen a woman who wasn't Madeleine.

Julian's helpless laughter wrapped him in doubt. "I hardly think this is America's fault, Papa."

"Then your American fiancée." He threw his hands in the air. "You would never have run out on a dinner party before."

"Before what?" Julian's temper flared and fueled him with confidence. He wouldn't tolerate anyone badmouthing Camille. Not even Papa. "Before I became bewitched by the seductive American? Before I passed on Madeleine? Before I grew up?"

Papa's nostrils flared.

But it didn't stop Julian. "Which is it father?"

Julian knew Papa didn't like it when he used that cold tone and called him *father*, any more than Julian liked being called *boy*.

"Which is it that's really got you so upset, Papa?" Julian dared to make demands upon his father.

Papa stared at him with those typically vacant brown eyes filling with the resentment of defeat.

Seeing concession in Papa's eyes bolstered Julian's poise. "How could you bring Madeleine here, knowing I was bringing home my fiancée?" he asked. "She'll be my wife by the end of the week."

"End of the week, huh?" His eyes traveled a slow journey to meet Julian's gaze, and suggested he knew Julian's secret.

"End of the week." Julian reiterated. It was true. Technically. She would be his wife by the end of the week, according to French law.

"You're losing your touch, boy." Papa's sneering laughter fractured Julian's composure.

There he goes again. Julian bit back the frustration. "All you need to know, Papa, is that Camille and I will have a traditional French ceremony at the end of the week. And until then, we will refrain from living together as husband and wife."

Papa's face lit with hope. "Does this mean your American marriage was not consummated?"

Julian knew what Papa was thinking and he couldn't let that happen. "No, father. Our American marriage is quite legal."

He challenged his father by standing first. This was usually Papa's step. It indicated the conversation was over. Julian turned his back on his father and moved toward the door, not waiting for Papa's customary dismissal.

"Where are you going?" Papa bellowed, his eleventh-hour attempt at re-seizing control.

Julian wrapped his hand around the doorknob and paused, looking over his shoulder. "I'm going to find Andre, Papa." He opened the door. "I'm sending him to America to get Camille's friend."

"Are her parents coming to the wedding?" Suspicion raided Papa's words.

"Camille was raised by her grandmother, who's no longer with us." Remorse crept around Julian and threatened to suffocate him. "She never had the opportunity to meet her parents...that she can remember." He bowed his head and moved into the hallway and shut the door.

Julian was always careful in his choice of words when talking to his father. He made it a point never to tell the man out-and-out lies. This time was no exception.

He passed Monique in the hallway. Claudette had assigned the housekeeping assistant as Camille's attendant. Julian agreed. It was a good choice.

"Have you seen my brother?" he asked, moving past her.

"Yes, sir. He's in the smaller, east dining room."

"Very good. Thank you."

The unplanned pleasantry surprised Julian as much as it must have shocked the maid. He didn't show graciousness to the servants. Why thank them for doing their job? They were duly compensated. Wasn't a monetary gain thanks enough? Julian had always thought so. But he'd gotten so used to Camille offering thanks to virtually everyone during the last couple of days that it seemed to come naturally. She had a kind word for anyone who was remotely nice to her, no matter the circumstances.

Camille was definitely having an effect over him. Whether or not it was good remained to be seen.

Julian stopped at the dining room's entryway and found Andre, Lecie, Claudette, and Camille having breakfast. No one seemed to notice him. Either that, or he was being ignored.

Andre was laughing, Claudette was gushing, and Lecie was declaring Camille's sentiments as, "the most romantic thing ever."

Good lord, what had she been telling them? Julian cleared the fear out of his throat.

Everyone glanced up and stopped.

"Julian." Lecie was the brave one, rising and coming to his side. She laced her arm around his and led him to Camille's side at the table. "Camille was just explaining why you two missed the dinner party last night."

She pushed him into the empty chair beside Camille.

"I guess you really can't fault a man when he's that romantic." Claudette smiled and flashed Julian her *you're forgiven* face.

Julian looked at Camille, smiled and winked. Whatever she'd said to get him back into his step-mother's good graces—he could kiss her. Again.

"Julian," Lecie smiled, returning to her seat at the table, "Mother and I are going to take Camille into town to arrange some wedding details."

He glanced at Camille, hoping that was okay.

"It's going to be fun." Camille assured him with confidence.

"All right." He checked his watch. 8:30 am. "Could you please have her back by three?" he said to no one in particular before turning to Camille. "We have plans this evening."

She inspected him with a questioning look. He leaned in and kissed her cheek and then whispered in her ear. "Don't worry. I'm looking out for you." Julian paused beside her ear, brushed his lips over her cheek again and moved away.

A weak smile turned the corners of her lips. "I'll be here."

Julian focused on Andre. "I need you to take the jet to California."

"California?" Andre grunted. "I don't want to go to California." The behavior reminded Julian of Andre during his toddler years.

"It's not up for discussion, Andre."

"Why am I going to America?" Andre did nothing to temper his dissatisfaction.

"You're going to pick up Camille's friend, Tasha."

His face brightened. "Is she married?"

"No," Camille said.

"Is she cute?"

"She's very cute." Camille paused, a bit of pity for Andre washing over her. Especially if Tasha saw him as entertainment while she was visiting. "You have no idea just how cute."

"Guard your heart, little brother." Julian stood and dropped his napkin on the table. "She will steal it."

"She didn't steal yours." Andre noted.

Julian looked at Camille. "My heart was already spoken for." He grabbed her hand and prompted her to stand. Tangling his fingers around hers, Julian kissed her sweetly. Not passionately. Just sweetly.

Everyone stopped talking abruptly.

Julian froze, his lips just a breath away from Camille's. He cut his eyes toward the table. Andre, Lecie, and Claudette were fixated on the dining room's entryway.

Madeleine.

Chapter Nine

MADELEINE THIBAULT WAS beyond gorgeous. The kind of woman that made Camille shrink into a cocoon of doubt and insecurity in the shadows of her basking beauty. But the look in her eyes—heartbroken devastation—had the opposite effect over Camille.

It was clear Madeleine was far more envious of her than Camille could ever feel in return. Still, the two could end up having far more in common than either imagined. But right now, Camille was on top and she had to be the bigger person.

She sucked it up and stepped toward Madeleine, extending her hand. "Hello. I'm Camille Chandler."

"de Laurent. Camille Chandler de Laurent." Julian corrected her.

Madeleine's face tightened. If Julian meant to discourage her, he was succeeding. Her cold hand gripped Camille's with the effectiveness of a wet noodle. "Madeleine Thibault," she said, her voice cracking around her queen's-English accent.

"Have you had breakfast?" Camille gestured at the table. "Would you like to join us?"

Madeleine's sad smile looked bereft and bleak. "Yes." She surveyed the table and moved toward the buffet table. "I think I might."

Julian, who moments before was excusing himself, sat back down. Camille eased into her chair, her spirits sinking to the floor. She was just about ready to throw a pity party for her competition.

Madeleine approached the table and snagged the empty seat between Andre and Lecie. She avoided looking at Julian.

Who could blame her? "So, Madeleine." Camille was not going to be the mean-spirited, so-called winner. Far as she could see, there were no winners. Not where Julian de Laurent was concerned. "Have you lived in Marseilles all your life?"

"No. I was born in Paris." Madeleine's words came slowly and reluctantly, like she didn't trust Camille's sincerity. "I spent much of my school years in England—" That explained the British accent. "—It wasn't until I'd met Julian in Nice a few years back, that I began spending time in Marseilles. I have a small apartment there." Madeleine held her head high, keeping her pride intact.

So why was she here? Why wasn't she at her small apartment in Marseilles?

But who was Camille to question the de Laurent family? She'd just have to make the best of an awkward situation. She made a mental note...when the time came to get married for real, she'd discourage an invasion of her bridegroom's old flings.

But this wasn't real. She couldn't forget that.

"I envy you." Camille admitted.

"Envy me? Whatever for?" Madeleine doused her with an annoying glare, as if she thought she was being mocked.

"You're so traveled." Camille remained calm. "I envy your firsthand experience of having visited so many places."

"I doubt that'll last long." Madeleine's wall of dignity began to crumble. She avoided any further eye contact with both Camille and Julian. Instead, she focused on Claudette. "Maurice said you were going shopping today. Might I perhaps tag along?"

Claudette's attention darted around the table and settled on Julian. "To tell the truth, Madeleine...Lecie and I are taking Camille into town to settle wedding arrangements."

"Ah..." Madeleine's voice tapered off. Her eyes glistened with unshed tears. "I guess nobody wants me to tag along for that."

Why would you want to? Camille didn't have the guts to say that out loud, but it didn't stop her curiosity. Why would anybody want to stick around and watch somebody they loved get hitched to someone else? Camille would be on the first plane, train, bus, or whatever.

"If Madeleine wants to go shopping with us," Camille said to no one in particular. "I have no objections."

Julian cleared his throat and rose from the table. "I'm sure you ladies will work it out. I must be going." He glanced at Camille and stretched out his hand. "Walk me out?"

Long, extended fingers drew her like a magnet. Their touch bathed her in an appealing gentleness. She hurried after Julian as he rushed into the hallway like a speed walker.

"What's going on?" Camille whispered. "Is she for real?"

Julian stopped just outside the door. "Madeleine Thibault has never been that considerate in her whole life."

"Well, she is heartbroken." Camille reminded him. "Thanks to you."

"Heartbroken?" His abruptness shook Camille, awakening her senses. "She's up to something. You be careful."

Budding fear swept through Camille. "Once again, I don't have to be worried about my physical safety, do I?"

"Madeline's not the physical kind." Julian dashed down the stairs. "She's more devious," he said, with Camille following him. "More backstabbing than that. She's more apt to discredit you. Make you appear unworthy, incapable of fulfilling the position my wife would assume in European society."

Geez, he made being his wife sound so hard. What had she gotten herself into?

At the front door, Julian brushed his lips against her cheek, and Camille forgot all about her insecurities. "Remember—" His tone held a mixture of order and suggestion. "—If the excursion gets to be too overwhelming, just call Soren and he'll bring you back to the house."

"Where are you going?" She wasn't being nosey. Just curious.

"I have an empire to run." He opened the door and headed outside.

"I thought that was your father's job."

"He leads the family. I run the business."

"Oh." Her response flittered off her tongue. His revelation surprised Camille, maybe even impressed her a little.

He moved toward the car and Sebastian opened the door. Julian stopped and glanced over his shoulder. "I'll be back around six," he said before disappearing into the limo.

Six? Didn't he say something about four at breakfast?

Camille had a lot to learn about the interworkings of a multi-billion dollar family and its very enigmatic, but oh so sexy, second-in-command.

Clouds sprinkled the morning sky like wisps of cotton balls. She was getting married in a couple of days; was this a bad sign?

Hell no. There aren't any signs, good or bad, for arranged marriages.

The car drove away and Andre appeared from inside the house, as if he'd been waiting for Julian to leave. He looked at her and smiled, slipping his hands inside his pockets.

"Camille. Is it all right if I call you Camille?" he asked, a little too friendly-like.

"Yes." She hesitated, unsure of his motives, and erected a sober reserve. "Do you work with Julian? He's left already."

"I work *for* Julian. And we rarely ride in together. He's always got me off running errands." His tone was free of animosity. Not only did Andre appear to know his place, he seemed content with the position.

"And you like that just fine." She realized out loud.

"Hell yes." He grinned, openly amused. "He's always stuck inside the office, making business deals and whatnot." Andre's tone illustrated his distaste for his brother's post. "I, on the other hand, am always off globetrotting. Visiting new and exciting places. Wining and dining clients...and friends," he said, with a wink. "He can keep his job. I like mine just fine."

"Well, then..." A covetous feeling of contentment swept over Camille. "I envy you. To love what you do for a living is a godsend. A luxury not many people can afford."

"Speaking of my job..." He chuckled. "It's my job to retrieve your friend in America. You might want to contact her. I'll send a car for her."

"She can meet you at the airport."

"I wouldn't hear of it."

What a gentlemanly thing to say. It reminded her of Julian. Always thinking of someone else's comfort and ease. Maurice and Claudette had taught them well the art of courteous behavior.

"It's no trouble at all." Camille raised her tone with insistence. "There's no need for you to go traipsing all over L.A., just to bring Tasha to the airport."

Andre's laughter cascaded across the wind whipping past. "Ah, yes, Americans...so independent."

She glanced at him through narrowed eyes and then looked away. "Which airport?"

Andre studied her with raised eyebrows.

"Which airport do you want her to meet you?"

"Which is more convenient for her?"

"Let's ask her." Camille pulled out her cell phone and began texting Tasha. Within seconds, she had an answer. *LAX. Where 2 meet?*

Camille showed Andre the cell phone screen and waited for his response.

Andre snatched up her phone and began pressing buttons. When he was done, a satisfied look warmed his face and he returned the device to Camille.

She studied the phone a moment, half-curious to know what he'd texted to Tasha.

"Ooh..." Andre smacked her arm lightly with the back of his hand. "Tell her to send a photo," he said, a flicker of amusement lighting his face.

Camille's phone chimed. "Hang on." She raised a finger at Andre and took the call. "Yeah."

"Chéri," Julian's voice, anxious yet comforting, poured over the phone. "Has Andre talked to you about bringing your friend over?"

"As a matter of fact, we're just discussing that right now." She glanced at Andre. "He wants her to text him a photograph...so he can recognize her at the airport, I suppose."

"Let me speak with my brother, please." Julian's tone, short and to the point, reached across the airwaves and wrapped Camille in an icy chill.

She shoved the phone at Julian's brother. "He wants to talk to you."

Andre drew a heavy breath and rolled his eyes before laying the phone against his ear. Even so, she still heard Julian's higher-pitched voice loud and clear. "No, Andre. There will be no pictures of Camille's friend. You're not going to get her for your own amusement, so get that out of your head." Hope fell from Andre's face as he listened to Julian's orders. "Just bring her here and be on your best behavior."

Andre disconnected the call and handed the phone to Camille. "Spoil sport."

"He's your brother."

"And your husband. I had no choice in the matter." An easy smile played at the corners of Andre's mouth. "You, on the other hand, could have and should have run far, far away." He nodded and slipped into the backseat of the car.

Oh, I know I should run. But Camille didn't have the desire.

She laced her fingers together behind her back and waited until Andre's car disappeared down the long, winding driveway. Hands still clasped behind her, Camille was ready to return to the house when another limo rolled up in front of the house.

As if right on cue, Claudette, Lecie, and Madeleine exited the house. The three women looked like an expensive fashion ad for Europe's finest designers. She glanced down at her own attire, a casual ensemble of white capri pants and a matching print blouse. Camille's clothes cost more than two weeks her normal pay, and she felt ill-qualified to wear them. She didn't do the outfit justice, especially up against her companions in their trendy styles.

"Are we ready?" Claudette asked, not giving the same attention Camille had to her attire.

Sure. Why not? Camille shrugged her misgivings aside and climbed into the limo.

The morning passed quickly as a high profile wedding planner led them around the city, stopping at places like the florist and the caterers. Claudette was more than willing to weigh in on every aspect, but ultimately and respectfully left the final decision to Camille. Lecie gave no arguments to anyone. Loving everything, she only looked for the romance. Madeleine remained quiet but observant.

At lunchtime, they stopped at a sidewalk café and dined on a buffet. Lecie had excused herself and gone to the restroom. Claudette had gone back for seconds, saying, "I try to watch my figure, but one or two meals a week, I just let loose."

Camille watched her sashaying away, contemplating Claudette's age. She had to be at least forty-five. Damn, she carried it well.

"Camille," Madeleine drew her attention away from Claudette and back to the awkwardness of the situation. "May I call you Camille?"

"Sure." What else would she call her?

"I hope that despite the circumstances...you and I can remain civil to one another."

"I don't see why we can't, Madeleine."

"Well, that's very big of you." The kind words were there, but so was the nettling insolence. "Most wives aren't so accommodating."

"Accommodating?" Camille wasn't quite sure what Madeleine was insinuating, and she wanted clarification.

"Well..." She looked away scandalously, then back at Camille. "He's put you *by* his side, but did he tell you about his plans to keep me *on* the side."

Camille tried to keep her jaw from falling, and failed. "I don't even know what to say to that."

"I can understand your reaction." Madeleine said, as if they were discussing a business deal. "A month ago, I thought I might fill your shoes. But then, I find out Julian's been swept off his feet by some bitch in America...pardon my English." She smirked, shrugged and perched her hands in the air. "And now I'm relegated to mistress."

"Guess I have a lot to learn about French culture." She paused and nodded absently. "Where I come from, we call that a demotion."

Camille displayed a picture of calmness for Madeleine's benefit, but she didn't understand Julian's reasoning and didn't like the idea that he wouldn't marry the girl, but he'd continue to sleep with her after he married someone else. Even if it was just a business deal.

♡

Julian scoured the house, looking for Camille, overwhelmed by his desire to hear the details of the shopping trip. He didn't trust Madeleine, mainly because he didn't trust his father to mind his own business. If Papa had his way, there's no telling what kind of corruption he'd hold over Madeleine.

After having no luck inside the house, he headed for the gardens. He didn't know Camille well enough to guess which direction she'd gone, so he took it methodically.

The scent from the roses called to him. Maybe it had done the same with Camille. The women in his life, first his mother and then Claudette and Lecie, were mesmerized by the fragrant flowers. Between the two mother-figures, he'd learned the meanings of all their colors at an early age.

In the garden, he snipped a lavender bloom, because he'd been enchanted with her at first sight and a blue bud because he figured she was pretty much unattainable—just like his mother had been.

His mother. Was that where she'd gone? The place his mother used to bring Julian and Andre to play.

The grove seemed to be one of the few areas left to look, even though Camille's finding it made no sense.

He turned sideways and squeezed into the shrubs, scraping his shirt as he reached the clearing—a place he hadn't been in over fifteen years. It looked the same, weathered with time but not necessarily neglect. Four windswept benches were centered on each side of the perimeter, four shrubs and the lawn they cornered were manicured, and various vines had spread across the trees behind the hedged borders.

To see her sitting on the bench, much like his mother used to do with her legs crossed at the ankles, warmed his heart. He cleared his throat and moved toward Camille.

Her gaze traveled up and met his, accompanied by a warm smile.

"How did you find this place?" he asked, taking a seat and leaving plenty of breathing room between them. Julian didn't want to invade her space without an invitation. Anybody who'd search out this place was definitely after seclusion.

"Just my wandering curiosity, I guess." She shrugged and draped her arms along the back of the bench, her hand nearly touching his shoulder.

Camille had learned to conceal her pain, the hurt carved into her heart over being abandoned by her parents. But here in the late afternoon sunset, her face, well modeled and feminine, gave away her secret.

Sadness twisted into a painful knot inside Julian. A take-charge man, he was used to getting his way and he wanted to remove her pain but didn't know how. His inadequacy hammered at him, made him feel helpless.

"It's funny that you should seek out and find this one place over all others."

"Why's that?"

"Andre and I used to play here as children."

"Really?" She gave him one of those looks that said *you're kidding, right?*

"It's the truth." He nodded, his thoughts wandering off toward his childhood memories. "My mother...my real mother...showed me this place." He'd opened a door that'd been locked for over twenty years, immediately assaulted by an acute sense of loss.

As if sensing his grief and despair, she removed her arms from the back of the bench and laced her hands together in her lap. "What happened to your mother?" she asked, encasing her words in a careful tone.

Julian leaned forward and rested his elbows on his thighs and absently caressed the soft petals of the roses in his hands. "She, ah..."

He stopped. Talking about his mother was hard; mentioning it meant he'd have to acknowledge the flaw that had consumed her sanity. Weakness. And what if Camille thought that had somehow rubbed off on him? What if she assumed it meant he was also weak?

Did it really matter what she thought? Last week he was sure the only thing that mattered was his wife staying put for the agreed time. After that he didn't care what happened. But that was last week. Now he wasn't so sure.

"She killed herself." Julian continued on, hoping Camille's presence would continue to bring him peace. "With a bottle of pills." He hated the helplessness piling around him. "I was five, but I'll never forget walking into her room and seeing her lying there on the bed." He looked away, the words snagging in his throat. "I thought she was sleeping."

Camille closed the gap between them and drew him into her arms. "Aw, Julian...I'm so sorry."

Instinct, and maybe need, pushed Julian to embrace Camille and hang on as if she'd float away otherwise. A rush of vulnerability swarmed around Julian and he pulled away.

Okay. We can stop this now. He handed her the roses, hoping that would sway her in another direction. "Here, these are for you."

She took the flowers and draped her arms around him again. Julian wished she wouldn't do that. He didn't like how good it felt, but he didn't try to stop it either. Instead, he welcomed her comforting embrace, even if it did mean he was losing his touch.

♡

Camille didn't know what to say, so she said nothing, did nothing but hold onto the magnificent man in her arms. She didn't want to acknowledge the magnetism building between them, but she had no choice. It was there dominating her mind, body and soul.

Julian pulled away and her heart reacted like it'd been electrocuted. She swallowed hard, trying to devour the lump lingering in her throat.

"How was your shopping trip?" he said smoothly, stoic faced.

The memory of her conversation with Madeleine shuddered through Camille. "Hm...your Madeleine is something else."

"My Madeleine? She's not my Madeleine."

"She thinks she is." Jealousy snuck up against Camille and she tried to divert the unwanted sensation.

"Is that so?" He smiled, like he saw right through her.

"She told me that I may be marrying you, but she's going to be sleeping with you on the side."

"She said those exact words?"

Camille couldn't tell if he was astonished or pleased to know he'd have a warm body waiting any time he wanted.

"Precisely," she said.

"Huh. Wow." He tempered his shock with amusement. "Papa's really pulling out all the stops to run you off."

"Then I guess the joke's on them." A sensation of tired sadness passed over Camille. "Considering our arrangement...it's really none of my business who you sleep with."

A hint of regret clouded his eyes for just a second, and then it was gone. "But that's our secret," he said, and winked.

"Yes, it is." She forced herself to look at Julian. "I'll be discreet if you are." She bargained in a teasing manner, the only way she knew to hide the reality of her discomfort.

"Really?" he said, half intrigued, half put-out. "And just who is on our radar?"

She stood and sashayed toward the shrubbery maze. "Wouldn't you like to know?" She giggled and ran inside.

Julian followed her. "You're serious, aren't you?" he asked, as if he'd been snubbed. "There's someone you want to sleep with?" He stopped her and backed her against the wall of shrubs.

They stood inches apart. Julian staring at Camille, her gaze glued to his. Their breaths increasing, mixing, intermingling. He looked her over seductively.

It left a tingling in the pit of her stomach that riveted out to her fingertips and toes, allowing her to break the visual connection. "I should go inside." She slipped to the side and put some space between them. "It's getting chilly out here." Stepping away, she let her fears quicken her steps toward the hidden passage in the hedge.

Camille's heartbeat amplified and coursed desire through her like an awakened river. Her head screamed *no*. Falling for Julian wasn't smart. Her new husband intended to remain the bachelor about town and no marriage would alter that—least of all theirs.

But her heart had already said *yes*.

Chapter Ten

By the time Andre returned with Tasha, preparations for the wedding were well underway. The flowers had arrived. The rented chairs, tables and tents had been delivered and now a crew of hired workers were setting the scene for the reception behind the rose garden. Claudette and Camille had agreed it was the perfect place with a spacious area amid the roses for a makeshift dance floor. Of course, it was also the location of Claudette and Maurice's wedding reception twenty years ago.

When the car arrived, bringing Andre and Tasha from the airport, Camille had been gazing out the west dining room's wall of windows. She raced through the hall and down the stairs, stopping halfway when her best friend entered the house and paused just inside the entryway.

Thank God. Camille no longer felt alone.

"Tasha." Camille trotted down the stairs and embraced Tasha as she reached the bottom step.

"Here she is," Andre said with a grand gesture. "Safe and sound."

"Yes, your new brother-in-law took a personal interest in my well-being." She smiled at Andre and winked. The gushing was almost sickening.

Julian barged in from an opposite hallway. "Where have you been?" he asked Andre in particular, offering no smiles. No welcome home. No 'thanks for the favor'.

"Tasha and I stopped over in London." Andre's flat tone offered no indication that an explanation was forthcoming.

Camille supposed it was his way of standing up to big brother.

Julian was silent for a moment. His frustration worked his bottom jaw and after a bit he made a conscious effort to stop. "Did you stop in Paris?" He remained focused on Andre.

"Yes, big brother, we did." Andre winked at Tasha. "Marie promised the dresses will all be delivered this afternoon. A full two hours before the ceremony."

"Two hours. Aren't we pushing it a little?" Tasha asked, in a comical tone.

Boy, I'll say. If this wedding was real, Camille would be nearing the breaking point.

"Well, we had to move up the wedding day." Julian smirked. "We think Camille is pregnant," Julian added, his tone drenched in sarcasm.

Camille smacked him.

He rolled his eyes and let them settle on Camille, his expression softening. "Why don't you get your friend settled in and then you can show her around. There's nothing much for you to do at this stage."

"You want me to show her around?" Camille said in a casual, jesting way. "Who's going to come find us when I get lost?"

Andre raised his hand. "I can do that."

Tasha looked at him like he was a white knight. "Everybody loves a hero."

Julian huffed and took a couple of steps away before turning back to Camille. "Chéri, I've got some things to attend to, but I'll be back in plenty of time before the ceremony."

Camille considered just what business he could have, but decided not to ask. Maybe he was going to pay Madeleine a visit, as most bridegrooms expected certain things to happen on their wedding day. Maybe Julian was arranging his wedding night bliss. It just wouldn't be with the bride.

There was a little something unsettling about that notion, even though Camille knew precisely where she stood with Julian. She didn't need to be reminded that they were in a business arrangement. Assuming it could turn into anything more wasn't smart, and she'd just be setting herself up for heartbreak.

"Come on," Camille grabbed Tasha's hand. "Come with me. There's an empty bedroom right beside mine."

"Like you're going to be in there." Tasha laughed as Camille pulled her up the stairs. "Thanks for the ride, Andre," she said, without looking over her shoulder.

"My pleasure, Chéri." He called out. "Remember, if you need anything. Anything at all. I'm your man."

Camille stopped Tasha at the top of the landing. "Look—" She pointed an accusatory finger at Tasha. "—Andre is not your play-toy, okay." It was no question.

"How about my boy toy?" She snickered. "Can he be my boy toy?"

"Tasha." Camille issued her best warning tone in hopes of stifling Tasha's amusement. "This is not funny."

"Lighten up." She eyed Camille with one suspiciously perched eyebrow. "God, you're so uptight. Geez, isn't that scrumptious man of yours taking care of you?" She breathed in a shallow, quick gasp. "Don't tell me this family is that old fashioned." She sighed, disappointed. Clearly, she'd set her sights on bagging Andre while she was here and she thought family principles might spoil her chances.

Maybe it was best to let her think that. Then maybe she'd leave Andre alone. "You can't argue with tradition."

Monique's silent footsteps went unheard until she was standing at Camille's side. She paused silently until she wasn't acknowledged.

"Miss Camille, you're needed in the downstairs library," she said softly. "Mrs. de Laurent needs your approval on some last minute arrangements."

Camille sighed and bit her tongue, the urge to swear growing. "All right," she said to the maid and turned to Tasha. "Just go ahead and get settled in. I'll be back in a few."

"Well don't leave me stranded here too long," Tasha's words chased her down the hallway. "I'll never find my way out of this place."

Leave it to Tasha to infuse a little humor into this zany situation. Camille snickered and hurried down the stairs. Knowing Claudette, her dilemma was probably nothing more than where to place the orchids in relation to the roses. Not that Claudette was superficial. She and Camille just lived in very different worlds.

♡

Sometime later, when Camille had finally garnered a spare moment away from the hustle and bustle of planning an impromptu wedding, she headed for Tasha's room only to find it empty.

Where was that girl? Hopefully, she hadn't found Andre's room.

Camille glanced up and down the hallway. Searching for Tasha meant she'd run the risk of running into Maurice, or worse yet, Madeleine. The last thing she needed right now was hearing Madeleine bragging about satisfying Julian on his wedding day to Camille.

She opted for her room across the hall instead, with thoughts on taking a nice, hot shower.

The shower was refreshing, but Camille was still left with a sense of unease. After the terrycloth robe had drained the excess moisture from her body, she slipped out of it and into the silk robe Julian had given her. She liked the feel of the smooth fabric against her bare skin.

She was getting married this evening, but she couldn't help feeling something was going to go wrong.

♡

The owner of the finest salon in Paris had been flown in to doll up the wedding party. Jean-Jean was attractive and hip and definitely not gay. He'd flirted relentlessly with Tasha the whole time he worked on her hair. He'd agreed to style Claudette, Lecie, Tasha and Camille's hair, saving the bride for last. He'd brought along an assistant to tend to everyone else.

Camille wanted to ignore the dark clouds rolling across the sky, but Jean-Jean had turned her toward the window to keep her from watching him in the mirror as he styled her hair.

She was faced with letting that nagging feeling that her wedding—as fake as it was—was going to get rained out consume her.

"Are you sure?" she asked Jean-Jean of his suggestion, more like insistence that he style her hair up off her shoulders.

"Leave it to me," he said. "I am the beauty expert."

Yeah, well, that's debatable. But that was just her own insecurities talking. Actually, Jean-Jean was the epitome of style. His high-end designer jeans and tee-shirt underneath a leather vest, off-set by those snakeskin boots, was the embodiment of cool. But still, a look Camille would never shoot for. She was much too conservative. Or as Tasha would say—drab.

Tasha meant well. There was no maliciousness in her at all. Not where Camille was concerned. Tasha had often tried to 'color' Camille up, but she just wasn't interested.

"If I don't like it," Camille told Jean-Jean of her hair, "I'm going to take it down."

"Oh, no." He paused, perched a hand on his hip. "You must not deface a creation by Jean-Jean." He used his comb as a pointer, admonishing Camille.

She didn't take her overbearing hairdresser seriously. He was overshadowed by the clouds outside as they thickened and darkened.

The door opened. No knock. No request to enter. From a diffused reflection in the window, Camille saw Tasha stormed in, wearing a mid-thigh length robe.

"What is up with that Madeleine chick?" She dropped onto the bed, and eyed the red silk robe Camille was wearing.

Jean-Jean snorted, but continued to work on Camille's hair.

Camille groaned, wanting to look at her hair but Jean-Jean refused.

"What's her deal?" Tasha said again. "She's awfully pissed about something." She toed out of her slippers and lay down on her side, propping her bare feet on the bed.

"She's not the bride." A smart-alecky tone escaped Camille.

Jean-Jean laughed.

"Seriously?" Tasha sat up and dangled her feet off the side of the bed. "She's Julian's ex?"

"Well, according to her, she's not an ex."

"In her dreams," Jean-Jean said. "She's never been anything more than a booty call."

"According to her and Maurice," Camille said, "she's just what Julian needs."

"Yeah, maybe if he's hard up." Jean-Jean snickered.

All three laughed.

"Man, I need to steer clear of her." Tasha stated.

"Well, good luck with that one," Jean-Jean said. "She's finagled her way into indefinite guest status here."

"Boy, I tell you..." Tasha shook her head. "I just don't understand French customs."

"Oh, honey, it's not a French thing," he said, waving his comb in the air. "It's a bitch thing."

"That's true." Camille agreed, recalling their lunch date. "She leaves a lot to be desired when it comes to tact."

"So, how many of Julian's ex-girlfriends are coming to the wedding?" Tasha's dramatic flair centered in her contemptuous laughter.

Only Camille. This could only happen to her. Who else would end up in a beautiful chateau in France, about to marry a billionaire—one that wasn't too hard on the eyes—but only as a business arrangement, and with his concubine staying in the same house with them. Any minute now, she'd awaken.

Jean-Jean giggled. "I like you," he said to Tasha. "You can stay."

"Cool." She turned to him. "So where do you hide all the hot French guys?"

"Oh, we keep them in during the day." His friendly bantering came across in a relaxed manner.

"Ooh, they come out at night?" Tasha pressed her fingertips to her lips.

Whatever. So long as Tasha left Andre alone, that's all Camille cared about. She didn't want to spend the next six months listening to Julian bitching about how Tasha broke Andre's heart.

Camille stared out the window at the unfolding scene on the lawn. The guests were starting to arrive. And she still didn't have a dress. It should've been delivered an hour ago. She glanced at the sky, thick and heavy with some of the blackest clouds she'd ever seen. Great. If she was the suspicious kind, and she was getting married for real, she'd say the day's uneasy events were starting to look like a sign.

She went to Julian's door and knocked.

"Come in." Madeleine's voice, velvet-edged and sickeningly sweet, filtered through the walls.

Could this day get any worse?

Camille plastered on the face of indifference as she opened the door. Seeing Madeleine sprawled out on Julian's bed was enough to push even the sanest of women over the edge.

She drew in a breath and forbade the claws to emerge. "Where is Julian?" Camille asked, staying in the entryway and hanging onto the doorknob.

"Shower." Madeleine's snarky tone and her expression irked Camille.

Camille tilted her brow and looked at Madeleine with ambiguity.

"Well," Madeleine laughed at her, "You don't want him standing beside you, declaring to keep himself only unto you, while he reeks of me, do you?"

She thought about backing out of the room. She thought about asking Madeleine to pass on a message—like that would happen. She thought about barging into Julian's bathroom. Camille opted for the latter.

"Hey?" Madeleine objected as Camille headed across the room. "You can't go in there."

Camille stopped at the door, her hand resting on the knob, and glanced over her shoulder. She tried to stop it, tried not to stoop to Madeleine's level, but her pride interjected. "There's nothing in there that I haven't seen before."

She didn't wait for Madeleine's response, just opened the door and hot steam rolled out. "Julian?" she called out, entering and closing the door behind her.

"Chéri?" Laughter chased his enduring term for her. "Have you come to join me?"

God, what nerve. She wasn't about to take Madeleine's sloppy seconds. Not today. But it was nice to know Julian was so virile. At least, he thought he was. And Julian wasn't the kind of guy to start something he wasn't certain he could finish.

Camille thought about what he'd told her about Madeleine making sure Camille caught them in bed. She wasn't sure if he meant that literally or figuratively. And she didn't have the courage to ask him. Whether or not Julian was sleeping with another woman wasn't any of her business.

"Julian!" Camille stomped her foot on the tile. "My dress was not in the delivery from the designer in Paris."

The water stopped. "What?" His hardened tone shredded the single word inquiry.

"My dress—" All her hopes for a trouble-free wedding were crushed in her diminishing, barely audible voice. "—It's not here."

By the time Julian opened the shower door, he'd wrapped a towel around his waist. Her disappointment was overshadowed by the view of his torso. Rippling muscles engraved on his bronzed skin, defined his manliness and nearly floored Camille.

Julian grabbed his cell phone off the nearby counter and hit the speed dial. He waited for an answer on the other end, and Camille got caught up in the water droplets dangling off his wet hair. Finally, they dripped onto his shoulders and followed well-carved paths down his chest. She tried to fend off the overwhelming desire to grab a towel and 'dry him off' with long, slow sensuous strokes.

He spouted words in French, pulling Camille out of her wishful thinking. She had no idea what he was saying, but by the tone of his voice, she'd say it wasn't good. He paused every so often and with each gap his ensuing tone softened. Finally, she thought he'd apologized just before he disconnected the call.

That surprised Camille. It wasn't in Julian's makeup to administer apologies.

He laid the phone on the counter and looked at Camille with sorrow shading his eyes. "Marie insists the dress was in the delivery." He spoke as if the words weighed heavy on his family's good name. "It's disappeared since arriving here." His face winced and the frown set into his features.

"Who would do such a thing?" Camille asked, even though she had a pretty good guess.

"I'll find your dress," he said and stormed out.

Camille followed him into his room.

Surprise, surprise. Madeleine was gone, right along with Camille's dress.

Chapter Eleven

CAMILLE CHANDLER DE LAURENT had been the picture of grace and poise during a wedding disaster like no other. First, her dress had disappeared, but she'd graciously gone to her closet and picked out a simple peach evening gown that Julian had bought her in London.

Claudette's hairdresser had done an excellent job of fashioning Camille's hair on top her head and leaving loose tresses framing her face and resting on her neckline. Between the dress and her hair, she reminded Julian of a goddess holding court on Mount Olympus rather than a woman he should be fortunate enough to wed.

Then the rain came. It destroyed her perfectly coiffured hair and drenched her designer gown, which would've shrunk several sizes had it not been forced to retain some of its shape by her womanly figure. At the reception, though, the dress had begun to dry and now brimmed several inches above her ankles.

Julian hated that he hadn't been able to find Camille's dress. He'd failed his new wife, but he was determined to win her forgiveness. Why he felt this way, he didn't know. Their marriage was nothing more than a deal and she was being well-compensated for her share. Still, to those on the outside, it looked like a personal disaster for the bride, and that was unacceptable for Julian.

Soren. *Where is Soren?* He would help Julian fix this, or at least make it seem less painful. With Soren's help, he'd find a way to ease Camille's embarrassment.

Finally, Julian spotted Soren directing the servants in the makeshift kitchen.

♡

A crew specializing in weddings had turned the inside of a rented tent into a temporary haven of enchanted opulence. Camille sat in a stiffened pose, trying to appear as regal and confident as possible, but detesting every second of her time at a table in the center of the pavilion.

She wasn't sure if she could pin the rain on Madeleine—unless the French had found a way to control the weather. If anybody could, Camille's money was on her new father-in-law. But the wedding gown? That mystery had Madeleine's name scribbled across it in big red letters.

Julian and Soren standing on the edge of the pavilion caught her eye. The two men were in a deep conversation, like two thieves plotting their next heist.

What were they up to? Camille's curiosity soared, and landed somewhere in the vicinity of tonight.

Not that she expected to have a night of wedded bliss with Julian, but the thought of him sleeping with another woman on this night just didn't seem right. Even though they weren't consummating the marriage, somehow she thought tonight should be about them. Camille and Julian. Not Julian and Madeleine.

On the other side of the bride and groom's table, Andre and Tasha sat whispering into one another's ears. One of Andre's arms rested on the back of Tasha's chair, and he was caressing her upper arm with his free hand. She, in turn, had laid her hand on his chest and leaned in toward him as she whispered into his ear.

Camille had told her not to do that. She didn't need Julian's dejected brother added to the mix. Keeping herself on the path of an unbroken heart was hard enough, especially now that the path had begun to narrow.

And if she thought this day couldn't get any worse, right on cue, Madeleine invited herself to sit in Julian's chair. She looked at Camille and gave her one of those fake smiles that makes you want to smack the girl across the face.

"Are you enjoying yourself?" Camille asked, determined to keep a civil tongue.

Madeleine frowned. "You poor dear." Her face skewed into a crooked smile and she followed it with laughter. "How ridiculous you look. No wonder your husband is clear across the room."

Camille played with the diamond-studded bands Julian had placed on her ring finger. Her way of pointing out something that Madeleine lacked. "I guess ridicule is in the eye of the beholder." Camille shrugged, well on her way to losing the fight with her pride. "How'd it feel to watch the man you want to marry, wed someone else?"

"Pretty much the same way it's going to feel when he stops coming to your bed at night because he's wrapped up in mine."

Camille's throat tightened and she hesitated, fighting for control of her temper. A thousand comebacks shuffled across her mind. If she didn't confront this challenge right away, the next six months would be hell. "Fancy yourself a permanent room here at Pacifique de Lumière, do you?" Camille flashed her a look she hoped was bathed in mockery. "You'd be surprised at how much influence a wife has over her husband where the mistress is concerned."

Madeleine's brittle laughter gave away her waning confidence, and she grabbed a glass of champagne off the tray of a passing waiter.

"Make no mistake, Madeleine," Camille said, her self-assurance continuing to swell. "You and I will not be living in the same house."

She hadn't seen Julian approaching the table, and was a bit startled when he leaned down between them but spoke to Madeleine. "I do hope you're not thinking of making a scene."

"Of course not, darling." She trailed her fingertips longingly over his cheek. "Your new bride and I were just setting some ground rules."

Julian turned to Camille and plastered on a smile. "Will you excuse us for just a moment, Chéri?" He didn't wait for her answer. Instead, he latched onto Madeleine's arm and forced her from the chair. His expression gave no sign of tolerance and Camille was certain Madeleine wasn't being guided willingly.

Hopefully, Julian didn't want a scene anymore than Camille. But he had to understand, she wasn't about to put up with Madeleine's rudeness. Not for any amount of money.

♡

Julian practically dragged Madeleine in front of him by the time they cleared the tent's entrance. Outside on the rain-drenched lawn, they stepped in a mud puddle. Madeleine scoffed and stomped her foot, splashing them both with dirty water.

"How dare you." She chastised him with one of those evil-eyed looks she was so famous for. "How dare you treat me like a casual and indifferent acquaintance."

"Madeleine, you are a guest at my wedding." He ripped out the words through gritted teeth. "Not my choice, but you are here. So let's be civil and do me a favor?" he asked, but didn't wait for her response. "Stay away from my wife."

Not that Julian liked being hostile to Madeleine, or any other woman, but he knew this one too well. Civility meant something more than its true purpose in her eyes. Thanks to his meddlesome father, Madeleine actually thought there was still a chance for some sort of relationship between them. And the last thing Julian wanted was Madeleine still hanging around with stars in her eyes after Camille had come and gone.

"Julian…?" Desperation invaded her voice and pushed her plea out. "She cannot give you what you truly need. I'm the only one that can do that. You know I know what satisfies and pleases you."

Well, she had a point, little did she know. Julian's wife had made it clear that he wasn't getting what he needed from her, but that wouldn't stop him from trying. The one thing he did know was there was no place for Madeleine in this scenario.

But he wasn't about to confirm that to Camille. He thought he'd seen a hint of jealousy in her eyes, more than once, over Madeleine. And where there's jealousy, there was also a chance for seduction.

"Have some dignity, girl." His less-than-friendly tone chilled the air around them. "I chose someone else. Move on."

He hated the hurt in her eyes, but it was necessary. Necessary to keep her away when Camille left and Julian played the dutiful, but abandoned husband. He neither needed nor wanted any comfort from Madeleine. Hopefully his treatment of her now would compel her to disregard him when the time came.

"You'll change your mind."

This was worse than he'd thought, and required drastic measures. "Pack your things. I want you gone by the time I get back."

"Get back? Where are you going?"

"On my honeymoon."

She glared at him for a moment, like she had something else to say, but instead, picked up the hem of her dress and trotted across the lawn toward the house.

Good. Now that that's taken care of....

Julian turned and faced his guests. Scanning the crowd, his bride was gone too. He checked his watch. Soren was probably on his way back by now. If he'd had trouble carrying out his mission, he would've called. A semblance of relief reassured Julian. At least something was going to go right today.

He stepped back inside the tent's entrance just in time to see Papa swoop into Andre's empty chair and commandeer Tasha's attention. Julian didn't trust Papa, not entirely. Stealth mode was the best course of action. Julian walked around the perimeter of the tent and slipped in through the back entrance. He paused, unnoticed, behind a wall of flowers next to the bride and groom's table.

The sweet scent of lavender overwhelmed him, but he didn't find it nearly as offensive as Madeleine's perfume.

"My dear, it was so nice of you to drop everything," Papa said, "and join us for Julian's wedding at the last minute."

Papa had left Camille's name out on purpose. But Julian had a feeling Papa's innuendos were going to be wasted on Tasha.

"Well," Tasha said, in a serene voice. "Nothing's more important than my best friend's wedding."

Good. She's keeping the conversation amiable and neutral.

"I hope your boss doesn't feel so inconvenienced that it will affect your job."

Papa was fishing. Julian hoped Tasha didn't bite.

"Well, I do freelance work," she said politely. "And I'm between gigs right now. So, there's no worries."

She's really good. It would serve Papa right if Andre did manage to steal her heart.

"You are a delightful girl, Tasha." Maurice's tone took on an air of indulgence. That worried Julian. It was Papa's lure of choice when the fish weren't biting. "Where prey tell did you and Camille meet?"

Her answer came after a split-second of silence. "Camille and I met in an acting class."

"Well, now...you don't say."

Julian slid his hands in his pockets and emerged from behind the partition. So what if Papa found out Camille was an actress. Big deal.

"Papa..." he eased up to the table and sat next to his father. "You're not pestering this young lady, are you?" he asked in an offhanded and joking manner. One he knew Papa would recognize for its hidden gravity. Julian was pretty sure the man had invented it himself.

"Me? Pester a lovely young lady?" he asked, as if that was a ridiculous notion. "Absolutely not." He added his boisterous trademark laughter, knowing it intimidated most people.

What Papa didn't know was that it hadn't intimidated Julian for quite some time. He'd been waiting for the perfect moment, and decided the time had come for his demands.

Julian leaned closer to his father. "When I return from my honeymoon—" His soft whispering tone tangled with the hardened stare he was caught up in with Papa. Julian didn't blink. "—I want Madeleine out of the house."

"Boy, don't presume to tell me what or who to invite into my home." Maurice kept his voice low, but stern.

"Either she goes, or Camille and I will move into town." Julian played his hand, but it wasn't a bluff. He was prepared to move out of

Pacifique de Lumière because the only thing Maurice de Laurent hated more than being told what to do, was being abandoned by his family. Julian smirked and leaned back into his chair. "I do believe Claudette is looking for you."

Papa's head crooked around, as if in spy mode, searching for his wife.

Julian leaned closer before Papa had the chance to escape. "You wouldn't know what happened to my wife's dress, would you?"

Papa looked stunned. "You think I had something to do with that?"

Julian studied his face. "In a word...yes. I wouldn't put it past you."

"Julian, I swear to you..." he said, raising a hand in the air as if giving an oath. "I had nothing to do with the disappearance of that wedding gown. Claudette would have my head."

That was true. Claudette didn't mess around when it came to fashion, and high-priced fashion at that. Julian doubted Papa would risk the doghouse just to upset Camille. No, this had to be Madeleine's doing.

Camille appeared in his peripheral vision, headed toward him, still wearing the same length-shrinking dress. She'd let her hair down, and he found the look, although a bit on the wild side, just as pleasing as before the rain. The perfect picture of grace, she greeted their guests with polite smiles and gestures as she passed them by. Julian swelled with pride.

He stood, pulled her chair out and waited. She smiled as she sat, and something in her manner soothed him. "I wondered where you'd gone off to," he said, returning to his seat.

"Just freshening up a bit." She surveyed the crowd around them with a quick glance. "So what's on the agenda for this evening?" She settled her gaze on Julian. "We do need to talk."

He chuckled. "We'll have plenty of time to talk about whatever your heart desires. There's going to be nobody but you and me for the next ten days...well, you, me and a small crew."

Camille studied his face. No doubt trying to figure out the mystery surrounding his elusive clue. But he wasn't telling.

"Am I going to regret this?"

Julian pretended to consider it. "No," he said, shaking his head. "I can pretty much guarantee you're going to love it." He smiled and winked.

"Full of yourself, aren't you?" she asked, half-serious, half-teasing.

"I'm getting to you." Julian caught her gaze and trapped her there.

"Not as much as you want to."

"Are you ready?"

"For...?"

"To...how do you Americans say...?" He paused, and searched his mind for the correct phrase. "Blow this pop stand?"

Camille giggled. "That's so 1990s." She looked at the bridal bouquet on the table. "But I haven't tossed my bouquet away yet."

"You're really going to throw that away?" He didn't understand the concept. Women were extremely sentimental and giving their bridal bouquet away made absolutely no sense.

"Well, this is not the one I carried down the aisle. It's a replacement to use specifically for tossing the bouquet." She reached for the flowers and cut her eyes toward Andre and Tasha.

Julian stole a look across the table. His brother was making a spectacle of himself. Julian managed to contain his amusement and kept the laughter to just a thought. He scooped up a handful of miniature mints in a nearby bowl and tossed them at Andre, tearing him away from Tasha. Julian's laughter escaped.

Andre glared at Julian and mouthed the word, "What?"

"You're on, little brother," Julian said. "Gather all the single girls around."

A smile spread across Andre's face. "I can do that." He stood and scooted Tasha up to the dance floor.

Once Andre had gathered a slew of single girls around Tasha, Julian reached for Camille's hand and led her to the stage in front of the dance floor. He turned her back to the crowd and winked, saying, "No peeking."

"You're incorrigible."

"Don't tell anyone," Julian said, as Andre hopped up onto the stage.

"Ladies, ladies...gather round." Andre coaxed with waving hands. "It's that time. Who's going to be next?"

"Andre, we want to see you front and center when Julian tosses the garter." An unidentifiable feminine voice came out of the crowd.

In spite of himself, Julian chuckled at Andre trying to charm his way out of this one. Andre landed his hand against his chest and followed it with a defining headshake. Baby brother was not interested in being next.

Andre turned his focus on Camille. "Okay, on the count of three." He paused and draped his hand over the microphone. "Just toss it over your shoulder. They'll do the rest."

Julian moved closer to Camille, targeting her ear. "Ten lira says he'll use this bouquet-throwing incident to seduce the woman who catches it."

Camille looked at Andre. "Ten lira. Is that a lot?"

Andre's laughter had a bite to it. "Okay, ladies...here we go." He cajoled Camille with a gentle nudge. "One. Two. Three..."

She tossed the bouquet back over her head and it sailed into the cluster of single women. The flowers bounced around as if on a springboard, rebounding off Tasha's head and sailing behind her into Lecie's hands...where it stayed.

Oh, Papa wasn't going to like this. Julian snickered inside. At least she was safe from Andre's charms.

"Okay, bud..." Camille hit his arm and waggled her hands. "Cough it up. Ten lira. Pay up."

One of the groomsmen passed a chair up to the stage. Andre directed Camille to sit. She glanced anxiously between Julian and his brother. Julian flashed her an assuring smile and leaned in toward her ear. "No worries, Chéri. I'm just going to tastefully removed your garter and toss it out into a group of uninteresting and undeserving members of the male sex." He kissed her cheek and she giggled as Julian dropped to the floor on one knee.

"He's already been there." Another nameless female yelled out, and all the other women howled.

Julian bowed his head and smiled at the mob, and that induced them to cheer louder. He slid his hands beneath Camille's dress and ran them slowly up her smooth, bare leg. The gentleman in him stopped when he found the garter.

"Remember," Andre said to Julian, "This is a G-rated show."

"I know that," Julian huffed under his breath. Did Andre think him a cad? He thought he deserved a bit more credit.

Julian slid the garter down Camille's leg and over her foot. He swung it around his extended forefinger like a hula hoop. When the crowd neared a frenzied state, Julian whipped it into the air like a prize.

The wedding guests cheered with catcalls and profane words in French. Julian slipped his hand around Camille's. He scanned over the crowd to see who'd caught the garter, but came up with nothing. He wouldn't care much, except that Lecie had caught the bouquet and these two people were supposed to dance.

He leaned toward Andre. "Who caught that?"

"Stephan Payette."

"You tell that little shit to keep his hands off Lecie." Julian ordered, trying to contain his ferocity and hint at it at the same time. He turned to Camille and she softened his mood. "Are you ready?"

She raised her chin with a cool stare in his direction.

"Trust me," he said.

She looked at him like she'd already done that and look where it had gotten her. Julian winked at her and squeezed her hand.

"Yeah, okay." Her expression of doubt changed to desire.

Julian winked at her again, his confidence growing. He tore his attention away from Camille and turned to their guests. "As much fun as this party is..." He laughed comically. "My wife and I must bid you adieu."

Julian hopped off the stage and swept Camille into his arms. He kept her there as he made his way through the crowd and to the limo waiting just outside the tent's main entrance. Soren was waiting by the car.

Good. He was back. That meant he'd completed his task.

Julian set Camille on her feet and Soren opened the car door. She slid inside, and Julian leaned against the opened door motioning for Soren to come closer. He inched toward Julian.

"Did you take care of it?" Julian asked.

"Yes, sir. It's in the safe on the boat." Soren folded his hands behind his back and a smile spread over his face. "She will be pleased, sir."

"Good." Julian slapped him on the arm and slipped inside the car.

"Have a good trip, sir," Soren said, closing the door. While Julian and Camille were honeymooning, Soren was taking his own, much deserved vacation. He'd earned it with his flawless loyalty.

Julian turned to Camille and draped his arm along the back of the seat.

"Are you going to tell me where we're going now?" she asked, intrigued.

"No." Julian grinned.

She sighed and smacked him on the knee. "Why not?"

"It's a surprise." Julian reached for the champagne bottle resting in the bin of ice. He snagged two glasses hidden inside a nearby compartment, steadied them between the fingers of one hand and filled them with the bubbly. He returned the bottle back to the ice and handed her a glass.

Suspicion held her gaze on him a little longer than necessary. She laced her fingers around the flute's stem, still looking at him. After a moment, she closed her eyes and sipped the champagne.

Julian took the opportunity to gaze at her while she wasn't looking and tried to evaluate her unreadable features. Failing miserably, he was somehow comforted by her nearness.

Her eyes opened slowly and focused on him. "So, why won't you tell me where we're going?" she asked again, more persistent this time.

"Already told you." He shook his head. "It's a surprise."

"Well, how long will we be gone?"

"About ten days."

"Ten days?" she echoed. "Are we going on a *honeymoon*?"

"Such as it is." He couldn't sound too eager. Women never found eagerness from a man appealing. "We have an image to uphold, Chéri."

"Yeah..." The single word trailed off into a long, low sigh and the smile on her face faded.

She was probably getting tired of all the drama. He couldn't blame her after the day they'd had. With any luck, he'd change all that with a short trip to the marina.

If not, it was going to be a long, lonely ten days.

Chapter Twelve

CAMILLE COULDN'T GET A BREAK. The rain had returned in another torrential downpour by the time the limo arrived at the marina. Curiosity over why they'd come here engulfed her, but she didn't dwell on it. She tried to peer out the car's windows, but sheets of rain distorted her view. All she could make out was blurred structures that she decided were luxury yachts.

"We'll wait a few moments for the rain to subside," Julian said, the car rolling up beside a massive ship.

"Then what?" Camille asked. She'd learned a long time ago not to make assumptions.

"Then we're going to get on the boat."

"Boat?" She tried to hide her enthusiasm behind a stoic expression, and wasn't sure if she'd succeeded.

Julian leaned toward her. She wished he wouldn't do that. Being this close to him was too tempting. Resisting his charms for the next six months might prove harder than she'd anticipated.

"Yes, the Naoma Louise," he said in a broken whisper.

"Well, that sure clears it up." She giggled, more at herself than anything else. She glanced out the window. The rain was still pouring. "Is it that one right there?" she asked, pointing to the blur they'd parked beside.

"Yes. That's the Naoma Louise."

"The Naoma Louise?" She stared unseeing at the distorted figure. "Does the name hold some significance?"

"My mother's name."

A faint flicker of sadness rattled through her, shaking her shoulders.

"Are you cold, Chéri?" he asked attentively.

"Not in the least," Camille said, wagging her head.

She glanced at her dress. It's not like it could get ruined anymore than it already had. And besides, the huge blur looked a lot bigger than the car she and Julian were caged in. She could get with putting some distance between them, and maybe a dry change of clothing.

"What the hell." She shrugged and perched her hands in the air. "Let's go for it." She latched onto the door handle.

He looked at her with surprise and intrigue. "Now? In the rain?"

"Come on...where's your sense of adventure?" They'd already gotten soaked once today. What could one more time hurt?

"All right." He finally came around. "But wait here. I'll open your door."

What a gentleman. She chuckled inside, pleased.

Julian opened his door and slipped out into the rainy night. Seconds later, the car door opened and a blast of cool rain bulleted Camille and the inside of the limo. She shielded her face with one hand and took Julian's with the other, climbing out onto the wet pavement and venturing into the storm. They ran, and she wished she'd taken off her shoes, afraid she'd slip on the slick surface.

Julian guided her aboard the ship and into the lounge on the main deck. He shut the door between them and the rain, and Camille released the breath she'd been holding.

They both dragged their soaked hair out of their faces and let their laughter fill the room.

"What do you say we get out of these wet clothes?" she asked, and immediately saw the desire to throw out some derisive comeback in his smile. "Into something warm and dry, I mean," she added, not wanting it to sound like a desperate come-on.

Julian rested his hand on the small of her back. "Our stateroom is this way."

Stateroom. As in single, just one. Camille's body vibrated with new life.

Consumed with rivaling sensations of anticipation and alarm, she was easily led toward an inside corridor. At the end of the hall, Julian opened the door to the ship's master suite. The room's size equaled that of Camille's L.A. apartment, but that was the only thing the two spaces had in common. The maple paneling was trimmed in beech and walnut veneers, and soft lighting gave the room a warm and pleasant atmosphere.

"You'll find clothes in the dressing room attached to the bath." Julian gestured toward a door on the other side of the room.

The sand-colored marble bathroom bathed her in warmth and tranquility. Mesmerized by the room's sleek sheen, Camille shut the door between herself and Julian.

"Chéri..." his voice mingled with a soft tap at the door. "I'm going back out into the main lounge. Please join me when you're ready."

"All right," she said, loud enough for her voice to filter through the walls. She hesitated and looked at herself in the mirror. Her hair was beyond help, having been drenched twice today. Her makeup had gone blotchy, some aspects withstanding the rain's wrath better than others.

All her toiletries had been laid out on the counter and placed in the drawers for her convenience. Everything had been pre-arranged, down to the last detail. She'd bet her clothes had already been unpacked and put away in the huge walk-in closet. What she hadn't expected to find was comfy sweats and oversized t-shirts. A smile spread from her heart to her face, Julian had remembered her chosen attire for relaxation.

Were Julian and his staff going to cater to her every need and desire for the next six months?

This was the life. But a life that she couldn't let herself get used to because it wasn't hers. She was not a permanent fixture in this lap of luxury. Still, there was no rule that said she couldn't enjoy it while it lasted. And that's exactly what Camille planned on doing.

She scrubbed the half-worn makeup off her face and applied a light layer of loose powder to get rid of the shine. Instead of going for lipstick she opted for a splash of flavored lip balm, more for its moisture content than anything else. She hated dry, chapped lips.

The damp dress's spaghetti straps slipped easily off her shoulders and she wiggled out of the gown and let it fall to the floor. She scooped it up and hung it on an empty hook next to a pair of plush bathrobes and a couple that looked like they were made of silk.

There was a small bottle of perfume on the counter and intrigue pushed her to examine it. The name was in French and she had trouble reading it, but she thought it had something to do with flowers or maybe the sun. She couldn't tell. She pressed the gold-tipped sprayer into the air and sniffed. The scent reminded her of orange blossoms.

Camille shrugged and sprayed it over her naked body. She thought about dressing in a pair of sweats and a t-shirt but grabbed the robe instead.

It is silk, she thought, wrapping herself in the soft luxury, enjoying the feel against her bare skin.

She went back to the bedroom and paused a moment. Did the robe make her look promiscuous? Who cares? She pushed the uneasiness aside and opened the door. Julian was her husband and they needed to at least look like they were intimate, especially to the staff—whom she had no doubt were reporting back to Maurice.

The red silk clung to her skin as she strolled through the hallway and out into the ship's main lounge.

A taupe couch hugged the far wall and rounded both corners, covering half the room's parameter. Dozens of pillows, the colors of creamy butter, crimson, and a pale green had been placed on the couch to provide guests with added comfort. Artwork hung on the walls above the couch, and artifacts, probably priceless ones, were displayed strategically around the room. Everything had a feminine touch to it. Claudette was better than most interior decorators.

Julian was sitting on a stool at the bar nestled in the corner, wearing nothing but a pair of sweats. The black fleece hugged his waist, the color didn't distract from the chiseled muscles rippling underneath his bronzed skin. His ebony curls, still damp from the rain, glistened against the soft lights illuminating the wet bar.

Camille surveyed the room one more time. The couch's center had a direct line to his stool and seemed like the best vantage point. She dropped to the sofa and covered a large portion with her long legs, crossing one over the other.

Glancing up, she saw Julian staring at her. Anxiety pounded her heart against her chest. Nobody had ever looked at her like that.

Thunder roared and vibrated through the boat and shook Camille's composure. She jumped up and charged toward the window, analyzing the rough seas. Hopefully, they weren't going to set sail in this mess.

She sucked in a deep breath and turned to Julian, pointing out the window. "We aren't going out in this weather, are we?"

"No." He shook his head. "We'll wait until the storm clears. Probably tomorrow." He drained his glass and poured another. "Can I get you a drink? Dinner is about half an hour away."

"Sure." She folded her arms in front of her and turned back to the window, mesmerized by the storm's ferocity.

Camille had a feeling she was going to need a drink. Lots of them. Between the boat thing—she'd never learned to swim—and a creeping desire for Julian—her husband in name only—she was going to need all the help she could collect.

♡

Julian rose and strolled behind the bar. He'd anticipated her need for a drink and put some champagne on ice as soon as he'd changed out of his wet clothing. His competitive nature enjoyed it when his hunches proved right.

Camille clutched her hands behind her back, fidgeting. Julian suspected the missing dress was to blame. It wouldn't surprise him. He couldn't censure her for thinking twice after what happened with her wedding gown and then the weather. She'd graciously and valiantly gone through with the ceremony, wet hair and all, in one of the outfits he'd bought her earlier in the week.

Julian still believed Madeleine had something to do with the missing garment.

It made Madeleine look like a fool, and a hopeless one at that. Imagine thinking a missing dress would stop the wedding. Thankfully, it was just a business arrangement and while Camille had expressed disappointment over not getting the chance to wear the dress, she had gladly and graciously agreed that any outfit would suffice.

He grabbed a couple of glasses from the rack, sat them on the counter and reached for the bottle of chilled champagne.

As soon as he figured out what Madeleine had done with the dress, he was going to retrieve it and give it to Camille as a gift so she could wear it when she was ready for a bonafide marriage.

And Andre thought Julian was selfish. *Shows how much he knows.*

Lightning flashed, casting a brief but welcomed glimpse of her beauty. Curves outlined her shapely figure beneath her silk robe as she approached the bar and hopped onto a stool. Loose tendrils of still damp blonde hair softened and framed her flawlessly stunning face.

Julian poured champagne and handed her a glass. "You were a great sport today, wearing a replacement gown at the ceremony."

She wrapped her fingers around the flute's stem. "Well, it's not like it was that important." She sipped the champagne. "Omens don't count for arranged marriages." She smiled girlishly, and the sight of it swept through Julian leaving him wanting to kiss her.

"Omens?" He moved around the bar and sat on the stool beside her.

"Well, if we were getting married for real...I would've called it a sign."

"Maybe it's still a sign."

"Nah, it doesn't work like that."

"Then how does it work?"

"It's only a bad sign if we were actually in love."

"Who says signs have to be bad?"

"A missing dress is bad." She slipped off the bar stool and moved to her original position on the couch.

"I can see why you'd think that." He followed her, draining his glass.

His empty champagne flute *clinked* as it made contact with the marble-top coffee table. Julian sat, leaving little space between himself and Camille, leaned back and looked at her. It's a shame a woman such as her—with all her beauty, wit and charm—couldn't have a real wedding night to go with the very legal ceremony.

"What do you think happened to the dress?" Camille's soft, sweet voice invaded his happy thoughts.

He'd give her three guesses and the first two didn't count. In a word—Madeleine. But without proof, Julian wasn't comfortable making accusations. "I could only guess, Chéri."

"Yeah, and your first two don't count."

What the hell? A manic, crazed feeling slammed Julian's heart to the floor. He swallowed the panic and lugged his heart up into his chest. "When we return to Marseilles," he said, commanding himself to relax, "I will find out what happened to your dress."

"Well, I guess it doesn't really matter." She shrugged, disappointed. "It's not like there was really anything to spoil by stealing it."

Her words left no guessing on the matter. She suspected, just as Julian did, that someone, probably Madeleine, had stolen the dress.

"But the dress is yours, Chéri," he said, stretching his arm along the back of the sofa. "No matter the circumstances. The dress was made for you. It belongs to you."

She smiled and seemed to soften, melting into a display of agreeability. "You're an awfully nice guy, Julian." A tremor touched her lips. "No wonder Madeleine's blowing a gasket."

Julian laughed. Partly because the last thing he ever wanted to be thought of was *a nice guy*, but mostly because he found her American point of view hilarious. *Blowing a gasket.* How amusing.

An attendant appeared in the doorway next to the wet bar. He waited until Julian acknowledged him with a slight nod.

"Good evening, sir," he said. "Will you and Mrs. de Laurent be dining in here, or do you prefer one of the dining areas?"

Julian looked at Camille. She shrugged, a clueless look shaping on her face. He thought about a romantic candlelit dinner up on deck overlooking the sea, but it was still raining. Eating in here in the lounge was out of the question. He didn't have many memories of his mother, but one of the few he had was about this place. She'd never allowed food in this room, beyond hors d'oeuvres.

"The dining room," he said.

♡

An hour later, Julian and Camille were finishing dessert dishes of chocolate mousse and fresh strawberries.

He reached for his glass of wine, needing to sate the fires ignited while he'd gazed upon Camille in the candlelight. Her crystal eyes sparkled in the flame's glow. Her mouth was inviting and begged to be kissed—long, slow, and hard.

Moaning desire charged up Julian's throat. He disguised it by clearing it out in a regimented cough.

Camille looked agitated. How was he going to get her to relax? What had her so wound up? Surely the dress wasn't an issue still. Granted, he saw how the whole missing dress episode could be unsettling, but he and Camille weren't actually committed to one another. It wasn't like it was a real omen. She'd pointed that out. Maybe it was all for show. A real bride would be devastated. And Camille was, after all, an actress.

But he couldn't help thinking there was something more to her anxiety. She'd been fiddling with her silverware. Cutting, poking and stirring the food on her plate all through dinner and dessert. Finally, she laid the fork down, the prongs resting on the edge of the dish, and raised her gaze to meet his.

"We need to talk." She rested her wrists against the edge of the table and rubbed her thumb against her forefinger.

Ah, perhaps I'm about to find out what's gotten her so upset. Julian sighed. If he knew what was bothering her, he could fix it. There was always a way to fix a woman's disappointment. You just had to know how to go about it, and Julian was an expert in that department.

"What's on your mind?" he asked, opening the door to any possibility.

"Look, I know where you and I stand on our marriage," she said provisionally. "But you yourself have said, more than once, that you want it to appear real."

That notion aroused old anxieties. "To everyone, including my family, our marriage must appear authentic." Obviously, she was worried about that and he needed to know why. "You think someone may not believe our authenticity?"

"Well..." She hesitated and shifted uneasily. "Some may doubt our sincerity, especially with your *booty call* hanging around."

"Booty call?"

She raked her fingers nervously through her hair. "I mean, I know it's none of my business and all, but, it's kind of hard to expect people to believe our marriage is real if there are noticeable indicators suggesting otherwise."

Somewhere in her rambling, she had a point. Madeleine was the whole reason for this ersatz marriage. That amplified Camille's point. But Julian had already realized that—which is why he'd taken steps at the reception to neutralize the awkward and problematic concerns.

To Julian's surprise, Camille was also coming across as a bit jealous of Madeleine, and he knew there was nothing quite so tempting as a man who was wanted by another woman. Especially when there was no love lost between the women. He was pretty sure Camille didn't think much of Madeleine.

"I can see your point." He leaned back in his chair and fed her his practiced, captivating grin. The one that charmed the ladies out of their good graces. "It's probably not a good idea to let a seemingly harmless idiosyncrasy poke holes in our otherwise perfect plan."

"Then you really need to get Madeleine in check."

Smart girl. She was getting rid of the thorn in her side and doing it diplomatically. Who could argue with the case she'd made?

"I've already taken care of that." It was best to let her know she'd triumphed over Madeleine. He was counting on it winning him points. "Either she's gone by the time you and I return, or we will be moving into town."

Just as he suspected, a victorious smile spread over her face. "Really?"

"You find that hard to believe?"

"Well, yeah. Kind of."

"Why?" He hadn't shown Madeleine any sort of particular favor since he and Camille had returned from America. Perhaps it had something to do with Madeleine being a guest at the house.

"Well, you know..." Her words drifted into a hushed whisper and she looked away shyly.

Julian laid his hand on the table, regretting they were so far apart that he couldn't touch her. "Chéri...?"

"Look, I know it's really none of my business who or what you do." Her tone was lit with a possessive desperation. "But since you're the one who wants it to look real, you probably should use a bit more discretion in your dalliances with Madeleine." She looked almost embarrassed.

Julian laughed. Camille thought he was carrying on a running affair with Madeline. And she was jealous. Huh. Imagine that. "Did she tell you we were...?" Or maybe she didn't like having it thrown in her face.

"Yes." Camille nodded. "In graphic detail."

No wonder she was angry.

"Chéri, have you forgotten...?" He paused, and managed to contain his laughter to just a thought. "Madeleine is the reason I married you."

A look of torment crossed her face. "I just don't get that." She paused, waving a gesture into the air. "Why didn't you just marry her? In your room this morning, she made it clear you'll be continuing your affair."

"What are you talking about?" He tried to hide his confusion, but it escaped in his coolly disapproving tone.

"She was in your room this morning."

"No, she wasn't."

"Yes, she was."

"When?" There was no way Madeleine was in his room, and he didn't understand why Camille thought otherwise.

"Oh, she was there. You were in the shower."

He shook his head, hardly able to believe Madeleine's nerve. "She must have come in when I got in the shower."

"Of course." Camille closed her eyes and seemed to be letting reality sink in. "You said she'd do this." She shook her head in a slow, rhythmic movement and looked at Julian. "I feel like an idiot," she said, almost laughing at herself. "She insinuated she'd been there all night."

A sense of sadness hung a long brittle silence in the air. He shook his head regretfully. "She's crazy. She was no more in my room last night than I was in yours."

"You did say she'd set out to have me catch the two of you in bed together," Camille said. "I just didn't realize it would all be a charade."

He felt bad now, that Madeleine—who thought the marriage was authentic—had thrown a faux affair in his wife's face.

"Chéri, I'm so sorry." He closed his eyes for a second or two and then looked back at Camille. "Even in a business arrangement, you didn't deserve to be humiliated."

Her cheeks reddened a tinge. He could see it, even in the dimly lit candles' glow.

Should he make his move? Or, should he bid her goodnight and let her contemplate all she'd learned?

He had to be very careful. Moving too quickly could ruin his chances forever.

Chapter Thirteen

AT SOME POINT DURING THE NIGHT the storm had passed and the Naoma Louise had set sail. The night had been restless for Camille. What possessed her to think she could pretend to be married to a guy like Julian de Laurent for six months and not develop a consuming desire to have sex with the man?

All night long, he'd invaded her thoughts, her dreams, her heart. The only place he hadn't invaded was her bed. And that was the one place she wouldn't have turned him away, even though it was the smart thing to do. But he'd slept on the sofa in their bedchamber.

She'd thought it looked uncomfortable, but he'd fallen asleep almost instantly and hadn't awakened, even after she'd started moving around in the bathroom that morning.

Sunshine and blue skies peeked in through the window. She slipped into a black bikini that fit like it had been made specifically for her body. Camille studied herself in the mirror, surprised at how good she looked. She grabbed a towel and her sunglasses and ventured outside.

Finding a swimming pool on the upper deck surprised and pleased Camille. She grabbed a lounge chair and made herself at home. For a while, she drank in the sight of the open sea, observing nothing but water and small dots of land off in the distance. Soon, drowsiness accompanied her into a nap.

She couldn't be certain how much time had passed since she'd fallen asleep, but footsteps fell over the deck and Camille opened her eyes behind her sunglasses. Julian in a pair of deep green boxer shorts jolted her heart. She swallowed hard. Acting on such an attraction—no matter how much she wanted to—would be perilous, because in six months he'd send her packing.

His eyes raked daringly over her, and his mouth softened. "Good morning, Chéri." He straddled the chair beside her. "I trust you slept well last night?"

Hell, no. She'd had the worst night ever. And how dare he tease her like that? "Fine, thanks." Fortunately, she had the shades to cover her eyes, which probably contradicted her lie.

"How about lunch? Are you hungry?" He extended his hand, his knuckles skimming against her bare thigh.

She inched her leg away and tipped her sunglasses, peering at him with one eye closed. "What's on the menu?"

"Whatever you want."

Whatever I want. A slight moan trickled up her throat. To stop it from blasting out in a full-blown expression, she lunged forward and threw her legs over the edge of the chair. "Lunch. That sounds like a plan."

Julian chuckled and stood, reaching for her hand. She draped her fingers over his, igniting a quick shiver that rolled through her. On the far side of the boat, a fully furnished table under an umbrella commandeered her attention.

He let go of her hand and seated her with her back to the sun. She worried about him as he moved to the other side, hoping the umbrella would provide him with shade.

The attendant, Jonathan, appeared with two lobster tails, fresh fruits, and various green and pasta salads.

Lobster tails? For lunch? "Oh, no," she said, thinking about the fat and calories that came as a packaged deal with all this rich food.

"What?" Julian asked, as if his feelings had been hurt. "You don't like lobster?"

"Oh, no...I like lobster just fine." She didn't want to sound ungrateful. "In fact, I love lobster." She paused, and while she didn't want to hurt his feelings, there were consequences for eating so recklessly. "But if I keep eating like this...in six months, I'll be as big as a house."

A flash of humor curled on Julian's lips. He grabbed his champagne glass. "Make a list of the foods you'd prefer to eat and give it to Soren when we return home. He'll relay your instructions to the kitchen."

"Man, you sure are accommodating." Camille dipped a piece of lobster in fresh butter. She popped it into her mouth and the flavors, sweet and rich, engaged her taste buds and filled them with immense pleasure.

"Well, I aim to please," Julian said.

They focused on their meal with bits and pieces of small talk about the weather, the Naoma Louise, and the Mediterranean around them. Afterward, Julian suggested they have dessert indoors, and they moved inside to an informal dining area.

She followed his lead and slipped into a chair at one corner of a very large table. Jonathan brought them each a covered tray. The dish was cold. Very cold.

"What is this?" she asked, pointing to the silver lid.

Julian looked at her with amplified innocence.

"Is it ice cream?" A sense of defeat swept over her. *Please, don't say yes.*

He smiled.

Damn. She was doomed. "You know, you've really got to start paying attention." She paused, trying to gulp down the lump swelling in her throat. "Big as a house. Remember that."

The smile spreading across his face was as intimate as a kiss. He lifted the cover, revealing an ice cream sundae. A diamond studded heart pendant on a gold chain was draped around the crystal bowl's stem.

"That's beautiful." Camille sucked in a breath filled with joy and then sorrow and disappointment. Disappointment that she hadn't been able to find a man such as Julian for real. Her very own Prince Charming. She sighed. "But why?" She summoned the courage to look at him. Their marriage wasn't real. Why was he baiting her with the actions of a *real* husband?

"After all you put up with yesterday," he said. "It's the least I could do."

The look on his face, genuine regret, softened her concern and eased her doubt. She wanted to hug him, kiss him, tell him she was his for the taking. But that wasn't wise. The only thing it would get her was some serious heartbreak time.

"You're very kind," she said, and dropped it at that. Filling with reluctance, she unwrapped the necklace from the dish.

Her heart pounded as Julian rose and moved around behind her. He slipped the trinket from her hand in a slow, seductive movement. Gentle strokes pulled her hair out of the way and he looped the bauble around her neck. No matter how hard she fought it, her desire for him intensified.

Julian's hands skimmed down her bare arms, patted them twice and then he returned to his seat. Of course he'd touch her like that, seductively, and then walk away.

She studied him with a calculated gaze. There was no way in hell she'd survive being teased by him for the next six months. No way.

She pulled her attention away from him and let it roam around the deck. Nothing. Not a thing to use as a viable distraction—except the inner cabin.

She pushed herself up from the table and sauntered toward the double doors. She hurried inside, met by a blast of cool air. A wall on the far side displayed a group of family photographs. Maybe there'd be one from his childhood...that she could poke fun at. That would lighten the mood.

She perched her hands on her hips and scanned the images. A picture of two boys sitting in a woman's lap caught her eye. The children were nothing more than toddlers, and Camille assumed they were Julian and Andre. The woman in the picture, presumably their mother, had a wonderful smile and laughing eyes that reminded her of Julian when he got really excited.

Pointing to the picture, she glanced over her shoulder. "Is this your mother?"

He nodded, a pleased look crossing his face. In an instant, Julian was at Camille's side and removing the photograph from its place on the wall. Stilling, he studied the picture, drawing a heavy breath. Finally, when he did move, he took the photograph and went to the couch on the other side of the room. Camille followed.

"This was taken just weeks before she..." His words faded, and he looked at Camille. The memory had stolen the laughter that usually resided in his eyes.

"Well, it's nice of Claudette not to complain about your mother's pictures being displayed here."

"While Claudette has been a wonderful mother-figure—" He almost laughed. "—This is not the family's boat. It's mine." He glanced around. "Much of what you see here...the décor, the photographs...it all belonged to my mother. These were her personal items."

"Wow." A frenzy of sudden, spinning sorrow toppled her poise. The tribute to his mother said something about what Julian valued in life. "This is a great way to honor your mother and keep her memory alive."

"Papa thinks I'm spending too much effort on the past," he said trivially, setting the framed picture on the coffee table. Julian shrugged and leaned back on the couch, spreading his arms along the back.

Camille relaxed, crossed her legs, and folded her arms over her chest. "I wouldn't say that." Phantom tears stained her heart. "It shows a devotion to your mother's memory. And that's a very appealing quality."

A lonesome sort of smile gave way to lips skewing into a tight pucker on his face. Clearly, the hurt over losing his mother was getting to Julian.

Physical need and a longing drove Camille toward him. A knot rose in her throat. She felt like a breathless teenager. The notion that this might be a bad idea slipped into her mind, but she cast it aside in favor of an inherent craving to comfort him—something she thought no one had ever attempted.

Camille snuggled up to Julian and trailed her soft, silk-like fingertips over his face. Her touch was affectionate and soothing and on the verge of becoming too powerful to resist. Julian closed his eyes and skimmed his hand up her arm.

She dropped her forehead on his chest and let out a pleasurable sigh. His hands trailed over her shoulder, as if they had a mind of their own, and explored the hollow of her back.

"If you're going to stop me," he whispered into her hair, "please have mercy and do it soon."

She lifted her head slowly and implored him with her eyes before leaning in and kissing him with a hunger that contradicted her outward composure. "I'm not going to stop you." Her lips brushed against his as she talked.

Julian caressed her untamed hair out of her face. "*Chéri* —" He traced his fingers along her cheek. "—if you become uncomfortable at anytime, just tell me and I'll stop."

"I want to be with you. That's all I know." She said, wrapping her arms around his neck. "I've never wanted anything so badly in my whole life."

Julian led her down onto the couch and trailed soft, sensuous kisses across her face and down the length of her neck. His hand brushed against the patch of fabric covering her breast. She sighed.

He grazed his pelvis against her thigh and felt himself growing hard. She turned herself toward him as if she wanted the contact.

Julian watched his own actions intently, pushing the triangles of fabric away from her breasts, first one and then the other, exposing her nakedness. He swallowed hard; he'd been wanting to do this from the first moment he'd laid eyes on her. Cupping her breast in his hand, he leaned down and teased her playfully, running his tongue over her nipple. She moaned and arched her back, trying to find him.

"Patience, *Chéri*." He gave her a smile born from affection, wanting to taste her lips now. He seized her mouth, kissing her hard and long. Watermelon. She tasted like watermelon.

Breathlessly, she locked her arms around his neck and pressed her naked breasts against his chest. Her nipples brushed firmly against his own bare skin. Urgent desire swept through him, catching him off guard.

He drew a deep breath, the sweet scent of her perfume—the Dior he'd bought her—invaded his senses. Julian grazed his fingertips over her stomach and down between her legs.

Camille let out a delightful gasp and a slight moan escaped her lips as his fingers touched her. She arched her hips, encouraging him to explore further. He danced playfully and she moved quickly trying to match his pace.

Encouraged by her, Julian's own desire throbbed inside his briefs, desperate to be let loose. As if instantly aware of the bulge pulsating against her thigh, she reached out and touched him, running her hand along the outside of his boxers.

She quickened her pace under his touch. She was too close to the edge. He stopped abruptly, pulling away.

He stood and removed his briefs. Her eyes sprang open and her surprise got tangled in her throat, escaping in a gritty groan.

Julian climbed back on top of her and paused, gazing down upon her angelic face. She flushed crimson. Their eyes locked and their breathing merged in unison.

"Do you want me to go on?" He gave her one last opportunity to back out, to be sure this was what she really wanted.

She smiled, pulling him closer. "Don't you dare leave me hanging now," she whispered, opening her legs.

Clearly an open invitation, Julian ripped the bikini bottoms away from her body and pushed his way inside her. She wrapped her legs around him, and he began gliding in and out, slowly at first, until his desires took over and he pumped faster.

Wave after wave of her delight burst rhythmically around him. "*Chéri...*" Julian muttered the endearment as he filled her instantly with his own satisfaction.

Feeling as though she'd claimed every ounce of energy that he had to give, he relaxed lifelessly on top of Camille.

"Wow..." she said softly, breathlessly.

"I didn't hurt you, did I?" He genuinely hoped he hadn't.

"No." She giggled slightly. "You didn't hurt me."

"That's good," he said with a bit of aloofness. He knew he should get up, but she felt so good. So right.

His manhood pulsed and slipped out of her as if it knew retreating was the best course of action. She moaned, as if disappointed.

"I'm sorry, *Chéri*." He paused for a moment, drinking in the striking afterglow shining on her face. "I shouldn't have let it go that far." He pushed himself off the couch, torn between culpability and contentment. "You've been more than vocal that this wasn't to be part of the bargain." He scooped his shorts off the floor and slid into them, positioning them comfortably around his waist. "Just say the word and it won't happen again."

"Look, I know this is not real. It's a business deal." She acknowledged. "But there's no reason why it can't be a business deal with benefits."

That wasn't exactly what he wanted to hear, and once he realized it, he found it disturbing.

Not to worry, though. In six months, he would have had his fill of her and be happy to see her go.

♡

Julian had breakfast brought into their stateroom the following morning. He'd anticipated, and was pretty sure Camille was in complete agreement, that they'd spend much of this day in bed. Not having to venture far for food was advantageous.

She been eyeing the plain black box, larger than the average jewelry case, with its gold ribbon tied around it in a neat little bow. It'd come in with the breakfast cart.

"Come here." He scooted his chair back and motioned her over with a lazy wave.

She sauntered around the small table and straddled his lap, awakening his loins.

He slid the box toward them and presented it to Camille. "This is for you."

She took it, giving him a narrowed glance and eased it opened. Finding a wallet-sized leather-bound checkbook and a credit card, both stamped with the name *Camille de Laurent*, she shot him a twisted smile. She opened it and fanned the checks before stopping to look at the check register.

Camille's mouth dropped open and she stared wordlessly. He'd guess she'd seen the amount on the liberal credit line.

She looked at him, her face etched with shock and surprise. "What is this?"

"You're going to need some cash at your disposal."

"A credit card isn't cash."

"It's pretty close."

"Why do I need this much cash available to me?" She paused, her look of surprise giving way to suspicion. "This has nothing to do with last night, does it?"

"No." He adjusted her in his lap, running his hands beneath her satin robe. She was naked underneath it. He enjoyed the feel of nothing but his silk boxers between them. "It has nothing to do with last night, this morning, or tomorrow."

"Good." She panted, her chest heaving. "Because I don't want to start feeling like a kept woman."

"Kept women aren't, by definition, wives," he said, exploring further beneath the soft, silky robe.

"What am I supposed to do with the checkbook and credit card?" Her arms enfolded him.

"Whatever you want. It's your money to spend." He pressed her against him. "I'm sure Claudette and Lecie will insist that you accompany them on regular shopping sprees. Buy whatever you want."

It's what was expected of his wife. And above all else, Julian couldn't forget the marriage needed to look authentic.

That's all it was. It just needed to *look* that way. And the sex? Well, like she'd said—it was a business transaction with benefits.

Yes. That's all it was.

Chapter Fourteen

CAMILLE WAS SADDENED when their honeymoon cruise ended. She had to keep reminding herself that it wasn't real, even if they had spent the last ten days having some incredible sex.

And, returning to Pacifique de Lumière under the cover of night felt like they were sneaking back in. But she refused to buy into those insecurities and fears. Instead, she let her mind wander to a place filled with possibilities as she followed Julian upstairs to their new suite, just a few doors down from Tasha's room.

Next morning, she realized she'd taken too much for granted when Soren gave her the news.

Camille charged into Tasha's room. Raw nerves bore down heavy in her gut at the sight of her only friend packing.

"You're leaving?" Camille's voice cracked. "Why are you leaving so soon? Did somebody do or say something to upset you?" Her fear of being abandoned gave way to suspicion. She wouldn't be surprised to find that Maurice or Madeleine, or both, were responsible for Tasha's decision to leave.

"When have you ever known me to shy away from a challenge?" Tasha said, as if that notion was the most ridiculous thing in the world. "It's just time for me to go home."

Camille didn't say anything, lost in a moment of deep pessimism.

Somewhere deep in her psyche she wondered if she could *will* Tasha into staying.

"This is your world now, but it's not mine." Her words cut through Camille like a sharp dagger.

Guess not.

"Mine's in L.A. Where I need to find work soon, or I'm screwed." She laughed as if it wasn't that big a deal, but Camille saw the worry in her vivid green eyes.

Julian had given her a "spending account" with a generous endowment. If she was going to use it, why not splurge on something worthwhile. She grabbed Tasha's hand and pulled her out the hallway and into her suite of rooms.

Tasha waited in the doorway, as if entering would have some ill-effected consequences. Camille grabbed her leather-bound checkbook from a desk drawer and used a nearby table to issue her first check. It ripped from the book with relative ease, and she waved it in the air at her friend.

"What's this?" Tasha's eyes danced anxiously.

"Just in case L.A.'s on a mean streak when you get back."

Tasha slipped the check between her fingers and glanced at it, her eyes widening. "Wow. Ten grand." She struggled with the silence for a moment and finally said, "I can't take this."

"Sure you can."

"I doubt I'd ever be able to pay it back." She shook her head. "I can't take it."

"It's not a loan. It's a gift. From one friend to another."

Tasha shook her head again, her mouth tightening. She closed her eyes. "No. I don't want to get you into trouble with Julian." She paused, and slowly raised her gaze to meet Camille's. "What'll he say when he finds out you're giving away money?"

"Julian gave me the money to do with as I please." Camille shrugged. "I choose to give it to you."

Tasha moaned and tapped her foot. "You let me know if he makes a fuss and I'll send it right back," she said, with a bit of reluctance. "Whatever I've spent, I'll find a way to pay you back."

"Don't worry about it," Camille said, taking her arm and leading her to the door. "He said I could spend it any way I wanted."

"I'm so afraid I'm never going to see you again." Tasha's words were drenched in angst.

"Oh, you'll see me again," Camille blurted out without thinking. "I'll make sure of it," she added, trying to cover her blunder with a well-meant declaration.

"Well, I guess so," she said, almost bitterly, following Camille into the hallway. "Your husband does have a fleet of private jets and he can take you anywhere you want to go." Immediately, regret cast a shadow over Tasha's face.

But Camille knew Tasha was feeling abandoned. She was losing her best friend to a husband half a world away. And Camille knew a thing or two about abandonment. There was no way to spin it to make the one left behind feel better.

"You know," Camille said as they descended the stairs, "You can always 'act' in France." She put it out there to see if Tasha would bite.

She didn't. "Are you kidding?" she shrieked. "Like they want to see some American on their TV screen."

"Jerry Lewis."

"Huh?"

"Jerry Lewis," Camille repeated. "He's an American. And the French love him."

"Everybody loves Jerry Lewis." Tasha snorted and then her face sobered. "I'm no Jerry Lewis."

She had a point.

They stopped at the entryway, and Julian came in through a door on the far side. His first move was to kiss Camille's cheek. "Good morning, darling."

"Ooh, darling..." Tasha's voice bordered on dreamy. "The honeymoon must've gone really well."

Camille smacked her.

Andre entered from a different doorway. Looking at Tasha with suitcases by her side, his smile faded. "Chéri...are you going somewhere?"

She sighed and got this poignant look on her face. "Andre, you have been a dear, really. But it's time for me to go home."

"Chéri," Andre slammed his hand against his chest. "You break my heart."

Julian took one look at Andre and another at Tasha. When his attention landed back on Andre, Julian's face turned into a scowl. "Soren!" Julian bellowed his valet's name.

Soren appeared from out of nowhere. "Yes, sir."

"You will accompany Miss Gordon back to Los Angeles."

"Me, sir?" Soren failed to hide the shock.

"I'll accompany her," Andre said.

"No." Julian stared at his brother. "You have other business that needs your attention." If looks could kill, Julian's came with a loaded nine millimeter.

Andre paused, slipped Tasha's hand in his and brushed his lips against it. "Chéri, I await your next visit." He bowed. "Do not make me wait long."

He gave her one of those looks that moved even Camille. It reminded her of Julian. Two heartthrobs in one family. The girls in France weren't safe. Neither was Camille. Tasha was the fortunate one; she was leaving.

♡

Julian leaned in and kissed Tasha's cheek, then moved immediately back to Camille's side. "Tasha, your visit was a pleasure." He smiled and rested his hand on the small of Camille's back. "I do hope you'll come back soon. Anytime you'd like to get away, just let Camille know and we'll send a plane for you directly."

He turned to Camille, wanting very much to run back upstairs with her. But Papa had said it was important. And it probably was, according to Papa. He could wait. At least a couple of minutes.

Julian grabbed Andre by the arm and dragged him into the west hallway. He closed the door and leaned against it, arm outstretched. "Are you insane?"

Andre remained silent. He slipped his hands inside his trousers pockets and waited.

Julian hated it when he did that. But it wouldn't stop him from admonishing his little brother. "Didn't I tell you specifically, do not sleep with Camille's friend?"

"In all fairness...I did not *sleep* with her." Andre defended his case.

"I'm in no mood for your play on words." Julian paused, drawing his hands into fists at his sides. "If you leave that girl brokenhearted, then my wife will become upset. If she's upset—"

Andre laughed. "I know, you don't..." Andre's words trailed off, as if recalling the last time he'd said something rude and risqué about Camille.

"Check yourself, baby brother," Julian warned.

"You've got it all wrong," Andre said, almost sulking.

"How's that?"

"I asked her not to leave."

"What?" Rippling waves of shock slapped at Julian.

He didn't know which was worse. Andre being a cad. Or Andre falling for Tasha. That's the worst thing that could happen. How could Julian walk away guilt-free at the end of six months if Camille's friend became his sister-in-law?

"I want you to stay away from that girl." Julian's finger popped up in Andre's face, accompanying his order. "Do you understand?"

Andre walked to the door and paused, looking over his shoulder. "Why do you get to have all the fun?"

"Apparently, I'm not the only one." Julian's thoughts lingered on Andre until he disappeared around a corner.

There was no putting it off any longer. Papa was waiting. Julian headed in the direction of his father's study. He whistled a jovial tune as he trekked through the halls and stopped at Papa's door. Summoning his courage, he knocked.

"Come." Papa's voice traveled through the walls.

Julian opened the door. Papa's bottle was already out of the drawer. An audacious move that desiccated Julian's confidence. If he was bold enough to flaunt the liquor, in the off-chance Claudette walked in, whatever had Papa so troubled, it must be bad.

"Papa..." Julian took to his pockets to keep from openly fiddling with his hands. His knees weakened as he progressed across the room, which seemed much too small today.

Papa gestured toward the empty chairs in front of the desk.

Julian hesitated and sank into one.

"How was the cruise?" Papa's tone was much too gentle and accommodating.

What's this? A trap? Julian hesitated. In the whole of Julian's life, Papa had never made small talk with anyone, not that he'd ever heard. His attempt reminded Julian of a spider stalking a fly that was on the verge of landing in his web.

That was a snare Julian wasn't about to fall into. "Fine."

Papa filled a shot glass and pushed it gently across the desk. Julian reached for it, feeling like a fly that was coming dangerously close to the spider's web. He pulled the drink toward him and left it sitting on the edge of the desk.

Take that. Two could play this game. Julian had after all learned from the best.

Papa saluted and drained his glass. Julian didn't have the guts to say, *should you be drinking that, and so early in the day?* But it was on his mind. His father's health worried him daily.

Papa opened the center drawer, pulled out a manila envelope and tossed it across the desk.

"What's that?" Julian asked, avoiding it. He wasn't playing.

"It's a dossier on your wife."

Julian tried to keep a stoic face. "Why?" His discomfort snuck out as awkward fidgeting.

Maurice's right jaw twitched. "See for yourself," he said, waving his hand over his desk.

"Why don't you just save me the trouble and tell me what you think you've uncovered?" Surely there couldn't be this much commotion over finding out Camille had acting aspirations.

Papa studied him for a moment with that cold, calculating glare of his, and pulled a box of cigars out of his desk.

Not the cigars. He brought out his trademark technique of smoke screening a weak accusation. On the surface, that looked like a good thing. But Papa could be brutal when he didn't get his way—and Julian wasn't about to let that happen.

The sweet scent of cognac followed the smoke as it floated about the room. Julian loved that smell, it reminded him of his childhood. But Papa rarely smoked the aromatic cigars anymore. Not because he couldn't afford them, but because Claudette's nose was stronger than a Bloodhound's.

She must be in town. Or perhaps Paris. Nothing else ever induced Papa to act so carelessly.

He puffed on his cigar a couple of times. "You've brought a wolf into the lion's den."

What? That made no sense. Julian searched his brain, coming up with nothing. Papa was losing his mind. "Perhaps you'd better spell it out for me." Julian met Papa's accusing eye without flinching. "I have no idea what wolf I've let into what lion's den."

Did this have something to do with a business deal? He'd wrapped up the merger—ala-takeover—of Dine Shipping nearly a month ago. Which is why he'd felt comfortable going to America to find Camille and then taking another ten days for the honeymoon. There was nothing pressing on his calendar.

"The lion's den would be this family." Papa's icy stare surrounded him with a chill.

This family? *What...?* Papa had nothing. It had to be so. Julian was always careful about what he subjected the family to. He may have let Madeleine down a little hard, but he'd never once put the family in harm's way.

"And the wolf is your wife." Papa looked like a cat with feathers in its mouth.

Julian's laughter echoed across the room. That was the most ridiculous thing he'd ever heard. "That's a stretch, Papa."

"Please tell me you had her sign a confidentiality agreement?" It wasn't a question so much as an opinion.

Confidentiality agreement? The thought hadn't crossed Julian's mind. Surely the attorneys had her sign one as part of the pre-nup.

"I'll take that as a no." Papa's voice faded and he glanced down at his lap. It was only a second or two, but it felt like forever to Julian.

No. He didn't say no. He didn't say anything. But, as usual, Papa had a way of reading Julian as if he were an open book. Julian rallied his desire to believe in Camille. "You have nothing to worry about."

"Nothing to worry about?" Papa snorted. "The girl works for a Los Angeles gossip rag called *Disclosure Magazine*." He paused, his face turning red. "I think we have plenty to worry about."

"There has to be some mistake." His voice weakened, right along with his confidence. Insistence and denial reeled through Julian's mind. *She's an actress. Not a reporter.*

"There's no mistake." Papa's accusing finger pointed to the envelope that Julian still hadn't touched.

But he had news for Papa—he refused to look at the information. Julian didn't believe it. Camille wasn't here under false pretenses. Whatever the truth was, he wanted to hear it from Camille herself. Not some suspect report given to him by his father.

"Find a way to handle this discreetly." Papa's voice cut through the silence.

"I'll handle it." Julian rose and paused in front of his father's desk. "It's not what you think."

"Just see to it that she doesn't do what I think she's come here to do." Papa's voice followed him to the door.

Julian hesitated, pushing aside the thoughts invading his head. The woman he'd poured his heart out to in the garden. The woman who'd rocked his world just last night. The woman who'd promised to be his salvation. She couldn't be here after a story.

Chapter Fifteen

CAMILLE STEPPED OUT of the marble-laid shower with its gold-plated fixtures and grabbed a hand-woven towel, the softest she'd ever seen.

She draped an equally plush bathrobe around her and tied the belt before tousling her wet hair. One last quick glance into the mirror, and she pushed herself toward the gigantic suite she and Julian had moved into after returning from the honeymoon cruise last night. The suite was like its own little apartment inside this huge old house. Camille saw no reason to leave the sanctity of its walls. Anything not to run into Madeleine or Maurice.

The glittering diamond necklace Julian had given her caught her eye. Before getting into the shower, she'd placed it on the table by the window overlooking the rose garden. She touched the pendant, aroused by its romantic inference.

Flashes of their naked bodies tangled together flittered through her mind. The thoughts made her smile. Camille had no disillusions where Julian was concerned. She knew this was temporary—well it had started out that way—but she had six months to change his mind—and hers. Julian was starting to grow on her, and she dared to entertain the notion that he could be her Prince Charming.

Camille dropped into the nearby chair and glanced out the window. The roses looked like someone had come along and splattered a green canvas with every color imaginable. The suite's décor with its yellows, golds, and reds had a pleasing and calming effect. She could get used to living in Julian's world—and in his arms.

A glass of champagne waited on the table beside her necklace. Someone, probably Monique, had placed it there while Camille was in the shower.

Man, these people are really into drinking. Bubbles floated up the amber liquid in relegated lines. *Just a sip.* Besides, she needed the extra edge to get her through the ups and downs of what was to come. She'd have to be careful not to become too dependent upon the crutch.

Granny Mae had said, more than once, that Camille's father was an alcoholic and it was a blessing in disguise when he'd run out on Camille and her mother. Camille didn't want to end up like that. Deserted and pregnant.

But if it did happen, she'd like to think she'd have enough wherewithal to stick by the child she'd created and not dump him or her off on the nearest relative. Not that Camille had that luxury.

The door opened and Julian entered. She glanced at him and sat up. He didn't look happy. Uh oh, what was this about. She hoped it had nothing to do with Madeleine.

He began pacing the length of the room. His head jerked away from her and then back to her every couple of steps.

Nerves pushed Camille out of the chair. "Julian?" She moved toward him. "What's wrong?"

His hands shot into the air, as if warning her not to touch him. He gave her a frown fraught with desperation. "Is it true?"

"Is what true?" Thoughts swarmed her brain and mingled chaotically to uncover his meaning. What had he discovered? Did he see right through her? Did he know of her secret desires now that they'd consummated their marriage? Did he not want to go there?

Julian elbowed his blazer back and perched his hands on his hips. "Are you or are you not an actress?" Every word came out of his mouth articulate and accusing.

That was not what she was expecting, and in fact, was the worst thing he could've asked. But did it really matter? Did he really care that much about her employment status?

She wanted to say what he wanted to hear, but she wasn't sure what that was. She hesitated and sighed.

"That's what I thought." He paused and glared at her.

He looked at her with such hatred it killed any confidence she'd built up during the course of the morning. Her pride and a fear of rejection wouldn't let her crumble. This was going to turn out just like every other time in her life when she'd been deserted. Julian had found a reason to erect an impenetrable wall between them. Okay, so she hadn't been completely honest but her intentions hadn't been malicious.

It wouldn't matter what she said. Julian had found his *out*, and she had to protect her heart from getting stomped on, once again.

"Just what exactly is your occupation?" His hatred lashed out at her.

Camille shoved the desire to sob back down her throat. "I am currently unemployed." That wasn't a lie. She had no job prospects, but she wasn't about to tell him why. No way was she going to make herself look like an even bigger fool.

Julian's accusing laughter raked her. "Does this mean it's for sale to the highest bidder?"

Huh? She fought the cobwebs of angst-filled confusion. *What's for sale?* She wasn't about to let Julian get the better of her, or make her look like an idiot. "Sure." She folded her arms and tapped red-tipped fingernails against her skin. "But there's a reserve on it." She paused, trying to read him. Trying to figure out what he thought she had for sale. "I'm not giving it away for free."

For a second he almost looked pleased, but that was quickly overshadowed by his hatred. "How much?"

Her pride concealed her inner turmoil. "How much for what?" Frustration poured out in her broken voice. "What the hell are you talking about?"

"You are a writer." His nose flared and his eyes bulged. "Are you not?"

He knew? Reality shuddered through her. Defeat escaped in her sharp sigh.

His lips tightened as if he was biting back the words of disapproval. He shook his fist and then pointed an accusing finger at her. His cold, hard stare froze her in place like a statue and left her quivering with fear. She wasn't afraid of him physically. Just emotionally.

Nobody else was going to desert her. She'd break this bond before he had the chance. "It really doesn't matter what I say," she said. "You won't believe me."

She wanted him to dispute that. She wanted him to say he wanted to hear her explanation. But he didn't.

"What do you say we dispense with the pleasantries?" It sounded like a question, but she knew it was an order. An order for something she couldn't define. She wished she knew what he was talking about.

"How much?"

"Huh?"

"How much will it take for the exclusive?"

"Exclusive?" She was starting to sound like a parrot.

"You're insulting my intelligence." He glowered and turned away.

"Look," she said, through the mounting pressure of tears. "Just tell me what you're talking about."

"Do you deny that you answered my ad as a staff member of Disclosure Magazine?"

Oh, that exclusive. No, she didn't deny it. "Why do you ask?" She bit back the hurt. "You've obviously got it all figured out."

"How much for the exclusive?" he repeated his question.

Camille stiffened, momentarily abashed. He'd never believe her story. She felt ice spreading through her heart. "What's it worth to you?" she asked, suddenly wanting him to share in her pain.

And damned if she was leaving. The way she saw it, he owed her five million bucks. She was staying until he paid up.

"How about one million dollars?" he offered.

She hesitated, torn by his audacious belief that everybody had a price.

He'd obviously read her silence as a bargaining tactic because he went into full negotiating mode. "I doubt that rag you were working for would pay that much. You Americans really don't care that much about what the crazy French are doing." He rolled his eyes and showered her with stinging laughter.

The accusation broke Camille's heart, but she held the hurt inside. How could he think so little of her? There were a ton of things she could say to defend herself, but none of them moved her stoned lips. Finally, a single word escaped. "Deal."

Julian's cold glare bored through her for what seemed an eternity before he stuck his hand out. She accepted it reluctantly. His firm grasp was cold and unfeeling, and elicited no fire, no compassion, no desire.

"There will be more papers to sign."

"I figured."

"I'll pay for the exclusive once I have your signature."

"That'll be fine." Her voice cracked but she held the pain inside. She swallowed the overwhelming urge to cry, holding her lips together tightly to keep the tears from escaping.

The glittering necklace, Julian's gift, sparkled, reminding her that his genuineness was not nearly as solid as the jewels clarity. She reached for it, clasped it in her fist for a moment before unfolding her fingers and offering it to him. "Here. I'm sure you'll want this back," she said over her aching inner pain.

Julian's cold stare squeezed her heart. He pivoted on one heel and walked away. The slamming door echoed through her.

Camille folded her fingers around the pendant and sighed heavily. She'd done it this time. Gotten herself into a real mess. One she was afraid she wouldn't be able to squirm her way out of. Damn.

♡

Julian slowed his pace once in the corridor leading to the main wing. An odd twinge of disappointment filled the empty cavity that used to contain his heart. He'd been deserted—again.

He should've known better. The minute he put his faith and trust in a woman, she turned out to be a liar and a cheat. Camille had deceived him, just like his mother had when she told him she'd always take care of him. How was checking out fulfilling that promise?

Stunned and furious, he fisted his hands at his sides. He struggled to hold his temper. *God, I'm so stupid.*

Julian took the stairs, two at a time, and headed for the side service door, preferring not to run into any of the family. He had to think.

"Julian!" Papa's voice assaulted him from behind.

Damn it. He thought about not stopping. But that was a bad idea. He slid his hands into his pockets, stalled a moment and then turned to face the criticism.

All sorts of things ran through Julian's head, none of them good. Not the kind of things you say to your father. He wished Papa hadn't been so hell-bent on destroying his marriage, as faux as it was, to Camille. This was one time Julian would've much rather been left in the dark. At least, until they were closer to the end of the six months. If Papa wanted to destroy it then, more power to him. But why'd he have to do it now, especially now that Julian and Camille had come to an understanding.

"Did you take care of our problem?" Papa asked.

"*We* don't have a problem."

"That's not the way I see it."

"How do you see it, Papa?" Julian dared to raise his voice to his father. "She's my wife and has no bearing on anyone else in this family."

"I might buy that if she weren't a reporter after a story about this family." His voice matched Julian's.

"What's the matter, Papa?" Julian's animosity escaped in his words. "Are you afraid some of your skeletons are going to come out of the closet?"

"You'd better worry about your own skeletons, boy." Papa looked ready to explode. "There is such a thing as bad publicity. And we don't want ours to start in some American trash magazine."

"I've taken care of that," Julian said, his tone calming. "From here on out you will say nothing, and I do mean nothing, about this to anyone."

"You presume to tell me what to do?"

"Papa...you wanted me to fix it. I did." Julian sucked in a deep breath. "Now, I'm asking you to drop it."

Papa studied him for a long moment, his way of bullying. It wasn't working. Julian was way beyond intimidation. Allowing the coercion would ruin his plan. He walked away.

"Where are you going?" Papa called after him. "Madeleine—"

Julian flung around and pitched his finger in the air at his father. "She'd better be gone."

"Julian..." Papa chastised him with laughter. "You can't really expect me to turn out an old family friend?"

"Fine." Julian paused, preparing to call his bluff. "Camille and I will leave."

"All right." Papa waved his hands in the air. "All right. I'll see what I can do."

Julian continued on, walking away. "When you figure it out—" He glanced over his shoulder. "—You can reach me at the Beauvau."

Chapter Sixteen

CAMILLE SAT ON ONE SIDE of the limousine, next to one door and Julian against the other. He'd made it clear, he wanted nothing more to do with her. She was there for a purpose, to help him avoid a 'real' marriage to Madeleine. And at the end of six months, he'd gladly release her.

Well, if he could walk away without so much as a second thought, she could reciprocate—even if she had to force herself.

She turned toward him but avoided looking into his eyes. "Is it too much to ask—where we're going?" Her tone carried no pleasantries. Camille rotated her gaze back toward the window and glued it on the quick-passing scenery.

"The Beauvau," he said in a flat monotone voice.

"The Beauvau?" She repeated his words and let her gaze take the slow journey to look at him. "Why are we going there?" she asked, overcome by guilt. "It's not because of me, is it?"

"You give yourself too much credit, Chéri." He sneered. "This is a war between my father and me. It has nothing to do with you." He looked disgusted by the sight of her and directed his attention back out the window.

Julian rested his hand on his thigh. Long bronzed fingers that had caressed her so lovingly yesterday tapped out today's irritation. There would be no gentle touches, no sweet caresses, no words of love.

If that's the way he wanted to play it, she'd be more than accommodating. Camille crowded herself against the door.

This was probably just his staged way out. Julian de Laurent had turned every aspect of his life into a life and death drama. He'd gone to great lengths to avoid a 'real' marriage. Whatever happened to...*"Sorry, Pops, but I just don't want to marry her"*?

Instead, he'd gone to America and hired her, a stranger, to pretend to be his wife for six months until his father got over his fascination. What kind of people did that?

Rich ones, that's who. People with way too much money at their disposal. People who are used to getting what they want. People who give no forethought to those they step on in the process.

The next six months was going to be hell.

"What pisses you off more?" she asked, without looking at him. "My seemingly ulterior motive? Or, that your father had to do your homework for you?"

She suspected she'd jabbed him good with that one and mustered the courage to look at him. For a split-second, she almost saw the hint of humorous appreciation trying to light his eyes. Soon it was overshadowed by his swelling anger, or maybe it was hurt. He chose not to speak, just stared at her with a dark, infuriated glare. It unnerved her, and she had a pretty good idea that was his plan.

Camille would love to *not* give him the satisfaction of letting him get to her, if she could just figure out how. But he had. When had that happened?

Julian blasted her with a quick dousing of French—which she didn't understand. But if she had to guess, she'd say it wasn't good.

She stared him down with what she hoped said *your-lecture-is-falling-on-deaf-ears-with-me.*

"Of course you don't understand French." He gave her one of those dismissive looks he'd kept in reserve for his servants until now.

"No. I skipped that class in high school."

"As if your high school French would've been adequate." Julian's obnoxious laughter bruised her ego.

Spiteful jerk.

"Look, I just want to know why we're going to a hotel."

"And I told you."

Lord, he was making this hard. Harder than it had to be. "Okay...if we don't want to stay at the house, for whatever reason." She paused, trying to reason the frivolous expenditure in her head. "Why are we going to a hotel? Why aren't we going back to the Naoma Louise?"

Julian shrugged. Obviously, he hadn't considered that option.

"I know it's none of my business. It's your money and all." Anxiety escaped in her nervous laughter. "But I just don't understand why you're spending money on a hotel when you've got a perfectly good yacht?" she said, even though she felt like she'd overstepped her boundaries.

Julian, on the other hand, looked like a light bulb had gone off inside his head. He turned to her, and seemed to be fighting a smile. "That's a really good idea." The anger and annoyance had deserted his voice, leaving behind nothing but indifference.

He nodded as if making the final decision and hit the intercom. "Sebastian, let's go to the marina instead," he said, and released the button.

The remainder of the drive passed in silence and the ever-growing presence of tension.

Was five million bucks worth all this? Was it worth six months of ridicule and hostilities from a man she could've easily fallen for? Was she seriously thinking she could survive that?

Not even close. No way.

♡

Sebastian opened the limousine's door and a blast of warm, salty sea air hit Julian. He would've enjoyed it, if not for the circumstances. His main objective was to get onboard the Naoma Louise and go below deck where he planned on hibernating until he'd recovered from this malady. Or maybe he'd drop Camille off at the Naoma Louise and then head on over to the Beauvau.

If it weren't for the reason he'd married her, to avoid a marriage with Madeleine, Julian would just give her the money he'd promised her and send her on her way. But that would put him right back where he started, and the one place he didn't want to be. Available.

Julian stepped on board and without thinking, stopped and extended his hand to Camille. For the first time in his life, Julian had been civil without an ulterior motive. The consummate gentleman. His mother would be so proud.

He knew he was probably smiling at Camille, and he remedied that right away by plastering on his hardest, practiced stare.

She looked vulnerable. He wanted to believe the best of her, but she made it hard. Falling back into her snare wasn't wise. Julian dropped her hand, letting it fall away.

He opened the door and again, subconsciously waited for her to enter first. Cool air wafted past as he followed her inside.

"The papers will be delivered later today, sealing our deal." He moved to the bar, ready to pour himself a drink but changed his mind.

"Whatever." She dropped to the couch, crossed her legs and played with her fingernails, which she'd changed to a bright red. Very different from the pastel shades of pink and orange he was used to seeing.

Julian searched the bar for water, opening several decanters and sniffing the liquids inside. All were liquor of some sort. Frustration balled inside him and knotted in his gut. What did a man have to do to get some water?

He grabbed the phone on the bar and punched in a number. "Soren. Can we get some water in here?" He didn't immediately hang up. Instead, he added, "Thank you."

That probably surprised Soren as much as it did Julian. Maybe he was getting sick. Figures. He'd caught a case of the pleasantries.

He leaned against a barstool, caressed his forehead and massaged his temples.

"Julian...?" She paused, hesitating.

He cut a stealthy gaze toward her. She looked like she'd been defeated. "Yeah?"

"I, ah, if leaving the house had anything at all to do with me." She stopped and drew a breath before continuing. "I know you say it wasn't me, but just in case I was any kind of factor." She dared to look at him. "I-I'm sorry, if I played even a small part in that."

Amazing. She looked genuinely sorry. How could she regret that and in the same breath, turn around and make a mental note to add it in her story?

It was probably just a ploy to make herself look better in the final copy. She was doing a good job of assuming the role of *victim*. If she wasn't an actress, she'd missed her calling.

"I told you," he said. "It has nothing to do with you."

"Then why?" she asked. "Why did we leave?"

Maybe he should tell her. Keep her off his back. Otherwise, she'd go on, incorrectly, telling herself that she had somehow played a part in this disaster.

"It's not about you." He smiled, feeling like he'd won some small battle. "It's about Madeleine."

"Madeleine?"

"Papa wants her to stay. I want her gone."

Camille nodded. "I can understand that, considering the lengths you went to, to avoid marrying her." She snickered.

Perhaps that hadn't been the smartest idea. His selfishness had allowed a member of the press to infiltrate the family, undetected. It's a good thing Papa still had his wits about him.

Julian stood and headed for the door, stopping only to glimpse over his shoulder at Camille. "Soren will come for you when the papers arrive."

He slipped into the hallway, needing to put some space between himself and Camille.

♡

Camille was awakened by the knock at the door. She lifted her head off the pillow and looked around groggily.

Oh, yeah. She'd grown tired of sitting in the upper deck lounge all alone, but remembered closing her eyes for just a second. Nothing made the time pass like sleeping your life away. She sighed and fell back on the couch.

The knock came again. More persistent this time. "Mrs. de Laurent?" Soren's voice floated through the walls.

"Yes." She sighed and closed her eyes. Maybe he'd go away. Doubtful. He worked for Julian.

"Mr. de Laurent asked me to come for you," he called through the door. "Your signature is required."

Camille pushed herself into a sitting position. "I'll be there directly."

Damn. She was starting to sound like Julian. Camille drew in a deep breath and sighed. *Okay. Time to face the music.* She just wished the musician played a more agreeable tune.

Having no other choice was the factor that pushed her off the couch. The plush carpet offered little comfort as she studied her messy hair in the mirror. Not caring about impressions, she ran her fingers through it a few times, straightened her blouse and headed out into the hallway where Soren was waiting.

Okay. So now she needed a chaperone? What? Did Julian think she was going to steal the silver?

Camille followed Soren to the top deck salon. Julian and his attorney—oh, what was his name? —were huddled over the bar enthralled in deep conversation. Julian looked up. She could tell when he'd seen her, his demeanor soured.

"Here she is." Julian offered no smile. His eyes didn't light up. In fact, he just looked annoyed.

"Okay," she said, dropping onto the couch. So he was going to be a jerk. Two could play that game. "Let's get this over with." She winced as the words poured from her mouth.

Julian shuffled across the room and sat beside her. Draping his arm around her, he whispered, "Now, darling." He called her 'darling' instead of Chéri. She didn't like that. "There's no need to be a bitch."

"No, that's your girlfriend's job." She flashed him a look that must have been effective because his confidence wilted, if only for a second or two.

"Good one." He winked at her and pushed himself off the couch. He stood over her, extending his hand. She took it, trying to erect a stronger guard against his charms.

Julian tugged her across the room, settling her at the bar where his attorney had a mass of paperwork laid out. She waited for an introduction. None came.

The lawyer handed her a fountain pen. She took it and looked at Julian. "You signed it already?"

He nodded.

"If you'll just sign here." The attorney pointed to a blank line beneath Julian's signature.

Camille snatched the papers off the counter and began reviewing them. Julian snickered. She ignored him. He was not as cute as he thought.

If she kept telling herself that, sooner or later she might buy into the notion.

The document read pretty standard. She was selling her story exclusively to de Laurent Enterprises. Pretty amusing, since she hadn't planned on writing one in the first place.

Camille signed all copies of the agreement and laid the gold-plated pen on the counter along with the papers.

"Is that all?" she said to Julian.

"For now." He winked at her and turned away.

Jerk.

Camille pushed off from the bar and headed for the door. There wasn't a reason in the world that she should put up with his asinine ways.

She let the door slam behind her as she left.

♡

Julian jumped and laughed comically. She was mad. Good. So was he. "How long before the money is wired into the account?"

"Tomorrow," Jasper said, gathering the documents. "I'll get these filed and bring your copies around tomorrow."

"Can you bring some documentation from the bank confirming the transfer?"

"Of course," he said, stuffing the paperwork inside his attaché. "Is there anything else I can do for you today?" he added, closing the case.

"No, I think that'll do it." Julian moved behind the bar and headed for the liquor. It was time for a drink.

He grabbed a glass and filled it with a generous serving of the closest bottle. Julian studied it for a moment before pouring it into his mouth. He swished it and swirled it around, letting the sting diminish before swallowing the tart liquid.

He slammed the glass down on the bar. It wasn't often that he got married and taken for a ride, all at the same time. There was almost something enticing about her outwitting him.

Almost.

Chapter Seventeen

WITHIN TWO DAYS Papa had moved Madeleine to town. For the first time, Julian felt he'd won in a battle of wills with his father. It wasn't often that Papa gave up, in effect admitting defeat.

Too bad Julian's victory was overshadowed by Camille's deception. But still, he had to honor his end of the bargain no matter what her motives were for accepting the deal. He didn't have to like it, but he had to accept the inevitable.

Camille had handled the constant shuffling between the house and the yacht like a champion. When he said it was time to go back to Pacifique de Lumière, she'd agreed without a second thought. She looked bored over the whole mess, more than anything else.

He'd been holding onto the filed papers and the bank transfer receipt for the last couple of days just because he could. Since they'd signed the documents, he wanted to see how long it'd take her to ask for the money. She hadn't, and he found that irksome.

She spent her time inside their suite or in the garden. Usually alone. He felt sorry for her and envied her at the same time over her aloneness and her ability to find solitude in it. Having no one to beleaguer or infuriate you must be great, yet lonely. If there's no one to bother you, there's also no one to love you.

But since when had that mattered to him?

He opened the door to the main parlor in their suite. She was sitting facing the window. Her still frame didn't move. She didn't acknowledge his presence.

He tapped the manila envelope against his palm and cleared his throat. She glanced over her shoulder, stared right through him and turned back to the window. After a moment of immobility, she pushed herself up and turned to face him. Her stoic expression gave nothing away about what she was feeling.

Camille clasped her hands together and raised her gaze to meet his. She didn't say anything, just looked at him with cold, hard eyes.

Julian vowed to show her just how little she affected him. He drew a breath and acknowledged the envelope in his hand. "I thought you might like these." He kept his voice calm, and on a low, even keel.

She shrugged and folded her arms in front of her. As if the distance across the room wasn't enough, she'd erected another barrier.

Part of him wanted to reach out to her, but it was smothered by the part that loathed her actions. Loathed that she'd come to him under false pretences. Loathed that she'd made him look like a fool.

Nobody got away with that.

"This is your copy of our agreement." He waved the envelope in the air. "The bank receipt is in here, too. Your acceptance of this money seals our deal." He paused, ruthlessness invading his tone. "Make no mistake, if you discuss this family with any outlets of the media, I will sue you."

She came toward him, her eyes darkening dangerously. Ignoring the envelope, she reacted with nothing more than a couple of pronounced blinks. Other than that, she was like a statuette poised in permanent indifference.

"Have you nothing to say?" His anger escaped in a harsh growl.

"What do you want me to say, Julian?"

He moved a couple of steps toward her and she backed up.

Julian's heart ached with defeat. He wanted her to say it was all a lie. But she wouldn't, couldn't do that. So what was the point?

"Can you say it's not true?" he asked. "Can you tell me you're not a writer and you weren't employed at some tabloid when you met me?"

The look on her face—guilt—said it all. "I thought so."

"You've already passed judgment on me." The vibrancy left her face. "Anything I say from here on out is just wasting my breath."

True. She had a point. He was beyond listening to or wanting to hear excuses.

Julian had to give her credit for having her own sense of self-respect, even if it was distorted.

It was going to be an awkward six months.

There wasn't much left to do or say. He looked at the envelope in his hand, then to the sofa before moving on to the coffee table to the left. One more glimpse of her cold, stoic face convinced him to toss the envelope at the table. It sailed through the air and slid across the tabletop, stopping in the center.

Julian gave her one last consideration. She hadn't moved or changed her expression. He was wasting his time. Irritation shoved his regret aside and pivoted him around, forcing him toward the door. He left, letting it swing shut with a bit of a slam. He winced and headed on down the hallway.

The next six months were not going to be pleasant ones. He'd find a way to conquer his affliction because, as bad as this was, being married to Madeleine would still be worse.

♡

Camille grabbed a pillow from the nearby chair and threw it at the door. She'd been wrong when she called him a jerk. He wasn't just a jerk. Julian de Laurent was a complete jerk.

Imagine, someone wanting you to defend yourself when they had no intention of listening to a word you said. Camille wasn't groveling at anybody's feet, least of all his. It would come to nothing because it was only for his own amusement.

The envelope he'd left on the table seemed to be his bargaining chip. Well sure, it contained the means to a million dollars. Or so he said. Curiosity pushed her toward the table. She picked up the envelope with casual grace and hesitated a moment before easing the flap open. The agreement didn't interest her as much as the bank transfer.

Seeing all those zeros next to her name made her heart skip a beat. In a matter of seconds, all her financial problems had disappeared. A million bucks might be chump change to a guy like Julian, but for a girl like Camille it could change her life.

But was the payment of five million worth six months of what she'd just endured? Could she stand six months of ridicule and rejection and dismissal from Julian. She'd have to if she wanted the money.

Wait. She'd decided to stick around because she needed the money. Not anymore. She was now in possession of a million dollars. Payment in full for a story she'd never intended to write. Why should she stick around and subject herself to Julian's BS when it was no longer necessary?

There was no longer a reason. Not anymore. And she liked the idea of being paid for a story much better than being paid for a marriage—even if it was less money. But hell, a million bucks was plenty for Camille. It would set her up nicely.

Okay, so all she needed to do was find someone to help her start the divorce proceedings. Julian wasn't the best bet. He'd try to talk her out of it since he had a little problem he liked to call Madeleine.

But Julian had—like Granny Mae used to say—made his bed and now he'd have to lay in it. He'd hurt her feelings and stung her ego and there was no going back from that. Why should she continue to help him? Not even five million dollars was worth sacrificing her dignity.

With that in mind, Camille knew she had to confide in at least one member of the de Laurent family. And there was only one who could come close to relating. Only one that might listen before judging. Only one that might agree to help Camille.

♡

Camille was thrilled when Claudette kept their lunch date that afternoon. It meant Maurice hadn't gotten to her, hadn't told Claudette what he knew. She hoped she was right, and her stepmother-in-law still remembered and understood what it was like to try to fit into this family of well-bred jackasses.

They opted for a little sidewalk café where the staff knew Claudette and were overly attentive to her every desire.

Camille had rehearsed what she'd say to Claudette a hundred times in her mind, but that hadn't helped to calm her nerves. What if she was wrong about Claudette? What if she was just as judgmental as the rest of them? What if...pigs could fly!

She pushed the silly anxieties aside. Nobody could be as judgmental as those de Laurent men. Maurice and Julian in particular.

Strategically, Claudette's induction into the family was the place to start. Take her back to what it felt like when she first arrived.

"Claudette..." Camille let her name amble off her tongue. "What was it like for you when you married Maurice?" she asked, playing with the food on her plate. "Did fitting in come easy for you?"

"Easy?" Claudette laughed, and rattled off a few words in French before returning to English. "I not only became the mother of two small children, but I had to follow in the footsteps of a woman who'd been put up on a pedestal and then devastated an entire family when she fell off."

Camille hadn't looked at it like that. She'd only seen Naoma's life and death from Julian's point of view. A broken-hearted son.

"I can't imagine what that must've been like for you." Sadness stabbed at Camille's chest. "I know it devastated Julian."

"Julian." Claudette's face softened. Clearly, she loved him like any mother would love her son. "He was such a dear, sweet boy. And so young, and broken-hearted over losing his mother." Her expression was one of quiet dejection. "It took a very long time to get him to accept my love. He was afraid I was going to leave, too."

"What about you and Maurice? Did he have trust issues?" Camille regretted it as soon as she asked.

Claudette snorted. "Still does." She rolled her eyes and a muscle quivered at her jaw. "Sometimes, I think Maurice doesn't even trust himself."

"He doesn't trust me."

"It's not that he doesn't trust you." Her words weren't bitter, just logical. "You made it impossible for him to get the daughter-in-law he wants."

Camille hadn't looked at it like that. Still, it wasn't her problem. "He has another son."

"Ah, yes. And a specific wife picked out for him too." A flicker of amusement flittered across her eyes. "And he's not likely to get that one any more than he did the last."

"Well, he shouldn't give up hope on Madeleine just yet," Camille said, with some remorse. "He's still got a chance. If he can convince Julian."

Claudette studied her with a scrutinizing eye. "Julian doesn't love Madeleine."

"He doesn't love me either."

Claudette's expression skewed into a "thinking face" that evoked her thoughts to the surface. "I think he does."

"I'm going to tell you something that is going to violate a contract." Camille paused. It was better to just say it and get it over with. That way the contract would be broken and she could go home. "Our marriage is a business deal. A marriage of convenience."

Claudette's mouth fell open. Clearly, a notion she hadn't suspected.

"Julian came to America looking for a temporary wife, so he could avoid being pressured into marriage with Madeleine." She searched for the next set of words that would make some sense of her reasoning, and not make her look like a villain. "He placed an ad in the L.A. Trades for an actress." There was something liberating about admitting the truth. "I, at the instruction of my boss, answered the ad. I was just supposed to see what Julian was up to. That's it. But my boss at Disclosure Magazine wanted a story, with all the dirt, on Julian de Laurent." She shook her head. Even she was starting to see herself as the bad guy.

Claudette didn't say anything. She just listened.

"There was something about Julian from the get-go. He makes you want to help him."

"He has that effect on most people."

"I told my boss I wouldn't write the story. She threatened to fire me. So I quit." Camille had no regrets about standing up to her ex-boss at Disclosure Magazine, but right now her ethics weren't making her feel any better.

"For a young girl, alone in the world, and having no job or viable job prospects...the world is a scary place." Claudette's expression softened. She did understand.

Camille sighed, relieved.

"I'm sure you were very afraid. And, the tiniest part of you probably wanted to help Julian."

"That's true. But it was more about me." She admitted with a regrettable shrug. "I was afraid for myself. I was afraid of ending up homeless."

"So you went to Julian and accepted his offer."

"Yes."

"And you didn't tell him about your boss or that you'd quit your job because of him."

"No, I didn't."

"And somewhere along the way, you fell in love with Julian."

"Well, I wouldn't say that." If she said it, that'd make it real. And it couldn't be real because she'd end up heartbroken.

"So what happened?" she asked, studying Camille. "Did Julian find out about your job?"

Camille nodded. "Maurice made it a point to dig up the dirt on me." She laughed at the irony.

"Of course!" She threw her hands into the air. "This has my husband written all over it. Jackass that he is."

"Julian is so angry with me," Camille said. "He thinks I'm here to get that story."

"And he's not going to believe otherwise. Unless you come up with a way to prove it to him."

Camille hadn't thought of that.

"That is the way of the de Laurent men," her spirited voice pealed on, "Loveable as they are...they're idiots when it comes to matters of the heart."

"I'm going to divorce Julian."

"It is the only thing to do," she said. "Especially if you want him back."

Camille came out of her despondence and looked at Claudette. "What makes you think he'd have me back?"

"Because he loves you."

Camille had given up on that when Julian lost the spark in his eyes. "Well, I don't think that's going to happen. I just want this to be over." The words shuddered through her. "I can't stand the way he looks at me now."

"He's going to have to lose you before he can appreciate you." Claudette leaned toward Camille. "But don't be foolish. Don't give him any ammunition to validate what he thinks is the truth. Take every piece of his so-called proof and ram it back at him before you leave."

Camille tried to think of how she could make that happen.

"Don't tell him you're leaving either. He'll talk you out of it," she said. "And you'll both lose if that happens."

"You're probably right." Camille wasn't willing to spend the next six months learning to hate Julian. She'd rather lose now, than have hatred attached later on down the line.

"I happen to know that Andre is planning a trip to the U.S." Her tone was born in suggestive innocence. "To see your friend."

Camille laughed inside. That would snap Maurice's sanity.

"Do you know someone who can draw up divorce papers quickly?" Camille asked, walking a tightrope of hope.

A thought, an idea came to her. It was risky. She'd lost all hope for any kind of solid relationship with Julian, but if she had any hope of proving herself to him, she had to take that chance.

Chapter Eighteen

JULIAN'S LIMOUSINE ROLLED to a stop in front of the house. The weather hadn't bothered to cooperate for his return from a business trip to London. Rain continued in a torrential downpour and he jumped out of the car without a second thought and faced the brunt of the storm head-on.

While away, he'd had plenty of time to think things through. Perhaps he'd been a bit hard on Camille. Sure, she'd come to him under false pretenses, but when had that ever stopped him? Where was his sense of adventure? Who said he couldn't change her mind, charm her out of her intentions? She'd come there for a story, but who's to say it couldn't turn into something more? Something meaningful. Something real.

He slinked out of his overcoat and shook the water off his hands and arms. Papa would want to see him, but Julian was more interested in talking to Camille and figuring out if there was a chance for them to salvage their amiable relationship or if he was just fooling himself.

There were only two places she would be. The gardens or their suite. And the rain cancelled out the first option. Julian headed up the stairs taking them two at a time.

"Chéri...?" he called out, entering their suite.

Nothing.

He moved from one room to the next, expecting to find her in each.

Again, nothing.

"Camille?" Anxiety knotted in his gut as he opened the door to the bedchamber, the only room left to examine inside the suite.

The bed was made, the room was empty and the bathroom door was open. Julian stopped, perched his hands on his hips and surveyed his surroundings. Where in the hell was Camille?

Maybe she was in town with Claudette and Lecie. They'd probably gone shopping and were likely to return in time for dinner. Along with a big hefty bill.

Julian laughed. He was beyond caring. He just wanted to see Camille.

He went back into the outer rooms of the suite and prepared to meet with Papa. He would've made it out the door too, if it hadn't been for the document lying on the table along with Camille's wedding rings and her necklace.

Curiosity pushed him to check it out. His heart rate increased as he reached for the folded document.

A Bill of Divorcement.

Her signature had been penned in black ink. All he had to do was sign it and he'd be a free man—free to get pushed in the direction of Madeleine.

The hell with that.

She couldn't do this to him. She couldn't throw him to the wolves. She couldn't pretend they'd never happened.

Where was she?

He tossed the document back onto the table and the bank receipt fell out. Julian snatched it up and looked at the paper.

One million dollars had been transferred back into its originating account.

Joy over the notion that she'd chosen him was overshadowed by the fear that she'd gotten a better offer for her story.

Oh, shit.

Julian's first instincts led him to the closet and her dressers. All her things—the things he'd bought her—were still there.

Good.

He stormed out into the hallway. She was here in the house somewhere, and Julian set out to find her. He ran into Andre coming up the stairs.

"Andre, have you seen my wife?" he asked, stopping just past his brother on the staircase.

Andre grabbed the banister and crooked halfway around and flashed Julian with a confused look. "Your wife?"

"Yes. Camille. Have you seen her?"

"You didn't know?" Fear darkened Andre's demeanor.

"Know what?" Julian asked, having little patience.

"I thought you knew." Andre paused, slinking up the stairs, outside Julian's reach.

Claudette appeared at the top and moved down between them. Julian didn't pay much attention to her and he didn't think Andre had either.

"I went to see Tasha while you were gone and Camille *hitched a ride* with me. Her words, not mine." He chuckled, seemingly amused by the axiom.

"What?" Julian's voice shrieked as he lurched toward his brother.

Andre backed up the steps. "She said you'd understand, not to mention agree."

"No, I don't understand." Julian huffed out his disapproval. "And, no, I don't agree."

"Well, don't yell at me."

"Why not?" Julian asked. "You took her away."

"What's the big deal?" Andre shrugged. "Just go get her."

Julian considered it—for a second. He shook his head. That's no good. What if she's gone to L.A. to sell her story? What if she didn't care about his feelings at all? What if she turned out to be just like his mother?

"If you're not sure you can trust her," Claudette said, as if she'd read Julian's mind, "you can always play the wait and see card. That way, you'll know."

That was a great idea.

Claudette headed down the stairs and a few steps from the bottom, she glanced over her shoulder. "But don't wait too long."

Julian stormed outside, where he hoped the rain had stopped. He'd talk to Papa later. Right now, he needed to think.

If he made it outside without running into Papa, he'd be happy. Just a couple of steps and he was home free. He laid his hand on the doorknob, expecting to hear Papa's voice spoiling his escape. The door opened in silence and Julian slipped outside.

Luckily, the rain had stopped.

Julian ran through the gardens until he got to the hidden clearing that not too many people beyond the gardeners had discovered.

He sat on the bench—the same bench he'd sat on with Camille just weeks earlier—and ignored the pool of rainwater.

The Roman goddess statue, the protector of the garden, offered no comfort today. In fact, the rain made her look like she had tears falling from her porcelain eyes. Julian hated that. It made him feel like his mother was crying since she was the one who'd put the sculpture in the garden.

Julian had to forget about his own feelings and consider the family's welfare. He had to figure out if Camille had come there looking for a story.

Only time would tell.

♡

Camille had never hated the sound of an alarm clock beeping incessantly as much as she did this morning. She awakened from her deep, dreamless sleep.

Reality set in; she was in Tasha's living room.

The last few days, hanging out and sleeping on her best friend's couch was a far cry from the luxury she'd experienced with Julian. But she didn't belong in Julian's world. Now she was back in her own, and it was a shock to say the least.

But not nearly as much of a shock as waitressing at the *4th Street Diner*. A couple of months ago, Camille would've never pictured herself working there. But Julian de Laurent had taught her a thing or two. First, she was capable of taking care of herself. And that brought her to the second—maybe writing wasn't quite so important to her, after all. Not if she had to compromise her principles for the sake of some tabloid's bottom line.

She sighed, threw the blanket back and swung her feet onto the floor. The clock said 10:30 am. She was due at work in less than four hours.

Oh, God. She dropped her face into her hands, fearful of never finding a way out of the fog between her heart and her mind.

How was she ever going to get off Tasha's couch, averaging a lousy two hundred and fifty bucks a week?

Tasha dropped into the chair kitty-cornered from the couch. "So, I'm thinking..." she said in that provisional tone that told Camille she was up to something. "Let's use some of the money you gave me to get a two bedroom apartment."

Camille wanted to send the money back to Julian—what was left of it, anyway. Using it was a bad idea.

"Just hear me out." Tasha's hand flew up. "We need a bigger place so you'll have your own bedroom. We can send Julian what's left, with an IOU for the remainder." She was optimistic about her plan, more so than Camille. "We can make monthly payments to him on the rest, which is actually more my bill than yours."

"But I *gave* you that money," Camille reminded Tasha. "I'm the one in debt."

"I'm not going to argue with you about this." Tasha's voice heightened and she leaned toward Camille. "Either we're both in debt, or neither of us is in debt."

Camille didn't like it. She didn't like being indebted to Julian for anything. She wanted a free and clear break from him. If nothing else, she wanted him to understand that she'd never set out to use or hurt him. She'd just wanted to help Julian. And if she was being honest, she wanted to help herself.

And in turn, her whole world had been turned upside down. But she didn't have time to worry about that. She had to get something to eat and get ready to go to work. Plus, if she didn't agree to Tasha's plan, she'd never hear the end of it. Nor could she keep living on her friend's couch. She'd have to go along with Tasha and hope Julian understood.

"Okay, okay." Camille pushed herself up and stumbled toward the one and only bathroom in the small, one bedroom apartment. "Can you get us a bigger place here?" That'd be convenient.

"There's a two bedroom available downstairs."

"Ooh, downstairs." The possibilities swarmed Camille's mind as she entered the bathroom.

She checked her reflection in the mirror, ignoring her disheveled hair and the dark shadows surrounding her reddened eyes. She'd made a mess of things. Who knew she'd end up actually wanting Julian's approval?

Camille squared her shoulders and lifted her chin. She'd have to make the best of the bad situation, and accept that her life was going to be lonely without Julian.

Chapter Twenty

JULIAN LAID THE FOLDER on his desk and pushed it inches away from him. The report on Camille had been enlightening, and disheartening. He drew a breath, taking in all her woes and troubles as if he could relieve her burden.

A soft knock at the door caught him off-guard. Who? It wasn't Andre...too light. Same for Papa. And his secretary had that two-tap rap going on, so it wasn't her. Who had showed up at his office unannounced? He had no appointments this afternoon.

"It's open," Julian called out, intrigue heightening his curiosity.

The door opened and surprise shook Julian as Claudette sauntered across the room.

"Claudette?" He stood and moved around the desk.

"Julian." She hugged him lightly and kissed his cheeks, one after the other. "I hope I'm not intruding." She scrutinized him. "I should have called, but it's a spur of the moment visit. Sorry."

Julian shushed her. "You know you're always welcome here." He led her to a chair and leaned against the front edge of his desk as she sat. "What can I do for you?"

She laughed. "So much like your father. Right down to business."

Julian crossed his arms in front of him. He didn't like being compared to Papa.

"Relax," she said, reaching for him. "I just came by for a friendly chat."

A friendly chat? Since when did he and his stepmother have friendly chats?

"All right," he said, knowing she was up to something and it behooved him to find out what. "Anything in particular that you'd like to *chat* about?"

"Have you made up your mind?"

"About what?"

"Your wife."

"My wife?" He was unable to contain the skeptical laughter erupting from his gut.

"She is still your wife, isn't she?"

"She left me."

"And..."

"And what?"

"Is she or is she not still your wife?"

Julian paused. It wasn't right to lie to Claudette. She'd stepped in when his mother checked out and had been a suitable replacement to both him and Andre. "Technically."

"Technically?" Claudette scoffed. "Either she is or she isn't. Did you or did you not sign the divorce documents?"

Julian had lost this battle and he didn't like it. "No," he said in a defeated manner. "I did not."

"Any particular reason why?"

Yes, there was a reason. Papa was still hanging around like a vulture, shoving Madeleine at Julian every chance he got. But the way Julian saw it, he couldn't get married if he already had a wife.

"Was it just a means to divert your father regarding Madeleine? Or is it something else?"

"What else could it be?" He laughed skeptically, to hide his anxiety that someone saw through his pretense.

"Maybe the bride herself?" Claudette asked. "Maybe you're not quite ready to let go of her?"

No. Julian wasn't going to admit that. Not out loud.

"The look on your face tells me everything I need to know."

She gave him one of those *you-poor-pitiful-soul* glances.

"That bad?"

"That obvious." Claudette hesitated and leaned toward Julian. "Did she sell her story?"

Julian snapped his head toward her. She knew? But how...? Papa would've never divulged such a potentially damaging thing to Claudette. Things that affected the family in an adverse way were never released outside the boardroom or Papa's study.

Julian examined Claudette with scrutinizing eyes.

"Well?" she asked, shrugging.

"No."

"Why? Did you buy it?"

He hesitated. "I tried, but she backed out of the deal."

"Backed out, huh." Claudette's stoic face gave nothing away about what she was thinking. "She tell you that herself?"

"No, but she turned down the payment at the last minute."

"Maybe she thought it was wrong to get paid for something she never intended to write in the first place."

Claudette stood and strolled toward the door. She stopped short a few steps and looked over her shoulder. "You know, de Laurent Enterprises isn't going to fade away if you leave for a while."

That's what Julian was afraid of, people finding out they didn't need him—for anything.

Perhaps Claudette was right, though. Perhaps he'd misjudged Camille. Perhaps she'd never intended to write a story about him and the family in the first place.

That was a notion worth investigating.

♡

Camille wasn't particularly pleased about being called in to work on her day off for some private party renting out the diner. Why couldn't one of the waitresses scheduled to work take the shift? Why'd it have to be her? And what kind of idiot rents out a run-down diner?

Camille wished they'd hurry up and get here because the sooner they did, the sooner she could call it a night.

She pushed the kitchen door open and went inside. There must have been something she'd forgotten, just as she did every day. Truth be told, Camille wasn't the best waitress around, which explained her employment here.

"Okay, so how many people are going to be in this party?" she said to her boss, doing a poor job of hiding her unhappiness and the fact that she was tired and just wanted to rest. But there wasn't any rest for people like Camille. The working class.

"Just two," George said, leaning against the grill, which wasn't turned on. There was nothing prepped.

Just two? So why was Ashley here too? Did George really think Camille couldn't handle serving two people? *What's going on?* No wonder this place sucked. George wasn't any better at running this joint than she was at waiting on the customers.

Ashley burst into the kitchen. "They're here." There was something in her voice, her tone and her demeanor that alarmed Camille. Ashley was too happy, too excited.

Camille scoffed. She wanted to strangle the girl.

"Come on, lighten up." Ashley came toward her with a wink and a friendly smile. "It's not that bad."

Of course it was that bad. Who was she kidding? The only way it could not be this bad was if Camille was a member of the dining party.

She sighed and shook her head. Julian's world had gotten to her. When was she going to realize she wasn't one of the fortunate ones? She wasn't lucky. She wasn't privileged.

Maybe Ashley was right. Maybe Camille should look on the bright side. Maybe this was her chance to score a hefty tip. One she could use to put a small dent in that massive debt she owed Julian.

"Okay, so where do I start. What should I do?" She turned to George. How was she supposed to 'serve' these people if George wasn't cooking?

"Why don't you go out and welcome our guest?"

"Okay." Camille rolled her eyes. Greeting the customers was useless when there was nothing to serve them. But who was she to argue.

She shoved through the door and out into the dining area. This was ridiculous. She'd probably end up biting the dust on this one. She'd been holding onto this job by a very thin thread as it was, and she got the feeling the blame for the fallout from this unorganized private dinner would ultimately land at her feet.

Out in the dining room, the place was empty. There was no one there. She ambled toward the front of the diner with slow, almost guarded steps, scanning both rows of booths lining the walls. Pausing at the front window, she looked outside but saw nothing unusual.

Hm.... Her hands landed on her hips and she gave the exterior one last glance before turning back to the interior. Leisurely steps took her back toward the kitchen. Somehow, this was going to bite her in the butt.

She paused a few feet from the kitchen door, near the last booth, and glanced over her shoulder to give the empty restaurant one last look. Weird. And just her luck. The customers probably took one look at the neighborhood and split.

Camille decided to go back into the kitchen and face George. He wasn't going to be happy about closing up shop for nothing.

A glittering twinkle on the last table before the kitchen, caught her eye.

Julian's necklace?

Her heart pounded. Camille sucked in a breath, as if that could calm it. She moved closer, inspecting it. It *was* Julian's necklace.

The kitchen door swung open, drawing Camille's attention.

Julian de Laurent stood in the doorway, looking handsome and humbled.

Camille's heart hammered against her chest. Fearing her mouth would fall open, she tightened her lips and forced them together.

Julian smiled one of those hopeful-looking smiles she was used to seeing from the diner's gracious patrons. Not a bad thing, just not what she was used to seeing from Julian.

She looked away, not knowing why he was here, but still fearful of losing her heart. "What are you doing here?" she asked, forcing her gaze back to him. "What happened? My check bounce?"

Julian snickered with a one-sided grin and walked toward her. "Chéri...I have missed you so." He scooped her hands in his. She stiffened.

"You missed me?" she asked. "That's all you have to say?" Camille yanked her hands free and turned away, more afraid this was some kind of joke than anything else.

Julian, as if he'd picked up on her weakness, stepped closer and guided her face, with gentle fingertips, until her gaze met his. His touch rekindled the hunger she'd been trying to smote. And those green eyes caught her, holding her captive. Undressing her. Caressing her. Tormenting her.

Camille wanted to break the gaze and called upon her anger for assistance. "No. I'm not feeling this, Julian." She backed away and shook her head. "What do you want?" she asked again, more forceful this time, stopping at the last booth before the kitchen.

He moved toward her. She braced herself against the booth, just in case her head swooned down into her heart.

"I came here to say I'm sorry." There was none of the usual arrogance in his tone. Only regret with a hint of hope.

That shocked Camille and scared her at the same time. "Apologize to me?" Her fingers landed against her chest. "A liar and a cheat." She hoped the words stung him. They had when she'd heard them pour from his mouth.

But her words didn't seem to faze Julian in the least. He moved within inches of her and fenced her in, latching both his hands onto the booth.

"Here." She tried to use the necklace as a barrier, holding it against his chest. That was a mistake. The feel of his muscular frame beneath his suit sent shockwaves of desire trembling through her.

Julian took the trinket and moved closer, draping it around her neck. She didn't move, in fact, she held her breath. He took forever to clasp the damn thing. The lack of oxygen squeezed her lungs and fogged her brain. Just when she thought she'd pass out, he trailed his fingertips over her shoulders and down her arms, stepped back and released her.

She siphoned a deep breath and a shudder of desire slipped in. His magnetism was so potent.

A smile quirked Julian's lips as he reached into his jacket pocket. "Close your eyes." The arrogance had returned to his eyes, like he knew he had her right where he wanted.

But Camille couldn't forget the hatred he'd dealt her back in France. "That's probably not a good idea."

He shushed her. "Close your eyes," he said again, with forceful calm.

She did it, against her better judgment.

Camille felt Julian's fingers engulfing her left hand and she started to get nervous. She yanked away, opening her eyes. "This is so not cool." Somehow, she managed to slink out of his snare and rushed to the other side of the restaurant.

As she suspected, he followed.

"Chéri, you're my wife," he said. "Can't you at least give me a chance to explain?"

She stopped. Irritation consumed her. She pivoted around and stuck a finger in his face. "First off...I'm not your wife. Not anymore." She paused, trying to contain the irrational behavior building up inside. "Secondly...as far as explanations go, I'll give you the same consideration you gave me."

She tried to move away, toward the kitchen. Julian grabbed her wrist and pulled her roughly, almost violently against him.

"First of all...yes, you are my wife. Still."

What? She'd signed the papers. They were divorced.

"I don't know about the rules in America, but in France a divorce takes two signatures."

"I signed." She looked away.

"I didn't."

"What?"

"I didn't sign. I couldn't."

"Oh, I get it." She sighed, disappointed. "You don't want to be divorced because then you'll be free to be pushed into marriage with Madeleine."

"No. That's not why I didn't sign." His tone took on a quality of mockery before it was overshadowed by remorse. "When it came down to it, I couldn't break our connection. Yours and mine."

He was good, she'd give him that. A passionate fluttering popped up in her chest. It was wise to ignore her heart and all it desired. Camille had trusted him before and look how that turned out. But he was looking at her with that look of his, the one that made her heart go pitter-patter.

She sighed, fighting that sinking, losing feeling.

"Please come home?"

"That's probably not a good idea," she said, shaking her head.

"Please, Camille. I realized something when you left." His voice drifted into a hushed whisper. "I love you. I need you to come home. Forever."

Love? Was he serious? She chewed on her lower lip and stole a look at him.

Julian shot her a mischievous grin before releasing her hands. He backed into the nearest booth and dropped her wedding rings onto the table.

"What are you doing?" she asked, his actions sending her pulses spinning.

"I'm sitting down."

"Why?"

"It looks like I'm going to be here a while."

She hesitated, blinking with bafflement.

"I'm not leaving until you agree to come home." There was something genuine and truthful and determined in his manner. Julian was serious.

Camille slid into the opposite side of the booth and laid her hand on the table. "Well, you've got a long wait ahead of you." She tried not to smile, but couldn't help herself.

"I've got all the time in the world." He reached across the table and grabbed at her fingers.

Camille ignored the blush burning her cheeks. She could hold out about ten minutes. Fifteen, if she tried really hard. When Julian turned on the charm, he had no trouble getting whatever he wanted.

Including Camille.

Epilogue

One Month Later

THE NAOMA LOUISE crept out of the marina, gliding toward the waters of the Mediterranean as the last, faint colors of day faded away.

Julian waited on deck for Camille. She'd said she wanted to slip into something more comfortable. He hoped that meant *sexy*.

They'd made a quick get-away right after the ceremony; she hadn't even taken the time to change out of her dress. They'd done the whole wedding-circus act last time. This time, it'd been just for them.

It seemed like the logical step after Soren had found her wedding dress in that little second-hand shop in Marseilles last week. It'd been a stroke of luck, actually, when Soren saw it in the shop's window while driving past.

After Julian reacquired the gown—and learning Madeleine had sold it to the shop—it only seemed fitting that he and Camille should renewed their vows so she could wear the dress that'd been made specifically for her.

They had done that today, and now, he was taking her on a cruise of the Greek Islands—a desire she had expressed right after he'd brought her to France the first time.

Julian looked at his watch, and back to the double doors leading below deck. *What's taking so long?*

Just when he was ready to go look for her, Camille emerged wearing a sheer black negligee over a bikini of the same color.

Desire swelled inside him, as quickly as a summer storm brews. Drinking in the sight of her, he stood slowly. "You look absolutely stunning."

A rush of pink stained her cheeks. Julian swept her into his arms. She sank into his embrace, saying, "Thank you for bringing my dress home."

"Anything to see you smile." He kissed her, savoring every second. "As far as weddings go, I think this one was by far our best."

"Well, you know what they say..." She looked at him with eyes that said she was ready to embark on the voyage of love. "Third time's a charm."

Julian laughed, and latched onto her hands. "I have something for you." He led her down to the chaise lounge chair and pulled her into his lap.

She snuggled her face into the crook of his neck. "You really don't have to give me presents."

"Well," he said, reaching for a folded document on the table beside them. "This is a special one."

He offered it to her; she took it and sat up, then unfolded the document and perused it. As she read, her mouth dropped open. She looked up at him, shaking her head. "Julian...?"

"You now own half of everything that is mine."

She glanced away, and remained silent for a time. It felt like forever before she sucked in a breath, and said, "Julian...I don't want your money." She shrugged. "Just your love."

"And that, Chéri, you have." He snuggled her closer. "No one will ever tear us apart again."

"You promise?" she whispered.

"I promise." He caressed her soft curves and she molded into the contours of his body. "Have I told you today that I love you?"

"Once or twice, my love. Once or twice." Her soft, whispering breath tickled his neck.

Holding Camille in his arms, Julian was the happiest of men.

Their marriage had started as a business arrangement, but somewhere along the way they'd fallen in love.

Destiny had certainly smiled upon Julian when she paired him with Camille—his perfect match.

- Please turn the page to read the novella The Memory Bouquet -

The Memory Bouquet
A Prequel to The Lonely Hearts Club

Sandra Edwards

PUBLISHED BY:
Sandra Edwards

The Memory Bouquet
Copyright © 2012 by Sandra Edwards

Digital ISBN: 978-1452492322
Kindle ASIN: B0073L7D40

Cover by Sandra Edwards
Photos used to make the cover obtained from fotolia.com

ALL RIGHTS RESERVED. No part of this book may be used or reproduced in any manner, or by any means (electronic, mechanical, photocopying, recording, or otherwise) without the prior written permission of the copyright owner, except in the case of brief quotations in reviews or critical articles.

This book is a work of fiction and all characters exist solely in the author's imagination. Any resemblance to persons, living or dead, is purely coincidental. Any references to places, events or locales are used in a fictitious manner.

Separate Ways

Ginger's Story

I'VE NEVER BEEN ABLE to cross over the Lost Creek bridge without thinking about Jeffrey Dean Ramsey. And it's impossible to get into the town of Cypress Falls off the Interstate without it—unless you take the long way around. But that involves a lot of back roads. And trust me, you don't want to get lost on some Louisiana back road in a rental car. It ain't exactly L.A.—which is where I live now.

I suppose there's some deeply-buried, lonely part of me that enjoys revisiting my past upon occasion. But a past with a guy like Blue—as his friends used to call him—is worth remembering. Especially when you've got a cad like Keith waiting at home in the here and now.

Tango's sits about a mile up from the bridge on the outskirts of town. That's the only place they'll let a bar exist around Cypress Falls. This one's been there since the dawn of time, I think. I can remember Tango's back when I was a kid. In fact, I got my first alcoholic drink there when I was seventeen—yeah, it wasn't legal back then, either.

Usually, when I come home, if it's not a family thing, it almost always has something to do with heartaches and regrets. This time was no exception. My husband Keith had gone off on one of his *business trips* again and the kids were away on a summer trip to Cancun—I should be so lucky—so there wasn't really much reason for me to sit around the house. Plus, I never was the kind of girl to sit around waiting for a guy to show up—even if he was my husband.

Times like this, I always liked to drop by Tango's before heading for my parents' home. A little liquid courage never hurt anybody, especially when you know what's waiting for you when you get to the house. Facing the ridicule of my mother was never easy—at any age. And my mother always has plenty to say about my marriage, even after all these years.

I tapped on the brakes and let the car roll to a stop near the front door of the bar. There were only a couple of cars in the lot. I was glad I wasn't likely to run into a bunch of people who'd be asking all kinds of nosey questions about my very famous twin sister or my failure to nab, and hold onto, a husband who was at best a second-rate actor.

I let out some of my frustration when I palmed open the wooden door. The inside was as empty as the parking lot. Tango was behind the bar wiping down the counter, and not looking much older than he had when he served me my first drink twenty-five years ago—God, had it been that long? It seemed like yesterday.

I approached the bar and he gave me a wink and half smile. "Long time no see, Ginger. What'll you have…the usual?"

"Sounds good, Tango," I said, claiming a barstool.

He reached into the cooler and grabbed a frosty bottle of Miller. "How's the world treating you?" he asked, setting the beer in front of me.

"It's a cruel world, Tango. Damn cruel world."

"What's the matter…?" A voice as smooth as Southern Comfort and as sensually sweet as a chunk of DeLafée's chocolate snuck up behind me. "The law business short on entertainment clients these days?"

My heart damn near stopped right then and there. Not because of what was said, but because of who said it. I looked over my shoulder. "Jeffrey Dean Ramsey…as I live and breathe."

His baby blues twinkled as he gave me one of his trademark grins. When he smiled, it was hard for a girl to resist. Then and now.

"Ginger..." he said my name and everything after that was a blur. At least that's the story I'm telling for how I ended up in his arms.

It wasn't as bad as all that though. It was just one of those friendly greetings between old friends that went on a little too long because we also happened to be ex-lovers. You see, Jeffrey Dean was my first.

He inched me an arm's length away and gave me a good once-over. "Ginger, you haven't changed a bit." Yeah, right. It'd been at least twenty years. "You're as beautiful as ever."

"And you're as good a liar as ever." We laughed and I climbed back up on my barstool.

"May I?" he asked, gesturing to the empty stool at my side.

"Be my guest." I shrugged.

Jeffrey Dean joined me at the bar and Tango served us Tequila Sunrises—in honor of those old high school days.

"Hey, do you remember when we met?" Jeffrey Dean elbowed my arm.

How could I forget? It was the night of the summer festival that had always taken place around the Fourth of July holiday. It was the break between tenth and eleventh grade for me. Jeffrey Dean was new to the area, and he was going to be a senior with his own car—plus, he was a hell of a baseball player. He'd infused new hope into Cypress Falls that year, and he didn't disappoint.

"Yeah," I said, feeling a little blue. The memories were bittersweet. Mainly because it was a time of such happiness, but it wasn't meant to last. "I remember that...and a lot more."

"It took a while to talk you up on that Ferris Wheel." He gave a little triumphant laugh, even now after all these years.

"Yeah, well..." I rolled my eyes. "You were gifted like that." I let out a snort and grabbed my cocktail glass. I could see this heading south at any moment.

Jeffrey Dean leaned closer to me. "I hear they still hold that festival every year at this time." He waited for me to look at him. When I did, he said, "You going?"

Images of my mother badgering me to go, just like she'd done on that fateful night when I first met "Blue", filled my head. "I hardly doubt I could avoid it."

He stared at me for what seemed like forever, just looking at me the way he used to—his eyes, like bright sapphires, effectively prolonged the moment. I was torn, knowing I should tell him to stop, but I was enjoying the feeling washing over me. It was a sensation I hadn't felt in ages, and right up until this very instant I hadn't realized just how much I'd missed it—him.

Needless to say, I was feeling pretty foolish about sinking back into those old high school daydreams. I needed to get out of there before I did something I'd regret. Well, maybe not regret so much as feel damned guilty about.

I looked at my watch. "Oh, look at the time." I grabbed my purse off the counter and pushed myself up from my stool. "It was nice seeing you again, but I've got to go."

I made it to my car without looking over my shoulder, and I was damned proud of myself for it. I hit the unlock button on my key fob and reached for the handle. All I had to do was get in the car and I was home free. So why'd I feel like prey being stalked by a highly effective predator?

"Ginger..." He called my name and then followed it with a bit of a laugh.

Get in the car, Ginger. My mental instruction did no good. I glanced over my shoulder.

The years had been good to Jeffrey Dean Ramsey. Shoulder-length black curls had me thinking about things I shouldn't. Broad shoulders, a trim waistline, and long legs all looked tempting on his tall, athletic frame. Geez, he was good to look at.

I shook my hair back out of my face and squared my shoulders—like that'd really help. "You in town for a while?" I asked, mostly because I couldn't think of anything else to say. But there was a little part of me that was curious about his plans. He nodded and tossed me a seductive glance. "Good," I said. "Maybe I'll see you around before I leave." I opened the car door, slid behind the wheel and slammed the door shut. Honestly, I was feeling pretty good about putting so much metal and steel between us, but I'd be lying if I said the thought to lock the doors didn't cross my mind.

As I turned the key in the ignition, I glanced up at the doorway and saw him mouth the words, "You can count on it."

♡

It's amazing how nearly twenty-five years of adulthood can dissipate in a matter of minutes when you're sitting at the dinner table with your parents. And it seemed like they were still arguing about the same thing—my older sister Risa. I had no idea what Risa had done this time, but considering that she'd been married and out of the house for over twenty years it did have me wondering.

"It's none of our business, June." My father's voice was calm, yet chastising, as he talked to my mother. "It's Risa's business. She'll deal with it as she sees fit."

Wait... "Deal with what?" I was curious now and very near the edge of panic. Was something wrong with Risa, Mike, or God forbid, my niece Lisa? That was all I needed to fall over the edge.

"It's nothing for you to get worked up over, dear." My mother took on her stern look as she rested her wrists on the edge of the table. "Mike and Risa have hit a rough patch. Nothing to worry about I'm sure. Risa's a smart—"

"June!" My father cut my mother off, and I can't say I was disappointed. When she goes off on her rants about Mike and Risa it always starts with something about a rough patch. I think that was more wishful thinking on my mother's part than anything else.

My father's trademark glare was enough to shut my mother down. She didn't say anything more about Risa. Instead, she turned on me. "You're not wearing that to the carnival tonight, are you?" She gave my attire—business casual—a quick once over and dismissed it with a critical frown.

"Well, gee, Mother..." I cleared my throat, trying to convince myself that I didn't need to answer to her. "I hadn't thought about going." But who was I kidding? It was a fate my sisters and I were cursed with. Each of us reverted straight back to our childhood whenever we were in the presence of our mother.

"Well of course you're going. What would people think if a Franklin was in town and didn't attend the carnival?"

Never mind that I hadn't been a Franklin in a really long time now. "I hardly think the world's going to fall apart if I miss the fair, Mother." Okay, so maybe that was a little harsh, but it wasn't often that I got a chance to outmaneuver June Royce Franklin.

My mother's face reddened and her eyes bulged wide. She shot me a quick glance and I swear I practically saw the daggers flinging my way, but then she cleared her throat quietly and repositioned herself in her chair. "Art..." She addressed my father in a hushed tone. "Would you please talk some sense into Virginia?"

Uh oh. She only called me *Virginia* when she was really pissed at me.

My father glanced back and forth between us several times before his gaze finally settled on me. "Ginger's more than willing to go to the fair." The look he'd shot me hardened. "Aren't you, Ginger?"

I almost burst out laughing. This was turning into a déjà vu moment for me. My father was bribing me, just as he'd done when I was sixteen years old. I wondered if the going rate was still twenty bucks. My mother hadn't known then, and I doubted she knew it now. "Sure, Daddy." Giving in was easy. I've always been a daddy's girl.

"Besides..." Devilish laughter played with Daddy's words. "She just might run into J.D. Ramsey."

"Art!" Mother's voice went into chastising overdrive. "Ginger is a married woman."

"Yes. And you keep calling that marriage a mistake." Daddy looked at me and winked. "Did you hear he's back in town?"

Yep. Already ran into him. "Is that right?" I asked, and dropped it at that. All-Star J.D. Ramsey was exactly the kind of son-in-law a guy like my father lived for. Blue had gone pro straight out of college, and immediately commenced breaking records by the dozens over the course of his twenty-year career in the Majors.

I hated the thought of disappointing my father, but the sad truth was Blue Ramsey wasn't any more interested in marrying me now than he was back then. All Blue had ever cared about was getting me into the sack. I prided myself on being older and wiser now. I wasn't about to revisit that fool's goal again.

"We all thought he'd take a sports casting job out in L.A.—"

Bite your tongue, Daddy! The last thing I needed was Blue out in L.A., tempting me every time Keith strayed. "Maybe he'll stay here, Daddy, and you can work on getting Georgia to marry him for you."

My mother's laughter snorted out through her nose until it finally broke into full-blown amusement. That was a great thing about my mother, she'd surprise me every now and then. She certainly had this time by seeing the humor in my repartee about my twin sister who was also my only unmarried sibling.

The fact remained that my mother wasn't going to let up about the carnival. She was fully expecting me to go. And I was wholly afraid to. Nothing good could come from putting myself in a familiar situation with Blue Ramsey.

♡

Summer nights in Cypress Falls were either hot and muggy, or rainy. Either way, it was wet. Tonight there was no rain in the forecast—thank goodness. I was glad I'd brought a tank top and a pair of blue jean shorts with me, even though Keith would have chastised me for even thinking about wearing them.

Keith liked to call it the over-the-hill syndrome, which he never failed to point out was happening solely to me. Not that I felt over the hill, although nearing the age of forty-two did leave me feeling a little like I was halfway up the steep side and once I crested the top I knew cruising down the backside would go much quicker than I'd like.

Course, it wasn't all that bad. I'd aged well. Even after two kids, I hadn't put on more than ten pounds since high school. Georgia was always telling me that I could still work a pair of jeans, but I'd often wondered if she was just trying to make me feel better. Judging by the reaction I'd gotten from Jeffrey Dean earlier, she might have been telling the truth. Either that, or Blue was a damned good actor.

I checked myself in the full-length mirror still standing in my old bedroom. My room, just like Risa's and Georgia's and our brother Ryan's, were like damned shrines. My parents were in serious need of a remodel.

Satisfied with my reflection—it's not like it was going to change—I headed for the hallway. Knowing my mother was waiting, I dragged my feet toward the staircase. I really didn't want to go, especially knowing Jeffrey Dean would most likely be there.

Nothing like jumping from the frying pan into the fire.

♡

There may not have been rain, but the humidity was high and it was leaving a clammy feeling on my skin as I milled through the fairgrounds. I cut through the maze of rides and headed for the midway.

I passed by several games, including the dime and baseball tosses, but it wasn't until I saw the dart game that panic tangled with my sensibility and held it hostage in my gut. I'd been at that very game, without much luck, when I met Blue way back when. He'd stopped beside me, gave me a smile, and asked if I'd *"like a few pointers?"*

Of course it'd taken a few seconds to compose myself after getting caught up in his baby blues. His smile and his eyes had been a lethal combination back then, and it hadn't diminished over the years.

By the time I was in front of the dart game I gave pause to recall the way it felt to have Jeffrey Dean's arms around me for the first time when he was "showing" me how to hit the balloons with the darts.

I thought about grabbing a bundle of darts and trying my luck, but why breed trouble? I'd best haul my ass on over to the nearest concession stand and get myself a corndog and a Coke, instead. After procuring my provisions I found an empty picnic table in the makeshift courtyard and settled in to tame my wandering thoughts with food.

I ripped open the mustard packet in one corner and squeezed a healthy line onto my corndog. As soon as I bit into it, I knew it was a bad idea. Unlike when I was a teenager, this delectable little treat would now go straight to my hips. I gave the consequences a second's notice and then took another bite.

From the corner of my eye, I saw someone walking toward my table. I hadn't let my gaze travel up to identify the face because I didn't need to. I knew who it was, and for that very reason I avoided looking up. If I didn't acknowledge him, maybe he'd go away.

"Ginger Franklin…" His voice carried more amusement than I was comfortable with. "Imagine running into you here."

Like a magnet, my eyes were pulled up to meet his. I tried, probably without much success, to plaster on a stone face. "I haven't been Ginger *Franklin* in a very long time." I let my eyes linger on him for a moment before I cut back to the corndog in my hand.

To my dismay, Blue helped himself to a seat across the table from me. "When's the last time you had some *fun*?" he asked, putting extra emphasis on the final word.

I gave a little shrug. "I have so much, I hardly know where to begin." I lied. If I was being completely honest, the more accurate response would've been, *"it's been a while."* But who wanted to say something like that to Blue Ramsey?

"Tomorrow morning. You and me. We're going up to the falls."

Readying myself to tell him, *no, we're not*, I glanced away because, let's face it, how could anyone say *no* while staring into those eyes? And that's when I saw them. Lisa and Ethan, strolling along hand-in-hand.

"Lisa and Ethan?" Surprise spilled out in my voice. "I certainly didn't see that coming!"

"Don't you think it's fitting that your niece and my nephew should get together?"

Hell, no. My niece—Georgia's niece—getting together with Tommy Dixon's son was a disaster waiting to happen, especially since

Georgia and Tommy had *unfinished business*. Lisa and Ethan were in their early twenties now, and the haunted past should've died away long ago, but it hadn't. Nope, those old ghosts were alive and kicking. Georgia's success, Lisa, and even Ethan, were all constant reminders of how life had taken an unexpected turn.

I stared at Lisa and Ethan. Lisa really favors her Aunt Georgia—did I mention that Georgia and I aren't identical? And Ethan, he really looks like his dad. It was almost like looking back in time and seeing what might have been if Georgia and Tommy hadn't been star-crossed. "This is so weird."

"Yeah..." Blue chuckled. "You should've seen my sister's reaction."

I hadn't thought of that. But hey, Kathy had had seven years to win over Tommy. That's how long they'd kept up the charade after Tommy married her because he'd gotten her pregnant. But I think everybody knew—including Tommy and Kathy—that the marriage was destined to fail. Even so, for as much as I'd always thought Tommy belonged with my sister, I couldn't help feeling sorry for Kathy. She'd loved a man who couldn't possibly love her back. And it was mean of her brother to take pleasure in her pain.

I slowly cut my eyes toward Blue. "Seriously. When did this happen and just how serious is it?"

"What's the matter, Ginger?" Blue gave me a wink. "Afraid we'll start sharing the same holiday dinner table?"

I felt my head shaking before my thoughts tumbled from my mouth. "It's not that serious?" I wanted it to be a statement, more than anything else, but I'm afraid it wasn't.

I glanced back at Lisa and Ethan, seeing them heading our way. They were still holding hands; both were glowing. Dread began to sink into my gut. This was going to freak Georgia out.

I stood as they approached the table, and Lisa fell into my arms. "Aunt Ginger! I had no idea you were in town." We parted, but her eyes—twinkling with the light of love—stayed glued on me. "Are you here for long? Did Justin and Diana come too?" she asked of my teenage children.

"No." I shook my head. "I just came in for the weekend." I'm not sure when I'd made that decision. In that instant, I guess. "Justin and Diana are in Mexico."

"And Keith?" Her tone grew chillier.

"Keith is away...on business," I said, as we all sat down at the table.

Lisa did a little half roll with her eyes and capped it off with a slight nod. She knew, as well as I, monkey business was more like it.

It's funny how family members can read a cad like an open book. It would've helped if they'd told me before I married him five years ago. Thankfully, he's not the father of my children. That honor belongs to my first husband, Rick. He stayed long enough to knock me up twice, and then split.

There were two other husbands between Rick and Keith. I have been called, upon occasion, a serial bride. That may be why I put up with a lot from Keith. Four failed marriages looks pretty bad on a dating resume.

I'm not sure exactly when I saw *it*, but it was right about then that I *noticed* it. The colossal diamond on a certain finger on Lisa's hand.

I guess my mouth dropped open because her hand inched across the table at me. "Isn't it gorgeous?"

"It's beautiful," I said. "When did this happen?"

"A few days ago. We haven't made a formal announcement yet."

Oh, God. "I hope your mother knows." If I found out before Risa, there'd be hell to pay.

Lisa giggled. "Yes, Mom knows."

"Well—" What else was there to say? "Congratulations to both of you," I said, glancing back and forth between them. My attention finally stalled on Lisa's new fiancé. "Ethan, how are your parents?"

"Fine." He shrugged. "My dad seems to have a lot on his mind lately."

Yeah, I'll bet. Like my sister, maybe, and how his son was about to marry her niece? I glanced over at Blue. Oh, Lord...fate had been a cruel bitch to both Georgia and me.

"Have you set a date yet?" I asked. It was better to keep the conversation out of the past. Nothing good could come from going there. Not in Georgia's case, and definitely not in mine.

"Not yet." Lisa smiled. "But when we do, you'll be the first to know."

I laughed, doubting that, but appreciating the gesture. We all stood at the same time, as if our minds had been tied to some universal mental cue.

Blue and Ethan exchanged some manly farewells while Lisa gave me another hug. "It's so good to see you again, Aunt Ginger. When we do set the date, I hope you'll come."

"I wouldn't miss it for the world," I said as she and Ethan locked hands again, preparing to leave.

"Please make sure Aunt Georgia comes too?" Lisa said in an almost pleading tone. She and I both knew she'd have to twist Risa's arm to get her to send Georgia an invitation. Risa had been mad at Georgia for so long now that I think my mother is the only person still holding out hope that Risa would come around.

"Georgia wouldn't miss your wedding for the world," I told Lisa. "Besides, you're her favorite niece."

"Aunt Ginger..." She giggled and turned away, leaving me and Blue standing there all alone. Nothing good could come from that either.

"Care to go for a walk?" Blue whispered against my ear.

"Where'd you have in mind?"

"Memory lane."

I'd be lying if I said I didn't think about it, seriously, and probably far longer than I should have. I looked sideways at Blue. It wasn't smart to look that guy in the eyes head-on. "I really should be going." I moved slowly away from him, hoping he wouldn't notice until I was long gone.

"Tomorrow morning, Ginger." He winked at me. "We're going up to the falls."

"Right. Tomorrow morning," I said turning away. Tomorrow morning, I'd be long gone.

♡

This may have been the first time my mother was actually happy to see me leave Cypress Falls. The farther she could get me away from

Jeffrey Dean Ramsey the better—for once I tended to agree with her. See, it's not that my mother's old-fashioned about fooling around so much as she is about appearances and scandals. Scandals are the worst thing that could happen to our family, from where she's sitting. Georgia and I have given her lots to contend with.

And while Blue Ramsey may have been my weakness—still—he wasn't the reason I was leaving. Nope, it was all about Georgia. Word was bound to spread soon enough, and it's better that she heard it from me. Or at the very least I needed to be there with her when she heard that her niece was about to marry Ethan—son of the man Georgia had secretly loved for practically the whole of her life.

I booked an early flight for the next morning, somewhere around the crack of dawn so I'd be long gone by the time Blue showed up at my parents' house.

When I got back to southern California my own home was eerily silent. The kids weren't due home until tomorrow, but I would've thought Keith would be back by now. I tossed my keys on the kitchen counter and headed for the back stairway with my cell in hand. I hit the speed dial for Georgia.

"Ginger..." Her voice poured through the earpiece. "How was Cypress Falls?"

"Scary."

"Uh oh. What happened?"

"Well, first off...Blue Ramsey is back in town."

Georgia's devilish laughter gave me a chill. "Talk about a blast from the past."

"That ain't the half of it. Where are you? How fast can you get over here?"

"I can be there in ten minutes." Good. She was home. All she had to do was hop in her car and zip around the corner.

I walked into my bedroom as I disconnected the call. Nothing appeared to be out of place, but still, something was off. I scanned the room. On my second run I saw the folded paper lying on the dresser. I walked over, scooped it up and opened it. Anxiety blew through me.

Ginger,

We both know this hasn't been working for a while now. I'll send the movers for the rest of my things in a day or two. I wish you the best and I hope you find what you're looking for, the thing that makes you happy. We both know that's not me.

Keith

Seriously? A note? Man, I sure know how to pick 'em.

My cell chimed. I looked at the display. A text message from Blue. God, that's all I needed. Against my better judgment, I cued it up.

I'll see you at the wedding, Ginger. You can count on it!

Heartbreak Time

Risa's Story

I LOOKED AT THE CLOCK. 9:30 pm. If Mike was coming home tonight, he'd be here by now. That meant he was with *her*.

He doesn't think I know about his little trollop. But there isn't much I don't know, except whether or not he started seeing her before or after he decided we should separate. The only thing I agreed to was a trial period after our daughter Lisa's wedding. Lisa's getting married in six weeks. I wanted her big day to be perfect. Separating parents would put a damper on it. And if Mike kept up with his late night carousing, he'd ruin everything. We live in a small town, but the rumor mill is running rampant. People will talk.

I heard the back door leading from the garage into the kitchen slam shut. Mike. It has to be him. Lisa's been living on her own for years. I stood, preparing to confront him.

He strolled in from the dining room and gave me that cavalier smile of his. It used to make me weak at the knees, but not anymore. Now it annoyed me more than anything else.

"What?" He threw his hands in the air and tried to turn on the charm.

"You promised that we'd keep this separation—" I gestured some finger quotes in the air just to let him know I was as naïve as I used to be. "—under wraps until after Lisa's wedding."

Mike elbowed his blazer back and perched his hands on his hips. "Do you really think it's a good idea to hide it from her?"

"Hell, yes, it's a good idea!" I clenched my teeth to keep from losing my cool. "Do you really want Lisa's wedding overshadowed by the gossip once it kicks into high gear?"

Mike kicked his head back and laughed. Not a jovial laugh, but one conceived from a smirk. "Who are you really worried about?" he asked. "Lisa...or you?"

"You promised," I said with a stern glare. I knew Mike well enough to know what was coming next. Promises meant nothing to him; they never had. Even so, I'd been hoping he'd keep his word, just this once, for Lisa's sake.

"You don't have to worry." He shook his head. "I talked to Lisa this afternoon."

"You what?"

"She knows." He gave me that smirk of his again. "And she didn't freak out the way you claim."

"Mike..." I cleared my throat, hoping that'd stop me from screaming. "I never said she was going to freak out." This was a losing battle, and Mike was going to make sure that I ended up looking like the bad guy. "I don't want anything to ruin Lisa's wedding. Why can't you understand that? I don't want her to have to endure the hushed voices when she walks into the florist shop, the bakery, the dress shop."

"Lisa's wedding is your excuse now. What will it be after the wedding?" he asked. "Some new drama that has to keep us living together under the same roof?" He shook his head. "I'm done, Risa." Mike shrugged and headed for the stairs.

I strolled to the landing at the bottom of the staircase and leaned toward it. "Make sure you take anything that's important to you with you tonight," I said, just above a whisper.

Moments later, he trotted down the stairs with a single suitcase in hand. "I'll send someone for the rest of my things in a few days." He passed me by, heading for the door, without so much as a sideways glance.

I stepped toward the door and closed it with my foot. "A few days, huh? A lot can happen in a few days." I ended my statement with a little laugh.

The next morning, I heard the doorbell but I ignored it. I was busy separating Mike's *things* from mine.

"Risa...?" Emily, a friend of mine, had obviously let herself in and was now looking for me.

"Up here," I called out from inside my closet where I had a pair of scissors in one hand and I was holding onto one of Mike's shirts, still on the hanger, with the other. I sliced about a foot up the middle of the shirt's back and shoved it and the hanger aside toward the portion of Mike's clothing that I'd already given my personal touch. I latched onto the next piece, one of Mike's favorite blazers.

Emily stopped at my closet door just as I chopped off a sleeve at the midway point. "Risa...?" Her voice cracked with worry. "What are you doing?" she asked, as I sliced the other sleeve so they'd match.

"I'm helping Mike pack." And then, for good measure, I cut the backside up to the collar.

"Pack?" She cleared her throat. "What's going on? And why are you destroying Mike's clothing?"

"The rat bastard promised he'd wait until after Lisa's wedding to leave." I grabbed the next shirt and started snipping. "He lied." I looked at her. "He packed a quick suitcase last night and left." I was pissed. When I get mad, I usually end up crying. But I didn't want to shed a single tear over his dumb ass. I clinched my teeth tight, trying to hold it in. "This is going to ruin Lisa's wedding." I shut my eyes and shook my head.

"He left you?" Emily's voice took on a high pitched, annoyed quality. I nodded. "Well, hell..." She shrugged and stepped into the roomy closet. "You need a hand?"

I started laughing, hard, which would've been okay except there was a very real chance that it could turn into tears at any moment. And any tears that I shed at this point weren't in honor of Mike. Nope. They'd be based in regret.

"After everything you've given up? For him?" Emily yanked a pair of Mike's good slacks off their hanger and took a pant leg in each hand, spreading them. "Here!" She shoved the crotch toward me. "Cut them where it counts."

Emily and I had a grand time redesigning Mike's wardrobe. Then we went downstairs and had a couple of drinks and I talked about cutting his face out of *all* our photographs.

"That could take a while," Emily said.

True. Mike and I had known each other a long time—since first grade—so there would be a ton of images to *fix*. "Maybe I'll just burn them all."

Of course, I knew I wasn't going to do that—mainly because of Lisa—but it was fun talking about it. A lot of fun.

Mike and I had been together for so long. In fact, it was hard to remember when I didn't know him. That was my whole problem. By the time Lisa had come along I wasn't sure I knew how to make it on my own. Well, that was a theory I was bound to test now.

This was a job for Tango's. "Let's go down to the bar," I said.

"I wish I could." Emily shrugged and grabbed her purse off the coffee table. "Jim's expecting me for dinner."

I couldn't blame Emily for deserting me. She and Jim had a good thing going. Most of our friends from high school were on their second and third marriages. Emily and I were a rarity—well, at least Emily was.

To be honest, I don't get down to Tango's much these days. But as you can imagine, I was feeling a bit nostalgic, longing for the old days, so I grabbed my purse and headed out at the same time Emily left for home.

I glanced at the clock on the dashboard as I rolled into the parking lot. 6:18 pm. Used to be, at this time the place would be filled with the happy hour crowd and I wondered if that still rang true. Tango wasn't much older than me when he took over the tavern from his father. Tango is his last name, not his first.

I got out of the car and ambled my way up the wooden steps that Mike had stumbled down a time or two back in the day. I really needed to stop thinking about all the things Mike and I used to do.

Trouble was, if I did that, I'd start thinking about all the things I'd missed out on, given up for Mike.

We used to play here at Tango's, the band, back in the day. Our mistake was letting Georgia in. My little sister, as it turned out, was loyal to no one. Then again, look where loyalty got me.

I found my way across the dimly lit tavern and claimed a seat at the bar where the stools on either side of me were empty. That suited me just fine. I wasn't interested in entertaining some middle-aged, menopausal man this evening.

Tango strolled toward me with a smile tipping his mouth. "Miss Risa..." He leaned against the counter. "How's that beautiful voice?"

That's the one thing I had on Georgia; I could out-sing her any day. For all the good it did me. She was the famous one, the one who got paid—very well—to sing while I was sitting here on my ass at Tango's, starting to wonder how I was going to provide for myself after the divorce.

Well, it really wasn't as bad as all that. I had plans to take Mike to the cleaners. Twenty-five years of marriage and the fact that I'd given up everything for him had earned me the right.

"It's been quiet lately, Tango," I said of my *voice*. "How are you doing?"

"All is well in the world of Tango." He chuckled. "What can I get you?"

"I'm feeling a little nostalgic." I nodded, giving it some thought.

He raised a finger into the air. "I know just the thing," he said. "Leave it to me."

"Fair enough." Normally, I wouldn't be so easy-going, but things were about to change and I needed to change right along with the times.

I didn't really pay much attention to the drink Tango was concocting, but when he set the glass down in front of me the cherry-tinted liquid stirred familiarity deep inside me. Could it be?

"Try that on for size." He smiled, pleased with himself. "I bet it'll spark some memories." He gave me a wink and turned away.

I sipped the drink. Tom Collins. I had to hand it to Tango, he knew his stuff. And he had one hell of a memory if he remembered that I used to drink them back in the day.

Next thing I knew, someone had sat down beside me, to the left. I sucked up a healthy swig of my drink through my straw—I'd need the confidence to shoo my new neighbor away—and then set the glass down before turning to meet my unwanted company.

Tommy Dixon—but people had stopped calling him Tommy years ago. Now he preferred the more mature *Tom*. But he'd always be Tommy to me.

As I stared into the face of Mike's best friend and the father of the groom, an anxious feeling sunk down into my gut. Tommy obviously knew everything that was going on with Mike, including that he was leaving me. That meant Tommy would think I was here drowning my sorrows. Not trying to say I wasn't, but I just didn't want it so blatantly thrown in my face.

"Risa..." Tommy nodded and grabbed the beer bottle Tango set down in front of him. "What brings you here?" He took a healthy drink of his beer. Probably because seeing me reminded him of the old days and how a simple twist of fate could change lives forever.

"I just wanted to get a drink." I shrugged, took a sip and cut my eyes toward him. "What's your excuse?"

"Happy hour. I didn't know I needed an excuse."

"Hey, I'm just here to have a good time."

He flashed me one of those looks that spelled *pity*. "How're you doing, Risa?" he asked. I was about to get pissed at him, but his tone was filled with such concern that it chased away my resentment.

"I'm fine. What'd he tell you?"

"Well I haven't talked to him in a couple weeks," Tommy said, taking another hit off his beer.

Couple weeks? I hadn't ever known Mike and Tommy not to *talk*. "That's very odd. I didn't know sheriffing around here took up that much time." I hadn't meant that to be funny, but I laughed in spite of myself. Tommy had been elected the local sheriff a couple of years back, and he also raised and bred horses, Arabians, I think.

"Let's just say I don't agree with what he's doing."

"What's he doing?" And then it dawned on me. "Never mind..." I turned away, embarrassment filling me up.

"I just don't think it's right, Risa. He owes her better than that."

"Yeah, I know," I said, thinking he was talking about Lisa and her wedding. "He won't listen to reason though."

"Well, if he doesn't make this right—" Tommy's tone hardened. "He and I are done."

Done? "You sure about that?" I asked. "You two have been friends for a long time."

"Yes, we have." He started shaking his head, looked at me and grinned. "I heard Ginger was in town not too long ago."

"Yes, she was. I didn't see her."

"So, do you think Georgia will come to the wedding?"

"I hardly think we'll be able to avoid it." I let sarcasm fuel my tone. I have no idea why Tommy was bringing her up. He knew how I felt about her.

"All things considered, I kind of wondered..." He paused, as if thinking about it, then he turned back to me. "But she wouldn't miss Lisa's wedding. Right?"

I shrugged and shook my head. "No." No matter what I thought about Georgia, she'd die before she disappointed Lisa. And it pissed me off that Lisa's own father didn't feel that way.

Tango strolled in our direction and leaned on the bar. "Hey, Risa..." He gave me a big, fake grin. "Any chance of getting you and Georgia up on stage while she's here for the wedding?"

I couldn't do anything but laugh. Me and Georgia onstage, together again? That'd be a cold day. "I think Georgia's probably outgrown us, Tango," I said with a measure of regret. Not that I regretted it, really, but I didn't want to hurt Tango's feelings. He was very supportive of the band back in the day.

"You two never patched up, huh?" Tango asked.

"No." I shook my head, and kept my tone even. "We never got past that thing."

"A lot of years have passed, Risa," Tommy said. "Don't you think it's time to let bygones be bygones?"

"I've *not* liked her longer than I've liked her." I looked at Tommy. "I'm too set in my ways."

"Well, I thought you might be feeling differently now, but I guess I was wrong." Tommy finished his beer and set the bottle down on the counter. "See you 'round, Tango." He looked at me again. "Risa...forgiveness is a powerful drug." His green eyes stayed on me for what seemed an eternity before he turned and headed for the door.

I just didn't understand why Tommy wasn't mad at her. If it hadn't been for Georgia's selfish ass, he wouldn't have had to spend nearly seven years of his life with a woman he would never love. Then again, if Georgia had chosen differently, it's unlikely that Ethan—Tommy's son and my daughter's fiancé—would even exist.

I glanced up at Tango. "Well, I guess I'd better head on home." I grabbed my purse and hopped off the bar stool.

"Hey, Risa," Tango called after me and I looked over my shoulder on the way to the door. "If you ever want to sing...just let me know."

I'd love to sing again. But that ship, like so many others, had sailed.

Pieces of April

Georgia's Story

EVERY WEEK, MY SISTER Ginger and I meet our friends Dana and Malibu for drinks and dinner. Dana's a daytime soap star and Malibu—I'm not even sure that's his real name—is a hotshot events planner for the stars and the privileged. He's in his mid-thirties, extremely gorgeous, and straight.

I've known them both for about ten years, and consider them two of the truest friends I have. Half of L.A. thinks Malibu and I are secretly involved. The other half—since it's a common known fact that I've chased away every man I've ever been involved with—thinks he's gay because he's still hanging around.

Ginger zeroed in on Dana, and asked, "Are you really dead?"

"Well, they did bury me." She scooped up her cocktail glass and drained it.

"So you're like unemployed now?" Ginger asked.

"Not exactly." She flashed a devilish smile. "I landed a feature film."

"Really?" I said. "Congratulations!"

"You know, Georgia..." Her words tapered off as she glanced away and then looked back at me slyly. "I think it helped that they know I'm friends with you." She stopped talking, but I got the feeling there was more.

"Glad I could help." I waited for the rest.

"Do you think you could maybe try writing something for the movie?" she asked, and I knew she was talking about a song. That's what I do. I sing, and write my own songs. I guess I'm pretty good at it. I've sold a ton of records and won a few awards.

"Yeah." I grabbed a tortilla chip and dipped it in the salsa. "Have them send me a script so I can read it. I'll see what I can come up with." I popped the chip into my mouth.

"As always, you'll come up with something great." Malibu let his gaze bounce between Ginger and me. "But I'd like to talk about this trip you two are taking. Is your past coming back to haunt you?" He gave me a one-sided dimpled grin.

That got an eye roll out of me, and it was quickly followed by a groan. "Trust me...the goings-on behind the scenes of the latest event you're planning—" I nodded my head. "—are far more interesting than anything that happened to me back in the day."

"Don't give me that, missy. There's a story in your past." He pointed a finger at me. "And I aim to find out what it is."

"Some old high school boyfriends perhaps?" Dana chuckled and looked at Malibu. "Wouldn't it be great to talk to those guys?" Her chortle turned into devilish laughter.

Malibu looked at Ginger and me. "Can we come too?"

I gave him a big, fat resounding, "No."

"Okay," Dana said. "If we can't go, somebody's got to dish." Her gaze settled on me for a few seconds and when I didn't say anything she turned to Ginger, and waited.

"Georgia casually dated a few guys in high school." Ginger shrugged. "But that's not really the story you want to hear."

"Do tell..." Malibu egged her on.

"Really, Ginger...?" I was annoyed, but I tried not to let it show. And I didn't want her embarrassing me either. You see, I knew the story she was aiming to tell. "Can we just *not* go there?"

"What?" Dana gave one of those incredulous laughs that told me she wasn't about to give up. She'd stumbled upon a goldmine and she intended to unearth it. "Uh uh. We're going all the way back."

"You guys are going to love this!" Ginger was enjoying this way too much. I had to cut her off at the pass.

"There's really nothing to tell," I said. "It's just your classic...I was in love with a guy who didn't know I existed." I tried to play it off, but that whole part of my life was still sharp as a straight razor, even twenty-five years later.

Ginger shook her head. "Georgia's leaving out the best parts..." My sister's voice trailed off and I could see in her lonely stare, exactly where her thoughts were headed....

♡

Twenty-seven years ago…

By the time I'd turned fifteen, I'd been in love with Tommy Dixon—a boy from my older sister Risa's class—for as long as I could remember. Some of my earliest memories included swinging in the backyard, long before I'd ever stepped across the schoolhouse steps for the first time, and being pushed in the swing by little Tommy Dixon who, along with classmate Mike Russell, frequently ended up at the Franklin house to play.

Standing in front of the full-length mirror in my bedroom on the second story of the Franklin family home, I wished I could hide away in those days when we all played in the backyard. But we'd stopped playing long ago. With Ginger and me starting tenth grade, and Risa, Mike and Tommy in their first year of college, we just didn't *play* anymore.

I glanced out the window. The swing set was still there; overgrown grass and weeds beneath the seats signified its idleness during the past few years. My mother refused to get rid of it, saying she'd have grandchildren to utilize it soon enough. That statement had heated my cheeks. I hadn't even kissed a boy, much less thought of doing anything else. I was saving myself for Tommy Dixon.

But here I stood, looking at myself in the mirror. I'd just turned fifteen and I still didn't have any boobs. It didn't help that Ginger did. Big ones.

But that wasn't the half of it; Mike and Risa were asking me to make a fool of myself in front of Tommy. I already knew he thought of me as nothing more than Risa's kid sister, and I didn't need that to turn into Risa's *pathetic* kid sister.

Damn Risa anyway for getting sick. Didn't she know she had responsibilities with that stupid band she and Mike had started? Now they expected me to come in and save the day—by singing.

Sure, okay...I play the guitar and sing a little, but I'm no singer. Not like Risa. And there was no way I could stand in for her either, without embarrassing myself.

But Risa had practically begged. If they didn't find someone they'd lose the gig, right along with the money, and they needed the money to make the payments on all that equipment they'd bought. If they didn't make the payments they'd lose the equipment. I couldn't exactly figure how this was my problem, but I'd been taught that it was right to help out family. So I agreed. Reluctantly. But that didn't stop me from feeling like this was going to turn out badly for me. It wasn't like it was going to be a one-time thing. Doc Ainsley has diagnosed Risa with mononucleosis, said it'd be weeks before she could get back on stage. Weeks?

A knock at my bedroom door made me jump. Mike's boisterous voice prompted, "Come on, Georgia! Let's rock-n-roll. We're going to be late."

Late was good. Granted, this was only a practice session at the bar, but I'd have to pass muster with the band. More importantly though, Tommy Dixon was going to be there because he was their sound and light guy.

On the drive over to Tango's, the club where we'd be performing that weekend, I kept my eyes glued to the scenery racing by outside the window of Mike's car. Every so often, he'd take his eyes off the road long enough to offer words of encouragement. This time, he tossed me a sideways glance and said, "Don't worry, Georgia. You'll do fine."

"Says you." I pulled my gaze away from the farm houses speckled along Chaney Road and looked at Mike. "How do you know I'll do *fine*? You've never even heard me sing."

"Well..." Mike looked back at the road and did a half-shrug, half-smirk. "Risa says you can sing. And if she says it, it's true."

"Well, yeah...I can sing. But not as good as Risa." I turned my head and settled my gaze back on the mixture of sassafras, magnolia, and cypress trees now lining the side of the road.

"Don't worry, Georgia. If you suck, I won't tell you until *after* they've booed you offstage this weekend." Mike chuckled as he pulled his '72 Pontiac LeMans into Tango's parking lot. Ronnie, the lead guitar player's car, a late 70s Camaro, was sitting just to the side of the door.

Mike hopped out of the car and trotted up the front steps, stopped and looked back at me. I was still sitting in the car. He paused and then headed back down the steps. Coming around to the passenger's side of the car, he opened the door. "Come on, Georgia." He gestured me out of the car. "Let's go."

I moaned while swinging my feet out and planting them on the ground. "If I end up regretting this—" Outside the car now, I slammed the door and charged up the steps. "So will you." I turned sideways and hit the wooden door with my upper arm, flinging it wide open before I stepped inside.

Everybody was already there. The guys in the band were lounging at the tables up front. Tommy was sitting in the booth at the back of the lower level, playing with the stage lights. I hadn't actually been to any of their shows because they were always in bars and I was too young to sit in the audience, but I'd heard from Risa that Tommy did double-time for the band on sound and lights, so I knew he was bound to be there. Even so, seeing him sitting there sent my heart into a frenzy. I trudged on awkwardly toward the stage.

Once Mike came in things got serious quickly. The guys took to the stage and I tried to find some enjoyment in standing in front of the microphone—Risa's microphone—but I found none.

A spotlight zeroed in on me and I looked back at Tommy in the booth, but I couldn't see him over the glare in my face. I screamed inside my head for him to *stop it!* But outwardly, I propped one hand on my hip and shaded my eyes with the other. "Is that really necessary?" I asked him.

I heard him laugh. "This is all about you, Georgia."

Then the other guys joined in on his revelry. I scanned the stage counter-clockwise. The guitar players Ronnie and Andy winked at me. Phil, the drummer, gave me a drum roll. Jimmy strummed off a scandalous run on the bass. And when I got to Mike standing behind the keyboards, he gave me his trademark *what's-the-big-deal* look.

"The crowd really likes it when Risa opens with something they can dance to, like *Dancing in the Moonlight?* You know that song?" Mike asked.

I nodded and mouthed the word, "*Yes.*"

Mike cranked out the keyboard intro and the rest of the band joined in. When it was time for me to start singing, I froze. Mike stopped playing first and soon after the rest of the band followed suit.

"Georgia...?" Mike said. "You okay?"

I glanced over my shoulder and twisted around to face him. "Maybe if I could just play the guitar first, for a song or two, and get comfortable with the stage?"

"Okay." Mike shrugged. "What's your pleasure? Lead, rhythm, bass?"

"Well, I really prefer lead."

"Lead it is." Mike looked at Ronnie. "Let her use your guitar."

I turned to Ronnie, who didn't say anything. He just pulled the strap over his head and handed the white Strat to me. I took the guitar, unhooked the strap and readjusted it over my shoulder and then refastened it. I made sure to stay back, away from the microphone, as I wasn't ready to sing just yet. I strummed the guitar's strings to get a feel for the instrument. It sounded good. I glanced over my shoulder at Mike and nodded.

"What you want to play?" he asked.

"Well..." I shrugged. What the hell...if I was going to end up looking like a fool, I might as well do it in style. "I've been into Chicago lately."

I didn't miss Mike's devilish laugh. "Chicago, huh?" He looked around and it seemed like a long time before he set his sights back on me again. "How about a little *25 or 6 to 4?*" It wasn't a question, and I sensed the smirk in his tone.

But I wasn't worried. "Okay." For as insecure as I was about my ability to fill Risa's shoes as a singer, I was just as confident about my abilities to play the guitar. I glanced up toward Tommy, and asked, "Can we kill the spotlight please?"

"You're going to have to have it sooner or later, Georgia."

"Can we ease me into it?" I asked. "Instead of shoving me into the deep end right off the bat?"

The spotlight went out and I heard Tommy chuckle. "Take it away, Georgia."

I hit the first chords of that very recognizable riff and I heard Ronnie say into the mic, "Not bad. Not bad at all."

I felt myself sighing a breath of relief. Don't get me wrong, I love to play the guitar and I know I'm pretty good at it, but I'd be lying if I said I wasn't a bit nervous—mostly over the fear of singing.

I knew I was playing a bit stilted at the beginning of the song, but by the time we were well into the second verse I was one with the Strat.

When the song was over, Ronnie stepped toward me and said, "Damn, Georgia...you play better than I do."

So I guess what happened after the practice was kind of like fate. We walked outside Tango's and what do you think—Ronnie's car was gone!

He started pitching a fit, kicking the side of the building and yelling and screaming and carrying on. It was no secret what had happened to his car. We all knew the volatile relationship he had with his girlfriend Peggy. She hated that he was in the band and she'd taken his car in retaliation while we were practicing.

Ronnie, Andy, Phil, and Jimmy piled into the back seat of Mike's car—it was a tight fit. Mike hopped into the driver's seat and Tommy climbed in on the passenger's side. There was no bench seat in Mike's LeMans. Just two bucket seats with a stick shift between them.

"Uhm, Mike...?" I said, standing next to the passenger's side of the car.

"Oh, shit!" Mike leaned over and looked at me through the window. He looked at Tommy and back at me again. "Sit on his lap," he said, pointing at Tommy.

"What...?" Tommy and I both said in unison.

"What else am I supposed to do with her?" Mike said to Tommy. "I can't put her in the backseat with them." He gestured toward the other guys. "Risa would kill me."

We all knew that was true. If he crammed me in the backseat with four guys, Risa would be pissed. As a big sister, she's a little overprotective. In this case, I can't say that I minded. But hell, that meant I was headed for Tommy's lap. Oh, God.

Tommy gave me a gesturing wave. "Come on, Georgia. Let's go."

"You behave yourself." Mike stuck an officious finger in Tommy's face.

"Yeah, right." Tommy pulled me into his lap and slammed the door shut. "I ain't no child molester."

God, that was embarrassing.

Mike turned over the key and started the engine. He put the car in reverse, throwing a few rocks around as he gunned it. "Where do you think she went?" he asked Ronnie, over his shoulder. "Home?"

"Nah...she's probably hiding out at Robin's house," Ronnie's said.

Mike hit the gas again, taking off toward the Tunston Highway, and my head hit the window. Reflexively, I clutched my head in my hand.

"Georgia...?" Tommy grabbed me. "You okay?"

Pretty much. "Yeah." My pride was hurt way more than my head.

I was still rubbing my head—milking it—so Tommy pulled me to his chest and I about died. He steadied me and then relaxed his hold, but he kept his arms wrapped loosely around me. Mortified, I buried my face against his chest.

"You sure you're all right?" he asked me again.

"Yeah. It just smarts. I'll get over it." I continued to rub my head because I didn't want anyone to see my face. I'm sure it was beet-red. I know my heart was pounding wildly, and for once I was thankful for the vibration from the car's Cherry Bomb mufflers. Not that I rode in Mike's car all that often, just on the rare occasion that Mike and Risa would give Ginger and me a ride somewhere.

Just as Mike rounded Dead Man's Curve, Ronnie's Camaro cut

the corner at intersection of Wells Road without stopping at the stop sign. The car charged up the road in front of us.

"There she is!" Ronnie tapped the back of Mike's seat. Mike gunned it and closed in on Peggy as Ronnie declared, "I should kick her ass. Literally."

"Should?" Mike snorted. The fact that he advocated the literal kicking of any girl's ass didn't set well with me.

Everyone was chattering and emotions were running high as we sped after Ronnie's car.

Mike took the Clampett Cut-off and roared up the brief shortcut, with the intention of heading Peggy off on the Tunston Highway, before she made it to the Interstate. Tommy tightened his embrace on me, knowing the curve would send me back into the window again. The feel of his arms around me was both exhilarating and exasperating. Not exactly a lover's embrace, but I was there just the same.

I closed my eyes as we neared the intersection at full speed. Just feet from our stop sign Mike hit the brakes and skidded into the middle of the highway. Tires squealed on both vehicles as each came to a halt inches from each other.

Mike jumped out of the car and let Ronnie out. Ronnie charged toward his car and the rest of us watched, shamelessly digging the drama. After a couple of minutes of Ronnie and Peggy yelling at each other, the rest of the guys filed out from the back seat of Mike's car and moved closer to the action.

Tommy opened the car door and when I didn't move right away, he patted me on the leg. "Hop up, Georgia."

I was still in his lap. Embarrassment flooded through me and I felt my cheeks burn. "Sorry." I pulled myself out of the car and took a step or two away. Thoroughly humiliated, I rubbed my temples, wondering if I'd ever live this down.

Tommy moved past me and stopped after a couple of steps. He turned back, looking at me. "You sure you're okay?"

I shook my head. "I'm fine." I turned away from him because I didn't want him to see my face in case it was red. I was already mortified enough.

Suddenly, Ronnie's voice became very loud. "You want to break up? Fine." The anger painting his face was more than I'd ever seen on him. "You can kiss my ass." He looked at Mike. "Will you take her home?"

"Sure." Mike shrugged.

"You go ahead and run off with your friends!" Peggy screamed at Ronnie with tears streaming down her face. "But you've got responsibilities and I'm going to make sure you don't dodge them."

"Wait..." Mike looked at Ronnie. "What she's talking about?"

"Nothing." Ronnie's tone held a measure of resentment. "It's nothing that I can't handle."

Mike yanked Ronnie off to the side, closer to Tommy and me. "Is she...?"

"I told you I can handle it," Ronnie insisted.

"By deserting her?" Mike's own anger was showing now. "Is that how you're going to handle it?"

Say what? Tommy and I looked at each other, our mouths dropping open. Ronnie had knocked up Peggy?

"You know what...?" Ronnie smirked. "Screw you, man."

"No. Screw you." Mike turned away.

"Get your own bitch in line before you start telling me how to handle mine." Now this was probably Ronnie's frustration talking more than anything, but that didn't carry much weight with Mike. He took two steps away and then spun back around and plowed Ronnie with an upper right hook.

Mike gave Ronnie, who was now on the ground, a moment's notice before shifting his gaze between me, Tommy and Peggy, and said to us, "You guys get in the car." He looked at the other guys while we did as instructed. "If he won't give you a ride, just wait at Sid's." He pointed to the gas station across the street. "Tommy and I will be right back for you."

Peggy and I were settling into the back seat while Tommy reclaimed his place up front. Mike charged around the car and stopped at the door. He looked at Ronnie who was picking himself up off the ground, and said, "And Ronnie...you're out of the band."

Tommy looked at Mike as he climbed in behind the wheel and slammed his car door. "What the hell just happened?"

"I think I just fired our lead guitarist." Mike glanced up into the rearview mirror, specifically at me, and fired up the engine. "You got a decent guitar, Georgia?"

"Yeah. Why?" I asked, uneasy.

"You're our new guitarist." Mike floored it, burning rubber as we left the scene.

♡

"Okay. Wai, wai, wait." Dana slapped me on the arm, bringing me back to the present, inside the L.A. restaurant. "Who is this *band* you played with as a teenager? Anybody we know?"

Ginger laughed. "No. Just our older sister and some guys from high school. None of them but Georgia made it in the music biz."

"Yeah, but you're getting ahead of the story." I looked at Ginger.

Ginger nodded and chucked. "Now she wants the story told."

"Hold up..." Dana's hand was in the air. "You said Tommy didn't know you existed."

"It's true," Malibu agreed. "You did say that."

"But we're thinking..." Dana said, "what with that car ride and all, that that's not entirely accurate." She interrogated me with arched eyebrows. "You still maintain that you never dated him?"

Ginger shook her head. "Georgia and Tommy never dated. They just mooned over each other in secret."

"Not true," I said.

"Come on, Georgia." Ginger gave me a chastising glare. "Everybody but Tommy knew you were in love with him...and vice versa." Sometimes, my sister has a perverse sense of humor.

"Let's focus." Malibu's voice deepened. "I want to know more about you and this *band*. What'd you do...desert them and head to California seeking fame and fortune?"

I was happy to change the subject, but I was naturally defensive about that period of my life so I bit back the urge to defend myself. "It was a little more complicated than that."

"Do tell..." Malibu looked at me, waiting for the particulars—which I might as well spill. Once he got started, it was hard to stop him.

♡

Twenty-four Years Ago...

I'd been playing lead guitar for the band for nearly three years when my senior year in high school was drawing to a close. We were pretty popular on the nightclub circuit, and during the previous six months or so we'd been playing at the legendary hot spots in New Orleans.

The weekend before my graduation we were scheduled to play at Tango's, but Risa had been feeling poorly for the past week or so. She and I were in the club's dressing room, and we were alone.

She sat down next to me and tried to smile. "I'm going to need you to do some of the singing tonight."

"Some?" I asked. I wasn't afraid to sing. I'd gotten over that long ago. But the truth was, people came to see me play the guitar and to hear Risa sing.

"Come on, Georgia." She shrugged and tried to play it off with a casual tone. "I'm just not feeling all that great. You've got to cover for me."

"Risa, are you okay?" I started to worry. Her bout with mono had started like this.

"I'm going to be fine," she insisted. "I just need some rest."

"Have you been to see Doc Ainsley?"

"No." She shook her head.

"Maybe you should."

"Why?"

"This is oddly reminiscent of when you came down with mono."

"I'm not getting mono again," she said, as if that was a ridiculous notion.

"How can you be so sure?" I, on the other hand, was genuinely worried. "Do Mom and Dad know about this?"

"God, no." She got serious. "You can't say anything to Mom and Dad."

"Why?"

"Because I don't want them to know."

Now she was starting to scare me. "If you don't tell them...I will."

"Okay, fine." She threw her hands into the air. "I don't have mono. I'm pregnant."

I felt my mouth drop open. "Pregnant?" I had to ask just to make sure I'd heard her right. She nodded. "How far along are you?"

"A few weeks. We just figured it out. We're going to get married. But I've got to find the right time to tell Mom and Dad."

I laughed out loud. "There is no *right* time to tell Mom that her single daughter is pregnant."

Risa laughed. Believe it or not, it lightened the mood. Then she looked at me seriously. "You won't say anything, will you?"

"No." I shook my head. "This is your secret to tell."

By the time we actually got up on stage, Risa was feeling much better. I think a part of her just needed to get it off her chest.

At the end of the second set a couple of suits approached us as we filed off the stage. "Excuse me." The taller one spoke directly to Risa and me.

She looked at him, at me, and then back at him again and started shaking her head. "She doesn't hang out in the barroom. Between sets she sits in the dressing room. We're told that's okay since she's in the band."

"We're not here to haggle over your sister's age." The shorter one chuckled.

"Okay. Then why are you here?" Mike said.

The taller one gave Mike a dismissive glance and turned back to Risa. "Can we talk in the dressing room, where it's a bit quieter?"

"Sure." She shrugged and headed back toward the only place I was allowed to be when not on stage.

Inside the dressing room the suits identified themselves as executives for the *Summer* record label in L.A. We were all shocked; you could tell by the silence and the jaw-dropping expressions.

"One of our scouts saw you in New Orleans last month. He said you were good, and we agree."

The guys in the band started crowing like banty roosters, but Risa and I just looked at each other and remained silent.

"I'm sorry, guys," the shorter one said, "but we're only here for the girls."

"What?" Mike bellowed.

"We're here to make contract offers, but only for the two of you." He gave a gesturing wave at Risa and me.

"That ain't happening." Mike shook his head. "We come with them."

"Ladies..." The taller one fished a small case out of his blazer and took out two business cards. "We'll be in New Orleans through next weekend." He handed a card to me and one to Risa. "We're offering each of you a bonafide record deal. This is not an opportunity that comes along every day."

Hell no, it wasn't! I knew who Summer Records was. Everybody knew who Summer Records was.

The card bearer looked at me. "You might want to have your parents contact us before you make your final decision."

The suits took their leave, and Risa and I stood looking at the business cards in our hands. Mike grabbed Risa's card, ripped it apart, and threw it on the floor. Next, he stepped toward me. But he wasn't about to get my card. I hid it in my hands behind my back, and I was honestly shocked when Mike tried to overpower me.

I was even more surprised when Tommy pulled him off me. "Mike..." he said to his friend. "You don't want to do that." His tone was calm but there was something in it, something inhibiting, that made Mike back off.

Mike glared at Tommy. "She's not accepting *that* deal."

"Well let's let Georgia and her parents decide what she's going to do." Tommy cast a quick glance and me and Risa and then looked back at Mike. "Truth is...we can't make the decision for either of them. They have to decide for themselves."

Mike pointed an accusatory finger at Tommy. "Bullshit." He

looked at me and then Risa and a snarl lifted his upper lip. "This ain't happening," he said to her. He cleared his throat before taking a step backward, and then spun around and stomped toward the door. He flung it open and disappeared into the hallway.

The rest of the evening spilled by with a lot of tension in the air. Time trudged on, but Mike's anger filtered out and engulfed the rest of the band. Suddenly, Risa and I were traitors, and all we'd done was take a business card from some record people.

At the end of the night, back in the dressing room, Mike skulked toward me. "I want you to tell me now that you're not going to take that contract." His tone was calm enough, but there was an anger in his eyes that, honestly, scared me.

"I can't tell you that." I wasn't going to make up my mind until I'd talked to my parents and we'd heard the actual offer. I'd be a simpleton not to listen to what the record company had to say.

"Find your own damn ride home then." He didn't wait for Risa to retaliate, instead he headed for the door.

"Hey..." Risa yelled.

Mike stopped at the door and glared at Risa. "Are you coming?" But he didn't wait for her response. He stomped out into the hallway.

"Don't worry about it, Risa," Tommy said. "I'll make sure Georgia gets home."

Risa looked at me with sad eyes. "You go with Tommy. I'll be home soon." She tried to smile but had little luck. "And remember..."

"Yeah, I know..." Mum's the word. But I kept that last thought to myself. I wasn't sure who exactly knew about Risa's *condition*, but I was determined not to be the one to give it away.

I'd never ridden in Tommy's truck before. It was a *beater*, but it came with one advantage—Tommy. We both were quiet as we drove down Chaney Road, heading for my neighborhood.

"You know the odds of Mike talking Risa out of accepting that contract are pretty damn good," Tommy said.

Considering Risa's current condition... "Yeah." I sighed.

"Don't let them bully you." He glanced at me. "You do what you want to do."

"Risa wouldn't try to bully me." Would she?

Tommy laughed and shook his head. "Georgia, I can just imagine the lines that Mike's feeding Risa right now." He looked at me and his amusement stopped. "All of which I'm sure you'll hear later on, with Risa claiming all of it makes sense."

I shook my head. This contract offer was starting to give me a headache. "I had no idea this was going to get so complicated."

"When a record company offers only part of the band contracts," he said, turning into my driveway. "Things always get complicated."

"I just don't get Mike. Why's he so angry?"

Tommy shrugged. "Well, he just found out he's not good enough."

"I don't think anybody actually said that."

"Yes, but what they don't say speaks volumes."

The porch light flickered on. My cue. "I've got to go," I said, disappointed. "Thanks for the ride," I added, and got out of the truck.

"Anytime, Georgia." He gave me a smile as I shut the door. He leaned over and rolled the window down. "Follow your dreams, Georgia. Go find your place in the world, cause it ain't here."

Encouragement from Tommy was great, but the words still stung. I didn't know which was worse: Mike trying to bully Risa into staying, or Tommy practically giving me a ride out of town. It was disheartening hearing Tommy say that I didn't belong in Cypress Falls. The sad thing was, I knew he was right. But when I left Cypress Falls, that'd mean I'd have to leave Tommy behind too. That thought didn't leave me feeling very cheerful.

Half way up the steps, I looked over my shoulder. He was sitting there in his truck just watching me. The look on his face was neither happy nor remorseful. I waved and he reciprocated. The truck's engine started and I saw Tommy shifting into gear. He stepped on the gas, backing up, and I headed inside.

I opened and closed the door with care, and tiptoed up the stairs. By the time I got to my room, I saw headlights rolling up the driveway.

Well, it was either Mike and Risa—unlikely—or Jeffrey Dean was bringing Ginger home.

Blue, as Jeffrey Dean's friends called him, was Ginger's boyfriend and had been for nearly two years. He was a good-looking guy and a great baseball player. Currently in his freshman year at LSU, everybody's expecting him to end up in the Majors. Where Ginger will fit into that picture I'm not sure. For now, she seemed to be living in the moment.

The car door opened—the vehicle's identity safely hidden behind the headlights—and to my surprise Risa stepped out. She closed the door, leaned down and said something to Mike through the window and then headed for the house.

Watching her trot up to the walkway, I wondered what Mike had said to her. Well, I supposed I'd find out soon enough. I had to time it to know when to expect her to appear in my doorway, all the Franklin kids had learned how to walk lightly at an early age. My brother Ryan was still learning, but he was only fourteen. I suspected he'd master it soon enough.

I sat down on my bed at precisely the moment I expected to see Risa in my doorway. I was right. "You're home early." I looked up at her and nodded for her to enter. All the Franklin kids had been taught to respect each other's privacy. We didn't enter our siblings' rooms without being invited first.

She came to my bed and sat down at the foot. "Mike thought it best that I come on home and talk to you."

"Why the rush?"

"Well, see Georgia, the way the music business works is..." She sucked in a breath, and I wondered if she truly believed the line she was about to feed me. I mean, I'm just a teenager from a small town. I know absolutely nothing about the music business. I suspected that Mike and Risa didn't either. "We just have to be gutsy."

I didn't say anything. I just looked at her, waiting for that reasoning.

"We can negotiate and make them include the rest of the band."

I laughed out loud. "How do you figure that?" I'm no expert, but I didn't see that we had that much to bargain with.

"Mike says that's the way it works." She said it like she really believed it. I wasn't sure what was fueling Risa's crusade for Mike—her love for him or the fact that she was pregnant.

"Well...I'm going to wait and see what Mom and Dad say before I make up my mind." I could sympathize with her. She was getting pressure from Mike, the father of her baby. "Given the circumstances, I'll respect whatever decision you make. I hope you'll do the same for me."

She nodded and tried to smile, but I had a feeling Risa thought she had only one option. But as for me, I was going to sleep on it and talk to my parents about what to do in the morning.

♡

Dana slammed her glass down on the table. "Wait...you don't have a *famous* sister." The realization that Risa may have missed her shot at success wiped the smile off Dana's face. I shook my head slowly, confirming her suspicions.

Malibu cleared his throat. "So your sister let Mike talk her into holding out and she got left behind too?"

"That's pretty much what happened," I said.

"And to make matters worse," Ginger added. "My parents thought Georgia should take the shot. So when she came out here, everybody—except maybe Tommy—was pissed off at her. They called her a traitor. Even Risa." Ginger shook her head. "Sad thing is...Mike and Risa are still mad at Georgia. They won't even talk to her."

Mike'll talk to me when it suits him, I thought. He didn't have any trouble talking to me when he wanted money to open up his own car dealership. He used my brother Ryan as bait, saying Ryan would always have a job. But truth be known, because of my sister and my niece, I didn't have a problem funding the venture. Mike had never told anyone, as far as I knew, where he'd gotten the money from, and I didn't either. It was supposed to have been a loan, but I've never seen a dime of repayment, even though the business has been wildly successful for years. Because of my sister and my niece, I didn't have the heart to call the loan.

"So what about your baseball player boyfriend?" Malibu, being a guy, was curious about the mention of a sports figure. "Are you telling me you dated the baseball player J.D. Ramsey in high school?"

Ginger nodded.

Dana sipped her drink before asking, "And what pray tell happened there?"

"Well, Mom came out here with Georgia at first. She stayed a few weeks and then I got accepted to Stanford and my parents thought Georgia and I would be okay out here as long as we were together." She shrugged. "I wasn't going to miss the chance to go to Stanford. Blue got pissed because I was so far away. Same old story. Distance is a bitch on relationships. Especially when you're young."

Ginger tried to pretend indifference, but I knew better. From what she'd told me about running into him on her last trip home, it was far from over. And now that she'd be attending Lisa's wedding as a single woman—thank goodness for quickie divorces—I suspected this was an old flame that might be revisited.

"Man...you guys got some crappy ass luck." Malibu reached for his beer and took a healthy swig.

"Blue recently moved back to Cypress Falls though," I said. "Ginger saw him last time she was there." I'll admit, I was instigating to keep the focus off me.

"So what happened...?" Dana giggled.

"Nothing." Ginger shook her head. "I was still married to Keith."

"So is Blue married? Involved?" Dana asked. "Does he still look good?"

"Not that I could tell." Ginger shrugged, like it was no big deal. "And yes, Blue still looks good."

"So what about you and Tommy?" Dana turned to me. "Nothing ever happened between you two when you went home for visits?"

Ginger laughed. "Georgia's not been home in damn near twenty-five years."

"What?" Even Malibu found that hard to believe.

"Nope." I shook my head. "I pissed off a lot of people when I left. My parents and Ginger were the only ones that didn't hate me."

"Tommy didn't hate you," Ginger said.

"Nevertheless..." I gave Ginger a hard glare. "It was just easier for my parents to come out to L.A." I shrugged. "Besides, Ginger was out here. Once Lisa turned a couple years old, they'd bring her out too, so I do *know* my niece. Risa would never come though."

"And now, our niece is marrying Tommy's son," Ginger said with lingering melancholy.

"Wait..." Dana said. "Tommy's married?"

Ginger shook her head. "No. He's divorced."

"Who is the groom's mother?" Dana asked. "Anybody we know?"

Ginger snorted. "Oh, yeah." Her eyes grew wide as she said, "Kathy Ramsey."

"Any relation to your ex-boyfriend?" Malibu asked.

"Sister." Ginger glanced at me. "Georgia here wasn't the only one harboring feelings for Tommy. The difference was, Kathy made hers known."

"Did Tommy date her?" Dana asked.

"No." Ginger shook her head. "Tommy never gave Kathy a second's notice...until Georgia split. You know, Tommy really wanted Georgia to go if that's what she wanted to do. I don't think he realized how much her leaving would affect him though." Ginger sighed. "A few days after Georgia left, rumors started flying that Tommy and Kathy had had a one night stand. A couple months later, Tommy was talking about going out to L.A. to see Georgia and then Kathy announced she was pregnant."

"So Tommy married Kathy," Malibu said without much feeling.

Ginger nodded. "And they had a son, Ethan, who's now going to marry our niece Lisa."

"So Tommy never made that trip out here to see Georgia?" Dana asked.

"Nope." Ginger looked at me for a second and then continued on. "Even though Tommy and Kathy divorced after a few years. He stuck close to home, not wanting to disregard his responsibilities to Ethan."

"Man, Georgia...you should go home and marry that guy." Malibu shook his head and downed his beer.

Me? Marry Tommy? Like that was ever going to happen. I'd been alone for the whole of my adult life. I'd been quite content pulling out the old *what if* card every now and then. It was better than playing the *rejected* card. It was much better to daydream about what might have been. In fact, I'd gotten more than a few miles out of it in my songwriting. I doubt I'd have had as much success with penning lyrics about unreciprocated love.

There was never any question about whether or not I'd finally make that trip back home to attend Lisa's wedding. If everybody still hated me, so be it. But there was no way I was disappointing that girl.

Cypress Falls…ready or not, here I come!

About the Author

Sandra Edwards is an award-winning author of romance. She has eclectic tastes, penning tales in a variety of genres such as paranormal (mostly time travel and reincarnation), contemporary and suspense. She lives in the U.S. (west coast) with her husband, two kids, four dogs and one very temperamental feline. Sandra's books often push the envelope and step outside the boundaries of conventional romance. For more info on Sandra's books, visit her website at www.SandraWrites.com, her blog at www.SandyWritesRomance.com, and her Facebook page at www.facebook.com/SandraEdwards.Author.

Printed in Great Britain
by Amazon.co.uk, Ltd.,
Marston Gate.